Return to Raby

Return to Raby

A New England Novel

J. P. Polidoro

Longtail Publishing

ISBN: 0-9677619-2-1
Library of Congress Control Number: 2002094014

Manufactured in the United States of America
Book production: Tabby House
Cover design: Incite Graphic Designs
Back cover photo credit: Alan MacRae
Front cover photos: Brenda Polidoro

Any resemblance to any person, either living or dead, or to places, in the novel *Return to Raby*, is purely coincidental.

Longtail Publishing
1391 Old North Main Street
Laconia, NH 03246
www.longtailpublishing.com

For Brenda
For reasons only she would know too well

Prologue

Bess Talbot knew that her nephew, Nelson Palmer, was thinking about retiring and moving out of the area. She had heard it from her friend, Ruth, who had visited her in the Willowbreath Nursing Home in Pennsylvania. Aunt Bess summoned Nelson to her room one Sunday to wish him well in his days of leisure. It was winter's end, but not yet spring. Because her health was poor, she was afraid that once he moved, she might not see him again. Aunt Bess wanted her family to remain in Pennsylvania, but at age ninety-four, she was keenly aware that no one stayed in one place anymore.

"Sit down, Nelson," she beckoned. "What's this I hear you plan to leave these parts and your dear old aunt to go to New England for good?"

He sat beside her rocker and held her hand. She loved him dearly and had teased him since he was a small boy. "Will you come back to bury me?"

Nelson was shocked by her bluntness. He did not answer directly. "Aunt Bess, you ain't goin' nowhere for a long time, my lady. Why, you're my *favorite* aunt!"

"Favorite? You, Nelson, are crazy . . . I'm your *only* aunt!" she chuckled. He was glad that she had retained her humor, despite her declining health.

"Then, that makes you even more special, Aunt Bess . . . bein' the only aunt," he said with a smile.

"Nelson . . . I wish you and Lydia well, no matter where you folks end up. New England is precious with the four seasons and all. It's the maples and oaks, ya know. They shimmer in the sun in October, they tell me. It's a natural painting . . . one of liquid nature . . . always changing . . . four seasons of wonder," she said with eyes closed for a moment, imagining.

She stared at a print on the wall in her room at the home. It was a five-and-dime photo of scenic Vermont, embedded in a molded-plastic, simulated-wood frame. The print was a famous barn and pasture scene in Woodstock, Vermont, complete with holsteins grazing. He noticed her stare. She seemed to perk up.

"Nelson! Is that New Hampshire?" she asked, pointing with her cane.

"No, Auntie . . . I'm afraid that is actually Vermont. It says so on the label in the middle of the frame. He held his reading glasses with one hand as he squinted at the now faded photo. His thick white hair made him look debonair.

"Yep . . . it's Vermont," he reaffirmed.

"Dang it! I was told it might be New Hampshire. We have our roots up there somewhere—somewhere in the south of the state. Can't remember the darn town . . . the name . . . my memory's gone," she said. "It started with an 'H' or maybe an 'R.' Fudge! I can't believe that it's slipped my mind."

"Roots?" he replied, surprised. "I thought you and your brothers were from Pennsylvania. That is what my own mother, your sister, led me to believe."

"Nah . . . she was confused, Nel," she said affectionately. "She never could keep the family tree straight. It was New Hampshire that the family ended up in, from England, I do believe."

Nelson was puzzled. He and Lydia were considering New Hampshire, along with several other New England states, as a place to move to in retirement. They had been drawn to areas near the ocean or Boston, where they had spent several nice vacations. In one month, he would be heading north to New England.

Although he tried to think of some more questions that might shake loose some additional memories of the ancestral New Hampshire town from Aunt Bess, she was tired now and couldn't come up with anything more.

Intrigued, Nelson now had another reason, besides the urging of friends in the northern part of the state, to make New Hampshire house hunting a priority—his unknown background.

"Aunt Bess, before I head out in a month, I'll be back to say good-bye," Nelson said, as he helped her back to her bed. "Don't worry, we'll stay in touch."

Aunt Bess died in her sleep at the home a week after his visit. After the funeral, which he helped arrange, Nelson placed Aunt Bess's limited belongings in a storage unit until he could make arrangements to move them. A few days after his official retirement, he began his drive to New England alone. Lydia respected his need to be alone. She had encouraged him to search on his own, and she knew the transition to permanent retirement required time for him to think and to plan. She knew that during this initial journey he would have her best interests in mind, as well as his own. They were both unselfish in that respect. She would join him later.

On the Jeep's passenger seat was the Vermont print that Aunt Bess had loved. It was a memento of her wisdom and their last conversation together. He promised himself that once settled in their new home, he would hang the picture in a special place. As he listened to the radio, he thought about their last conversation. He regretted not spending more time with her.

Next to the print was an old book that Aunt Bess had left to him. Her note indicated that the volume had been entrusted to her when she was quite young, by her elderly uncle, Clyde, who was also interested in history. Nelson believed the tattered volume might hold the only clues to his family's origin, and yet, it too was an enigma. Nelson had jotted down the letters Aunt Bess had mentioned on a bookmark in the historic compilation.

Nelson headed the Jeep north on the first leg of his New England search for a special building to renovate. His itinerary had changed after his conversation with Bess. He would not scope out Connecticut or Massachusetts first, but instead, headed straight for New Hampshire.

He stopped once for gas. Eight hours later, he crossed the state line at Nashua, New Hampshire.

One

It was a dreary Saturday in spring. A Jeep approached the dilapidated white building, slowed to a crawl, then stopped. Raindrops coalesced and formed small rivers on the windshield. Between the drops, the driver marveled at the historic church and graveyard.

"She's beautiful," he whispered. "She really is a fine, old place. Look at the trim on the soffits. They cared back then—carpenters really cared back then. There was no ticky-tacky construction like there is today," he continued, reveling in the beauty of the white clapboards and steeple.

The bell tower stood tall near the grove of pines that were well established over time. He knew that those pines were planted after the church had been built; yet, they were just as tall as the belfry. White pines rapidly grow tall and wide in New England. Their branches were uneven, unlike the blue spruce of the west that often displayed perfect symmetry. The pines had to be seventy-five to one hundred years old, but they were young compared to the historic church. The driver stood beside the vehicle and stared at the entire property—first looking right, then slowly left.

Nelson Palmer rubbed his eyes from the long ride and then approached the wrought-iron gate to the cemetery to the left of the church. Many of the earliest grave stones dated back to the 1700s, and were leaning. A few even predated those markers. Each stone told a story— the date of birth and death of all family members in the plot. The engraving often indicated the causes of death: diseases, hunting accidents, wars, drownings or other fatal events. Life was short. Adults died at age thirty or less and children often died as infants or toddlers, ages two or three. Violent deaths were common, including cabin fires, knife and gun incidents. Some people died when gunpowder blew up by mistake.

Cold rain fell on Nelson's faded, wide-brimmed hat and he adjusted the collar on his coat to block the wind and cold drizzle. The hat protected his shirt and neck from the damp weekend weather. A surreal mist covered much of the cemetery, creating an eerie sight, yet calm and serene. Nelson Palmer had already visited two other cemeteries in the general area that day. He had seen enough stones and markers all day to know that this graveyard would probably contain the memorial that he was looking for. It was his last hope. He felt like he had walked the countryside for miles. No one had bothered to mow the churchyard for quite a while. The graveyard, on the other hand, was a separate entity and had been maintained more recently.

Nelson carefully held *The History of Colonial New Hampshire,* written more than a century earlier. He had protected it from the rain by keeping it in a clear plastic bag. He panned the original fieldstone wall made from fieldstones that had been accumulated from the clearing of pastures and digging of graves more than two hundred years earlier. The large, well-fitted stones varied in shape and size, and surrounded three of the four sides of the graveyard. The fourth side was defined by a white picket fence and a wooden, double swinging gate, old, but fairly well maintained. The fence door of vertical slats was actually weathered oak, which had been painted white. Two swinging doors were needed for caskets and pallbearers to pass through upon entering the cemetery with the remains of the departed. This cemetery was the largest in the area and the final resting place for many local residents. The swinging doors were secured by handmade wrought-iron hinges. They were fastened to two vertical granite posts that had been hand-hewed at a quarry nearby. Nelson unlatched the metal swing lock and the rain-soaked hinges creaked when the doors were pushed open. He read some of the names that were engraved long ago. "Joseph Potter," he said deliberately and slowly. "Wife, Emma. Ah, there's Jessica Bridgestone and her children. Read of her in the book. Oh!

There he is—Ezra—Ezra Raby—Jesus! There were a lot of Rabys," he said slowly, with surprise. The surrounding stones of various heights revealed the immediate family of Ezra. There were descendants from over one hundred and fifty years.

The rain picked up as the dates and names on the moss and lichen encrusted stones became even wetter. Green parasites covered some letters and dates of the deceased. Nelson took out a Swiss Army knife and scraped Ezra's stone in order to read it better. His death, in 1751, was from consumption, it stated. His wife, Maybelle Carter Raby, had died the year before him from complications during childbirth. There was no other information on her death. Typically, when women died during childbirth, it was from difficult labor. A stone nearby suggested that there was an unnamed infant who died the same year as the mother. Perhaps it was the child that Maybelle was carrying.

Nelson was now soaked from the persistent storm. His shoes were saturated. Having looked down at many stones all day long, his collar was of little use in keeping the rain off his shirt and back. Before he got back in his car, Nelson copied down the phone number for Mountain Realty—800-271-LAND—from a sign. He had not noticed that old church was for sale when he first arrived.

He planned to contact the Realtor and then return to check out the inside of the church. If nothing else, he wished to see the quaint décor, woodwork, and beautiful stained glass windows. *I'll need to view the windows on a sunny day when they are naturally backlit and casting their colors across the floor of the church,* he thought. He had a gut feeling that the old church was beckoning him to return. He felt an attraction to the old building, an attraction so strong that he knew there and then, that he had to consider renovating her—perhaps into his retirement home. *What would Lydia think? Would she agree?* he wondered. He was flexible but he was not sure how flexible she would be in his desire to convert a house of worship into a home and move to the little New Hampshire town.

He climbed back in the Jeep, and leaned his head back against the headrest before starting the motor. He stared at the steeple and glanced back down to the front doors and granite steps. Streaks of rain blocked his view, creating a macabre distortion of the building.

He turned the key in the ignition just enough to have the wipers make one pass over the windshield. The horizontal clapboards became clear. He sighed, and started the engine. He drove slowly away from the front and began to think about the graveyard and church property. He would not rest easily that night. Ezra Raby had beckoned him there in the first place and was now calling him to return to the property. Nelson felt that he had found some of his roots and the little church on the hill was part of his ancestry. He felt a chill from the rain and the supernatural feeling.

Two

At sixty-six, Nelson Palmer was a trim 200 pounds for his six-foot-two frame and was in excellent physical shape. He had worked as a laborer when he was young and later became a successful businessman. An environmental engineer and consultant, he had traveled extensively prior to retirement. He had looked forward to retiring for two years and had started planning for his new life and relaxation when he turned sixty-five. He knew he could keep busy with his woodworking hobby and various sports, such as golf and skiing. New England offered all of these opportunities and life would finally be relaxing and uncomplicated. *Renovating a home himself might be fun,* he thought, as he threw away the solicitations for membership in AARP. He had refused to accept aging without a fight, and worked out in his exercise room at home, and took power walks. He dressed casually in denim and polo shirts ordered from L.L. Bean and Britches.

With his construction background, Nelson was an avid carpenter and cabinetmaker. He also dabbled in basic home wiring and plumbing. If the anticipated renovation tasks extended beyond his capabilities, he was prepared to hire whomever he needed to accomplish the task in a timely fashion. He had also studied stonewall construction from a friend who was an expert mason. The mason was an expert in building retaining walls and the repair of existing fieldstone walls. Nelson found the process artistic and therapeutic. He practiced creating small garden walls, which survived the trauma of ice and snow in winter. It was an art form to him—a New England art form.

With his knowledge of construction, Nelson was able to envision renovations without actually seeing the church's interior. If the basic structure were sound, the rest of the task would be cosmetic in nature. With a good retirement income, he knew he could make his next home a comfortable and unique residence with a lot of character. His environmental engineering background allowed him to envision the terrain and landscaping that would be needed for it. He was conscious of the fact that the world had altered most natural landscapes and replaced them with malls, parking lots, and office parks. He scorned strip malls. Cell phone towers were another pet peeve—the hated creations of modern man.

For a number of years, Palmer had hoped to find an historical building with potential as a home. He had looked at railway depots, old libraries, and other old churches. Nothing moved him quite like the Harvest church; no other properties had this church's impact.

Nelson's trip to Harvest was stimulated by Aunt Bess's thought that the town name may have begun with the letter "H," and because he could not find any reference to one that began with an "R." Harvest was one of only two towns in southern New Hampshire that started with "H." Until he visited the church graveyard in Harvest, Nelson had no idea how significantly the trip would impact his life. The visit to the historic site would ultimately possess him.

✠✠✠

"Hello. Nelson Palmer?" Betty Morrissey, the real estate agent, said on the telephone. "I got your message from my associate, and understand that you want to see the church property—the listing up on Bear Hill. I'd be pleased to show it."

"I think, when I called, your colleague indicated that you were out showing other properties. Yesterday was a messy one and might not have been a good time anyway," he said, searching for something to write on, as he pushed back his thick, white hair.

"I'm sorry. I was here all the time and could have met with you yesterday. Do you have time today?" she asked. "I am free this morning and we can spend all the time you need. There are a number of nice properties on the market besides the one you asked about."

"Yeah, today would be fine. Where shall we meet? At the church or your office?"

"How about at the church at . . . say 10:30 A.M.? I'll bring a listing sheet. It is a beautiful piece of property—and unique, to say the least. Someone special needs to own it—someone who can make it a home or a small business. It is approved for 'commercial' or 'residential utility' because of its uniqueness," she continued.

"See you then," he said. "I'll be at this phone number one more day. It's a Nashua hotel."

"Weatherman says sun for today, so pray for it. You'll be enamored with the brilliant stained glass in the building, when the sun hits it," she said.

✠✠✠

The night before, Nelson had stopped by the Harvest Village Store for a coffee. The cold of the rain had chilled him and he drank the contents out of a Styrofoam cup rather rapidly. He purchased a muffin and had the clerk warm it in the microwave behind the counter. He noticed the special monthly Lotto advertisement and threw a twenty dollar bill on the counter. He liked the idea of the higher payoff.

"Ten Quik Picks please," he said, as he paid for the one-dollar Lotto tickets, a muffin, and coffee.

"Annuity or cash?" the young clerk asked. "You want the whole shebang that they pay out over twenty-five years, or half the amount as a lump sum in cash?"

"Oh—that's how it works," Nelson said with a laugh. "Why not give me the annuity. Wouldn't want to spend it all in one year."

"Hope ya win, sir, and good luck," said the young man behind the cash register as he gave Nelson his change.

"Thanks, son. Hope we *both* win. They draw the numbers on the thirtieth, right? They look like good numbers there on the slip—the computer even printed my birthday in there—number 23, and the number 8 for the month.

Nelson left the store and headed for the Nashua Hotel twelve miles east of Harvest. The odds were ninety million to one that anyone would ever win this big lottery, supposedly for education. At the very least, Nelson hoped his Quik Picks would get him back his ten dollars in four weeks. If he had three of the six winning numbers, he would win seven dollars. That was good enough.

✠✠✠

Nelson Palmer initially had little knowledge of or interest in the town of Harvest itself. He was merely interested in a retirement home that was unique. The church appealed to him because it was not only historic and unusual, it had a direct tie with his ancestors. At his age, he figured the renovations would take up his time, not local issues or politics.

Realtor Betty Morrissey was quick to point out the positives of the town during their telephone conversation. The attributes she cited were not the people, but of its beauty and the remoteness of the surrounding areas. There were mountains, and lakes and streams with trout and bass. She was trying to sell him on the region; Nelson obviously saw potential in the church property. There was seclusion as well and he loved the fact that his nearest neighbors were some distance away.

Betty was smooth; she really wanted the sale, and her seven percent commission depended on it. Her sales pitch intensified. "You will love this little town," she told him. "People here stay to themselves and holiday functions are fun. The townspeople like parades on the Fourth of July and on Memorial Day. You can fish, boat, and snowmobile. There's lots of water and trails. The town even has an ice cream social once a year. It's old-fashioned and a great time."

"That's nice," said Nelson. "My wife, Lydia, and I would love that." His mind was wandering. He had little interest in nine-tenths of what she had said. Fishing was of interest, but the idea of attending community fairs, barbecues and firemen's musters hosted by the fire department bored him. Lydia no longer liked being involved in woman's club-type events. She preferred to read and garden.

"Is there a bar in town?" he asked, abruptly changing the subject.

"Why . . . yes . . . there is one," she replied, slightly surprised. "Why?"

18

"Well, I enjoy a beer or two on occasion and chatting with the locals. Need to have a beer with the boys once in a while," he said with a laugh.

"Well, there is the local pub at the restaurant. It has a small bar there and hunters and fishermen often frequent the establishment before or after their sporting activities."

"What's the pub's name?"

"It's the Three Pines Inn, but there is no *inn* there. It has a bar and pool table or two. It tends to draw a seedy crowd—like bikers and transients passin' through. Years ago, it had go-go dancers, complete with mesh chicken wire around the stage. The boys would get rowdy and toss Budweiser bottles at them. It was not conducive to the community's respectable image to have the exotic dancers there. The girls' safety was a factor as well. The town finally shut that part down."

"Too bad 'bout that. I would think that would be a draw in New Hampshire—bein' it's the 'Live Free or Die' state," he teased. "I'll be leavin' the hotel here in Nashua soon. I look forward to seeing the listing sheet for the church as well, and checking out the building."

"I will see you soon. Take the short route. It's more direct from Nashua. Exit 6 West will get you here," she said, helpfully.

He just knew in his mind that the property he was about to view would grab him, but he did not want to sound too eager with the real estate agent.

Shortly after Betty Morrissey, and Nelson Palmer met at the church property, they felt comfortable enough to use first names. They toured the property lines and then approached the granite steps. The church was on about a half-acre, excluding the adjacent cemetery.

"Betty, any ghosts in the cemetery? I mean—are there any real ones that wander in and out of the church and stuff?" He meant it as a joke, but she took him seriously.

"There are no indications of any sightings on the paperwork," she said. "If there were incidents that had occurred previously, it would be right here on the paperwork. They usually list them if they have been reported on the older properties."

"Really?" he asked. "They actually admit to them, if they have experiences in the past? That is cool."

"Yes, Nelson, on occasion we see listings with notations to that effect," she continued. "Often there are noises or footsteps that are cited on some listings. Just last week, I had a Victorian home up on Saw Mill Hill Road. It is known for the apparition of a sea captain's wife who was murdered by her sailor husband. She supposedly roams the house looking for her dead baby."

"Dead baby—dead wife?"

"Yes, both were murdered. Apparently, the seaman was away too long and came home to find his wife pregnant. He was not a 'happy camper,' so to speak. He knew it was not his child so he killed his wife with a hatchet. The baby died as well. Supposedly the baby was buried under a tree nearby but it was never found. The mother, named Liz, supposedly roams the grounds and home looking for her dead child."

"Really? People have seen her?" he asked, with wide eyes and raised eyebrows.

"Sure—they have seen her—many times. . . . She roams around almost nightly and has been known to throw kitchenware, like plates and stuff. She also turns lights on and off, and the gas stove as well. She is particularly mischievous on Mother's Day. No kidding!"

"Well, what about *this* place then? Anyone in the steeple or the reverend's quarters?" he asked, looking up at the roof. Just then a pigeon flew out from the belfry and fluttered off, startling Betty.

"Not that we have heard of, but you may be the first to witness something if you buy it!" she joked. "Are you a gambler, Nelson?"

"I gamble, but not on ghosts," he said. "Let's go in and check out this gem of a building." More pigeons emerged from the louvers above.

"Here we go," she said, with a spooky voice. She unlocked the double doors and allowed him to pass by her to enter the foyer first.

"Holy shit!" he said in amazement. "I'm sorry for the curse word . . . but this is a beautiful place. Just look at the cathedral ceilings and crown molding. The light coming through the windows is spectacular. This is better than I had envisioned."

"You're right, but it takes a special client and prospect to appreciate this structure. Not everyone is into old buildings and churches. It has so much potential and it is so well made. You seem to focus on the right aspects of the structure. Have you renovated a building before?"

"No, but I know what it takes for some of the chores, at least for the money and time needed here. These are long-term projects to make them work. As a home, it requires lots of prep and I know the basics of construction and landscaping, to move it forward. I really like this place! It has character, history, and ambiance."

Betty added, "A number of people have looked at it. Just last week, a family viewed it. They found it too much of a challenge, I guess. Price wasn't the issue. It was the insurmountable task of extensive renovation that scared them off. Glad you actually like it and also appreciate the task at hand."

"I do, and I know the wife will like it, too. She's back home in Pennsylvania and needs to see it. Can't imagine she would be opposed to this as a project. It's a beauty."

"If that's the case, why not hold it with a check or deposit? We can do a purchase and sales agreement with a minimum amount down. That would at least take it off the market . . . and give you time to have your wife see it."

"Hold on, young lady," he replied. "I haven't even seen the price of this place. Can I see the listing sheet?"

"Sure, Nelson, here it is." She fumbled with the paperwork as a pen hit the floor. Bending over quickly, she almost lost one breast out of her blouse. Nelson was impressed on how she covered up the potentially embarrassing moment. He smiled as her face flushed from the almost-certain exposure. *She is attractive, but not that attractive,* he thought.

Composing herself, she continued with the tour. Structurally, Nelson saw nothing underneath the building that was a problem. The enormous supporting beams were in wonderful shape. There was no apparent dry rot, no evidence of termites, and the structure could withstand the one-hundred-mile-an-hour winds of the occasional New England hurricane or tornado. The vestibule area, the steeple, bell, and internal walls were in fantastic condition. There were no negatives that he could see during the first viewing. All of the plumbing worked and the electrical service had been recently upgraded. He was unsure of what was behind the walls, but knew that the horsehair plaster, wooden laths, and stucco were original.

"I thought that you might like it," Betty said. "You have looked at things here that other people never cared to view. You seem knowledgeable and interested in a challenge of this nature. It certainly would be lovely as a home or business."

"Yes, you're right. It is a treasure. Structures like this need to be preserved and made functional again. A home here would be very feasible, at least in my mind. We could drop walls here and there and create a wonderful living area. A bedroom in the loft would be unique."

Betty adjusted her pantsuit; the flush was gone from her face. Nelson placed his hands in the back pockets of his jeans. He stared at the cathedral ceiling and said, "Well, I see where the heat used to go! Look at those three fans up there. I assume they were needed to blow the heat back down from way up there."

"Probably right," she said. "Can't imagine that they were functional for cooling," she added with some authority. "They seem too small for that."

"You're right. They look like they were needed to force the heat back down to the congregation on Sundays."

Nelson hated to dicker over prices of houses or cars. He crossed his arms in front of his red-and-black checkered shirt, making his collar somewhat uneven. "What are we talkin' here . . . price-wise? I think I could be 'that buyer' if the price was fair."

"The asking price is $125,000," she replied. "The owners do want to move it, so a reasonable offer might work." Nelson heard her, but did not respond. He had a figure of $79,000 in his mind, but he did not share that with her.

"I can see a living room here and a bedroom or two up there. The kitchen would look good over there and the master bath next to that wall. Looks like it could be three bedrooms if needed," he continued. "One in the choir loft would be neat."

She knew he was serious since he was already visualizing an interior plan, and right there in front of her. She had "room to move" on the sales price and still make a commission. *He will need to save money on the overall purchase price if he is to do all this renovation,* she thought. She planned to work on cutting him a deal, just to move the property. His eyes continued to gaze up and down and side to side. He noted all the little nooks and crannies that he could while he was there. In his pocket was a small, seven-dollar disposable camera, which he had purchased at a Nashua store the night before. Along the way, he took photos of the entire church and sanctuary to show his wife. She could then understand what he envisioned as a project and a future home.

"Let me call my wife," he said. "I need to discuss the pricing with her anyway. You said 125K, eh?"

"Yes . . . that is the asking price on the listing," she said. "However, we can work out a deal, I'm sure. Do you have an offer in mind, I mean if this all works out?" she asked, trying not to appear too pushy.

"Not yet," he replied. "I think it probably would be less than $100,000 though. There is much to be done here, inside and out, and with today's prices, this will be costly to renovate back to its original woodwork," he added. "Why don't I hold it with a $1,000 check, and then make an offer soon? I will need to see my banker as well."

Betty was inwardly excited. "One thousand dollars down will be fine. Why don't we initiate a purchase and sales agreement, and leave the offer amount open for now? We can at least take care of the basics in advance."

"A draft P&S would be fine," he said. "I need the deposit to be refundable and conditional upon my wife's approval of the property."

"That's fine, Nelson," she said. "We are merely initiating the process to take it off the market. Can you go back to my office? I can print most of the paperwork off the computer and that will save you time."

Nelson and Betty drove to her office, a short distance from the church and close to the center of Harvest. He felt good about the property. He saw nothing that he could not repair; structurally it was sound. He was not concerned that someone else might be interested. No one of significance had looked at it since it was listed eons ago, Betty had indicated. He knew that the deposit was refundable if any portion of the deal did not go through. For now, he could relax and stop looking at other listings. Nothing could match the church.

Three

The Three Pines Inn was located about one-half mile from the center of Harvest on Route 10. It was set back off the road about seventy-five feet. The weeds and grass around the building had not yet been mowed, so the property looked unkempt, like many parts of town. The unpaved parking area was full of ruts and potholes from the recent heavy rains. Crushed gravel had been used to fill some holes in the drive. When the parking lot was dry, cars pulling up to the front left a trail of dust. The restaurant did not generate enough revenue to have the parking lot paved. It was a catch-22. If the property was more attractive and appealing from the road, it probably would have drawn a better clientele. The food wasn't really that bad and the beer was cold. However, the place was only busy on certain days, and generally after work. The lunchtime crowd was nil.

Nelson Palmer had just finished with Betty, leaving a deposit of a thousand dollars with her. In a week or so, he would bring Lydia to New Hampshire with him to take a look at the church and land. He was confident that she would like it. Feeling upbeat, he decided to celebrate the day with a beer before returning to the Nashua Hotel. Although he figured from her comments that Betty would turn him down because she clearly didn't like the place, he asked her to join him at the bar. She quickly declined saying she had to show property to another client. And, she would need to finish the paperwork on his contract. He toyed with the idea of telling her the offer he had in mind—far below the asking price—but decided to wait until after Lydia was with him. There were serious renovation expenses required and he would need the money to accomplish the tasks that he envisioned. She knew that her commission would be impacted by the lower selling price, but she had a slow month and this check would carry her for a while if the deal was completed. The unusual listing had been an albatross, and the owners of the church were tired of paying $3,000 in property taxes. She hoped to move the property and be done with it.

"Shit," Nelson mumbled, as he stepped out of his Jeep into a pothole full of water. One of his Timberland boots was now soaked to its top.

"Couldn't they have filled the damn thing in?" he muttered angrily. *Why was it not paved near the front anyway? Even a couple of strips of asphalt would make the place look better,* he thought. Once inside the building's alcove, he passed through swinging doors and faced a small bar. The décor reminded him of a finished-off basement. It had dark-stained knotty pine paneling, with a few booths along one wall and small dining tables and chairs in the remaining open area. A pool table filled the center of the room with just enough distance around it for players to shoot comfortably. It cost fifty cents a game and the coin slot only took quarters. Above the center of the pool table was an imitation stained glass, horizontal light fixture advertising a beer company—a beer they didn't even offer at The Three Pines Inn.

"Greetings," Nelson said to the young female bartender, as he stamped his wet boot.

"What can I get ya?" she replied, while wiping down the top of the wood slab bar, covered with many coats of urethane.

"What's on draft, please?"

"Well, I'll tell ya. We got Bud and Bud Light, or Michelob in a bottle. What's your pleasure?"

"I'd like a Bud, please . . . in a frosted glass if you have it." The beer selection was clearly limited, but he wanted draft beer. He decided to keep it simple. That was a wise choice, because the Bud Light tap had just gone dry and she seemed in no real hurry to change the keg downstairs.

Looking around, he saw salt and pepper shakers on each little table. They bracketed the plastic flowers in each bud vase. Only two people were in the bar besides the bartender, but it was still early in the afternoon.

"I'm Susan," she said. She was washing beer glasses in the sink.

"Nelson, here," he said, shaking her wet hand. The hot water and steam from the sink surrounded her figure with a misty halo. She was cute and in excellent shape. Over his shoulder, two young men in their twenties played nine ball. They had consumed a few beers and were arguing over who was to "break" for the next game.

"My turn," said one man defiantly.

"You 'broke' last game," the other man chided his competitor for stealing a turn the game before. The last winner was supposed to break first.

"Settle down, you two," Susan yelled from afar. "You've been here too long and can't remember nothin'. Keep up the bickering and I'll cut ya off. You've had a few too many already."

Both men were quiet as they continued to play. Nelson was impressed by her command of the room, and complimented her on her authority. He then stepped away from his stool and threw a couple of quarters in the Wurlitzer jukebox. They were all hits from the 1950s, which seemed to fit the décor. Just for fun he pressed a Platters' tune and one by Elvis. The robotic arm of the machine grabbed a record and placed the 45 on the older spinning mechanism. A needle slowly lowered and began to play the tune. Art deco lights blinked around the glass front cover.

Susan refilled his glass of draft and began to hum the song. With a smile she asked, "Passin' through here on purpose . . . or just plain lost?"

"Neither," he said, returning the smile. "I'm thinkin' of retirin' here with my wife and I was out and about today lookin' for property. . . . Sort of like the area of southern New Hampshire."

"*Here?* . . . In *Harvest?* You want to live *here?*" she said, wiping the condensation from beneath his frosted glass in front of him. "What the hell for?"

Nelson said, "Well, I think I might consider it. Found a property today that would be a fun project—renovation-wise. I like to renovate old places."

"Really," Susan teased. "A worthwhile property in this town? Where? Up in the new development north of town?"

"No, actually, I'm looking at the old church up on the hill. You know . . . the abandoned one."

"You a pastor who drinks in bars or somethin'?" she joked. "If so, *I'll* be your new parishioner. That's my kind of church!"

"Not at all," he replied. "Do I look like a man of the cloth? I'm lookin' to renovate the building into my home—a unique home. Got the idea from a friend who did that in Connecticut. He now has a beautiful spacious building that he lives in."

"Wow!" Susan replied. "Now that would be cool. That place has been for sale for the better part of two years. Price keeps dropping. Imagine it's a deal by now," she added. "The church has been there forever it seems. It's one of the original buildings left from when they founded this shit-hole town, I think. Probably had lots of weddings, christenings, and funerals inside that old place. The damn cemetery was filled up years ago. All the stones are old, but I suppose you no-ticed *that* when you viewed the property. They tell me I'm related to a family in that cemetery . . . the Rabys."

"Really? You're Raby by descent?" Nelson perked up. "You know which Raby?"

"Nah. Not really. There was a preacher here a long time ago. Think it was his side of things. Really don't know. I never traced it. Don't much care. I hate this fuckin' town anyway."

Nelson was taken aback by her bitter tone.

"You don't *really* want to live here, do ya?" she asked.

"Sure—I mean maybe. Why not? It's quaint."

"Quaint? . . . Quaint, my ass! This place is a hellhole. We nick-named it 'Nasty Town' years ago. There's a reason for that," she said, pouring herself a shot of Tequila. "Think I'll join ya, mister," she said chuggin' the shot and biting into a lime slice. "I grew up here, Nelson, my man. That is your name, right? Nelson?"

He nodded yes.

"I've been here all my life. Nothin' ta do here but drink and screw as a teenager. The town has nothin' to offer anyone—especially kids—nothing!"

Nelson laughed, "Well then. That ain't so bad. Drinkin' and screwin'!"

"Right on mista!" said a pool player. "That ain't so bad."

Susan jumped in, "Well, drinkin's OK, but there ain't no normal person to screw in the whole town," she added, snapping a wet towel in the direction of the boys around the pool table. "Certainly, you two chain saw smelling dudes wouldn't qualify." The boys went silent. "Pencil dicks, I'm sure," she whispered to Nelson, cupping one hand by the side of her mouth, making Nelson laugh with her.

Nelson could sense that there was potential for a great conversation here. He might even be enlightened about the town and the rift Susan had with the residents and their politics.

"So, doll, how do you *really feel* about this place?" he teased. "You haven't expressed your true feelings." He took a long slow sip of his beer. "Why is it so nasty?"

Susan stood directly in front of him and stared. "This town is nothin' but inbreeds and old names. I'm even an old name by heritage. At least my old name is not filled with assholes. The people here suck," she said with disdain. She looked over at the pool players who were deep in thought. One lined up a shot and the other stood like the famed painting of the *American Gothic*. He held his pool cue like the farmer with his pitchfork.

"The town officials are the old names here. They and their friends run this fuckin' town. They care little about anything here—except themselves. I'm outta here as soon as my ol' man gets a job. He's lookin' in Boston today. He's a mason and they need stone layers for the Big Dig project down there. He hopes to work for the big construction companies there, and maybe live in Bean Town. At least there would be some money comin' in and I could get a similar job in a bar down there. People down there spend money, and they drink like fish. Up here, in this hellhole, people stay in their damn houses. No socializin' in Nasty Town!"

Nelson listened intently. He hadn't picked up any of this from Betty, but then he hadn't been interested in much information about the town either when they had talked. Susan hinted that newcomers were discouraged from settling there and old names hated them. He figured that Susan had a bone to pick with a couple of the locals. Perhaps she was alluding to something that was buried under the surface of the town's outward appearance. If she was right, perhaps he should talk with some other residents as well. He would spend a couple of extra days in the area before he brought his wife back to visit the church property.

But Susan was not done with her tirade. "You move here, Nelson my man, and you will regret it." She picked up the pool players' empties that had been placed on a small table.

Nelson interjected, "Well, young lady, if it's so bad here in Nasty Town, why did you stay here all your young life? You must be all of twenty-five, and have a lot of life ahead of you."

"Twenty-five, eh? I'm only twenty-one, thank you very much," she said, hands on her hips. "See what I mean? I'm lookin' older than I am already. Twenty-five? . . . Damn, Nelson! Do I look that old? It must be the water! Friggin' town . . . nasty little shit hole."

"Nah," he said. "I apologize for the miscalculation, my dear. I'm just bad at guessin' ages. You look much younger than twenty-five," he smiled.

"You saved yourself, you handsome man," she added. "Just remember . . . I'm only twenty-one."

Embarrassed, he decided to change the subject. "This area looks nice enough. I mean the town—it looks like it has potential to an outside visitor. What needs to change? Attitudes? People? The landscape?"

"All of it, dammit," she said loudly. "Look around you! See any patrons here? Nobody comes in here since they shut down the 'cage.' Nobody!"

"The cage?" he asked with confusion. "What cage?"

"The cage that we danced in. This place was once *the* night spot in town—the only one. I made good money here . . . dancin' go-go-style for years."

"Really? You danced here? Where?"

"Used to be right over there in the corner—the stage that is. See where the antique desk is and rocker? Right over there was a stage and chicken wire protective fence around it."

"Fence?" he asked. "Why a fence?"

"Well, people would come in and get liquored up. Me and Cheryl would be dancin' to the tunes and they'd get carried away with what they tossed at us. Was supposed to be money they tossed, but some assholes threw bottles and shit when drunk. Cut my lip once. Bled like a pig. See the scar?" she said, leaning into his face. Her breasts rested on the bar.

"Jeez," he said, sympathetically, "they threw bottles at you? I can't believe that."

"Believe it! This scar is proof that they were pretty rambunctious here. The money was good though. I'd clear two or three hundred bucks in a night from tips. A bit different today—money-wise. I mean with *your* tip, I might make fifteen dollars today. We get minimum wage, so you figure it out. It's not a huge day for me."

"Sorry 'bout that," he said to her. "Sounds like someone in town took away your sole income."

"Yeah, the assholes at town hall did it. The selectmen voted the entertainment license out. Practically shut down the inn for good. We can't make it here on burgers and beer. By the way . . . did you want to eat? I never asked you. Sorry."

"Nah. Just havin' a beer or two and headin' to the hotel. But thanks."

"If you eat, I'd get a bigger tip," she smiled, wondering about the good-looking stranger. She liked his quiet, somewhat humble manner.

Nelson was enthralled with the young woman. She deserved better than to be pushin' beer and watchin' two guys playin' pool all night. That was no life.

"Someday, someone will straighten this place out," she mumbled. "Need some new blood around here. We need to get rid of some of the putzes that have controlled this town for years. I'll be movin' on, so I don't give a shit anymore. By the way, want another brew? It's on me, Nelson."

"Sure, I'll have one more, thanks. That's nice of you," he replied with a smile. "I really hope things work out for you. I mean in Boston. Hope your friend has luck in finding a job. 'Scuse me a second."

Nelson went over to the pool table and placed two quarters on the rail. It was a way of tellin' the boys, whose eyes were glazed over from beer, that he wanted to play the winner of the current match. He wanted more local culture and needed to converse with the pool players, identified by Susan as loggers, who had been there for hours. Nelson had played the game well in his youth, and in the service, often winning money for beer and cigarettes. When his turn came, he grabbed a cue and rolled it on its side. It rolled true across the felt. He grabbed a blue chalk cube on the rail of the old Brunswick table and racked the balls. He managed to lose a few games to the townies, and on purpose. He then let loose, and cleaned the house for seven straight games, playing with a vengeance. Susan cheered every time he won, and brought him more beers. The two locals were stupefied at Nelson's shots. He made it look like it was just good luck, but obviously had not lost his touch.

After two hours, he was up two hundred dollars and decided to head back to the hotel. The loggers were pissed; they wanted to try and win back some of their losses. As Nelson gave Susan a hug, he palmed her five twenty-dollar bills and kissed her hand. She was shocked at his generosity and hugged him back. "No dance required," he said smiling, "and no wire cage!" With that, she smiled back at Nelson.

"You look like a good kid. Sorry for your tough luck lately. It will surely get better—here, or in Boston. If you don't move, let me know. I may need help with the church. You know . . . general maintenance, yard work and cleaning. My wife and I could use some help up on the hill if we buy the place. Lots for us to do. Might even need a mason to repair the walls and foundation. So keep us in mind. Give me a month."

"See you again, Nelson, and thank you. You are a sweet man." He made her night. "Nelson . . . what is your last name?" she asked hurriedly.

"OK, hon, the last name is Palmer, Nelson Palmer, and I just might be your new neighbor."

"Don't forget to tip the young lady," he said to the boys. "She's strugglin' to survive." He then quickly and casually saluted them with

31

his index finger and headed for his car. He left them arguing over who had lost most of the games, and their money. Each one blamed the other for their misfortune. When they finally realized that they had been hustled, it was too late.

Outside, Nelson folded the rest of the bills and put the wad in his pocket. He drove up Route 10 and then east toward Nashua. It was dusk now and he was laughing at the enlightening, entertaining, and profitable afternoon.

Susan would not end up in Boston and her boyfriend never secured the job he applied for that day.

Four

Like most tourists who passed through Harvest, Nelson's initial impression was that it was charming, with its Victorian homes near the center of town, brick mills along the river, and mountainous countryside. The antique stores attracted tourists hoping to locate something special relating to the area. The church steeples, white picket fences, old stone walls, and country graveyards, including family plots on farms, were classic New England.

Harvest was a small community surrounded by larger towns within a twenty-mile radius. To the south was a northernmost town in Massachusetts, and forty miles to the west, Vermont. Because of its proximity, residents from the Commonwealth of Massachusetts came north on weekends to buy booze, cigarettes, and lottery tickets. They took advantage of the lower prices in New Hampshire because there was no sales tax.

The surrounding countryside offered many recreational opportunities due to its mountains, lakes, and ponds. The topography was similar to neighboring Vermont. Geologically, there were differences. Vermont favored the marble industry and New Hampshire, granite. The mountain ranges, from the Green to the White, looked connected.

Many mountains north of Concord, New Hampshire, were protected as part of the national forest. The White Mountain range continued north to Mount Washington, the highest elevation in the state, towering at over 6,000 feet. Portions of the range contained state- and county-run ski areas. They were limited to selected areas and did not abuse the integrity of the mountain range. Ski areas and summer resorts generated income for the state and drew large numbers of tourists in the summer and winter. The foliage in September and October drew thousands of "leaf-peepers," as they were affectionately called. The leaves changed throughout the state beginning from the top of the state down to Nashua in the south. The leaves of maples, poplar, birch, oaks, and sumac became brilliant reds, oranges, yellows, and fuchsia in the southern portion of the state, usually by the third week of October. Foliage was known to change as late as early November in the lakes region.

Located west of Nashua and in Keene and Jaffrey, the foothills included a portion of Harvest, New Hampshire. The peaks were only 300–400 feet tall, but were the beginnings of the White Mountain range. Below each peak were numerous lakes that dotted the landscape. The lakes were spawned by glaciers many years ago, and maintained by mountain runoff and melting snow pack in the spring or from natural springs and streams that fed them. Church steeples and quaint towns surrounded many of the lakes and their economy depended on the waterways for both industry and recreation. The landscape was one reason for the onslaught of tourists each year. It offered an escape from the bustle of Boston, New York, New Jersey, Pennsylvania, and Connecticut.

Harvest residents enjoyed looking at Mt. Massapot, which overlooked the village and a local lake. On the west side of Massapot Mountain was a view of Massapot Lake. Most New Hampshire lakes were Native-American names, translated into English descriptions of beautiful views and earthly features. There were others to the north— Winnipesaukee, Winnisquam, and Opechee.

Counting the occasional restaurant and antique shops, barber and secondhand bookstore, Harvest had a small town center. Besides the town hall and village store, there were a fire station, rescue squad and a gas station. An historic water trough graced the town center, but no longer contained water for horses. The horse-and-carriage days were long gone. In the spring and summer, geraniums, marigolds and zinnias were planted in the old circular trough, an elaborate pedestal of cast-iron. History was evident, but shopping was limited.

What was not evident to the casual eye, however, was the unfriendly nature of those who controlled the town. For years, Harvest had been a hotbed of issues. The "old names," as others called them, retained control of the board of selectmen, plus various clerk positions in city hall, despite the influx of newcomers. The old names used their power to make decisions about construction, development of industry, and environmental issues. Though it seemed difficult to prove, the officials seemed to be in cahoots behind closed doors.

Old names tried through every means, such as permitting and zoning, to discourage the approval of services and occupations that new residents might try to open in direct competition with themselves or established families. They chastised the potential development and competition through editorials in the local "rag" newspaper, owned, not surprisingly, by an old name. The paper contended that the old-timers had served the community for more than one hundred years—that the community needed to appreciate their tenure, not drive them into obscurity. Newer residents found their occupations to be encouraged or tolerated only if they planned to establish something other than what other longtime residents offered. With the negative attitude of its powerful citizenry, Harvest had not been able to retain a doctor or dentist, or other intellectuals.

The town was heavily Republican and ultraconservative. It often lacked foresight and vision. Myopic old names tended to see the town as their own private world and had no desire for change. Happiness was a cold beer, a snowmobile, and a Ford pickup. They preferred a gravel pit operation to a protected wetland. If you owned the land, they thought it was basically yours to do whatever you wanted to with it. Dobermans and German shepherds were the dogs of choice, and often seen riding in the back of a pickup, barking at the people as they passed. To knowledgable outsiders, Harvest was an embarrassing place of fools and belligerent codgers.

Harvest, small and inbred for many years, was chilly toward those who were not natives. Its people had a longtime reputation for unfriendliness, beyond the reserved, and often misunderstood, nature of many New Englanders. Old names who dominated the community affairs, were adverse to growth beyond their self-imposed magic number of 3,000 residents; the population was already at 2,500 and growing. With the increased number of residents came added expenses to pay for new schools or expansion of existing services. This did not set well with the old names who did not want to have their taxes increased to pay for the unwanted outsiders.

New residents also brought fancy ideas with them—talking about how things were done elsewhere and arguing for improvements they felt were necessary to improve Harvest. Their ideas were clearly costly and immediately resisted by the old-timers in the longtime blue-collar community. It took about two months for newcomers to figure out the deeply ingrained politics of the town. Sometimes they noticed it early on, if they had unpleasant dealings at town hall with clerks. The attitude of the public servants was awful at best. It was even a hassle to reregister a car. Town officials acted as if they were doing you a favor by issuing a license for a dog. Even the town hall's hours of operation were inconvenient. The hours changed arbitrarily so residents could not get basic registrations completed without taking time off from work. For some residents, it was easier to go to the state capital of Concord for similar needs—and often it was quicker.

Nelson was aware of the fast-pace of the Nashua area, and some communities east of Harvest, which were more like Massachusetts. His longtime friend, Ed Hammond, had urged him to consider moving to northern New Hampshire where life moved at an easy pace. But Nelson needed to better understand what life was once like in the old days—the time Aunt Bess was referring to. Two hundred years earlier, New Hampshire might also have served as a slower-paced getaway for the people of Boston.

The mountain that shadowed Massapot Lake had once contained a small, privately owned ski area. It operated in the 1940s and 1950s and was a boon to the locals who did not want to travel to the north to ski. Many children learned to ski on that mountain. It offered a rope tow and J-bar for access to the top but it was a good practice slope for the locals. Its downfall was that its slopes faced south. The sun beat down on the five or six slopes and resulted in massive natural snow loss during the day. The rising sun from the east bathed the slopes until the sun set. Attempts to add snowmaking equipment were not lucrative. Eventually the ski area fell prey to economics and closed in the late 1970s. It was another blow to the Harvest community that had again lost something for the kids to do for recreation. Eventually, it became reduced to a hill for winter sledding and snow tubes.

Access to the mountaintop was by two routes, and those were basically dirt fire roads that were poorly maintained. They were overgrown with small bushes and trees, but were somewhat accessible by four-wheel vehicles, large and small. Kids took Jeeps to the top to "make out" or used the trails for ATVs in the summer and snowmobiles in the winter. Litter often marked the mountaintop. Beer cans, condoms, and cigarette butts were the remnants of their summer and winter escapades. Dirt bikes created ruts from their frequent use and caused minor erosion of the landscape, thereby threatening the stability of decades old white pines and birch trees. The runoff from rain and snow followed their path of carelessness and formed areas of extreme topsoil loss, creating rugged, but temporary creeks. Grass rarely grew where the kids went with their motorized mayhem. Ground cover had little time to recover or to establish root systems for renewed growth.

Harvest, New Hampshire, being located close to the northern Massachusetts border, had the "Mass-hole" attitude—a term that the Bay State residents disdained. Many lived in Harvest for the easy commute to jobs in Boston or to Routes 128/95—an industrial park beltway around Bean Town. The advantage was to avoid Massachusetts state taxes but still be able to work there. The Bay State taxed employees from New Hampshire, but it was refundable at the end of the year because they were nonresidents.

Those passing through quaint, little Harvest often said that the town reminded them of something out of *Yankee* magazine, but that was not the case. The famed publication would find little of interest about Harvest. Its historical buildings were limited and the *au natural* cosmetics of the town defied photography. It would be a stretch for the magazine to find something worthy of a feature, even though the publication office was only thirty miles away in nearby Dublin.

Tourists always noticed the churches, cemeteries, Victorian homes, and scenic lake. An occasional fruit or vegetable stand enticed them to buy blueberries, strawberries, or corn. In the fall, those stands changed their produce to pumpkins, squash, and ornamental corn. Newcomers knew otherwise. Underneath the facade was the stranglehold of the old names on the town. Trust was not a virtue in Harvest. Old names trusted no one new. They felt that they owned the town, by inheritance.

If author Grace Metalious had lived in Harvest, instead of Gilmanton, seventy miles to the north, she probably would have named her novel *Harvest Place* not *Peyton Place*. Her fictional account of small town life was equally applicable to Harvest.

Five

Darren Gooden had been Harvest's police chief for three years, and was considered a newcomer still. He and his staff of five officers and two part-timers covered the town. Chief Gooden, himself, was well trained and encouraged his staff to advance their training on a yearly basis. It didn't take long for him to clash with the town board. The selectmen often fought increases in his budget, even when justified. The antidrug program, DARE, was under-funded and often relied on special community events, such as fairs and rummage sales, to keep it operational. Even with those fund-raisers, it operated on a shoestring budget. The selectmen had refused to fund requests for new police cars or ancillary electronic equipment. They basically felt that there was sufficient equipment and police staff for the tiny town, and that increased funding was unnecessary. By the same token, the fire department often received its full budget requests. Old names controlled the fire department organizational structure and majority of staff. The police, on the other hand, had stepped on toes by arresting old name juveniles who were causing trouble.

"Why the need for all these expenses?" a resident had commented at a recent town meeting. "Towns bigger than ours have lesser police budgets."

Chief Gooden responded, "We have received many more 911 calls this year and the town residents are far more spread out now. It takes more manpower and more vehicles to cover the same area, especially on the outskirts. Without these budget increases, we cannot guarantee adequate police coverage for all areas. In times of multiple responses, like accidents and robbery attempts, we need to fund these occurrences. I have tried to outline the budget by line items. Not one item is unjustified," he emphasized, as diplomatically as he could.

"You had a substantial increase last year. Can't you live with that?" a resident asked, with an edgy tone in his voice. "Why are there more budgetary needs this year?"

Gooden was composed and firm in his assessment of needs. "Yes, you funded the needs of last year, but that was for additional officers and a new police car. Those needs were long overdue and the funding merely got us by last year. We need additional video equipment to reinforce our violation records in court cases. It also allows us a safety net when we pull someone over. The recording of road incidents is necessary on VHS, whether they are violations or accidents. It provides us with valuable data on suspects that may leave the scene of the infraction or accident. These may seem like minor or incidental expenses or unnecessary costs to the selectmen's committee, but they have a major impact in the court hearings of alleged perpetrators," he said.

The selectmen remained adamant about not spending money. They were unsympathetic to many of the chief's requests. They thought that the chief's thinking was "out of the box" or too extreme.

But Chief Gooden continued, "Just last week, we stopped someone in front of the sawmill down on Route 10. It turned out that he was wanted for numerous violations in Massachusetts. A video recording of the New Hampshire violation and the car's license plate would have supported the Massachusetts State Police's case and the Harvest police apprehension of the suspect across our border. Each police car needs the new device, just like our firemen need their infrared equipment to find victims in smoke-filled, burning buildings. They are professional tools of the trade in the modern criminal justice system. Surrounding towns have this equipment. Why not us?"

"Perhaps next year," the chairman of the committee suggested to the chief. "This year's budget is tight and the little league field needs new grandstands. The parents and grandparents have been complaining that they have to bring their own chairs or sit on the grass."

A second dissenting member of the committee concurred. "We need to take care of local issues, not be concerned with helping Massachusetts police apprehend their own criminals just because they crossed our state line."

Chief Gooden was perturbed but remained calm. He could not understand their reasoning or narrow-minded thinking in the twenty-first century. He had no choice but to accept the budget reduction, but was allowed to hire a new part-timer.

Gooden knew the politics of the town selectmen well. He knew that he only had one supporter on the committee, but that was OK. She was intelligent, sensible, and not part of the older local names that so often thought they were the "cat's butt" in town. Unfortunately, she was usually outvoted.

Gooden knew this was payback. He was aware that some council members had children that were often in trouble with the police—misdemeanors and vandalism charges. Gooden's officers had apprehended many of them in the past—mostly for their own good. They were often simple offenses that they had violated. Disturbing the peace or underage drinking issues were common. Kids bought beer with fake IDs or were caught speeding in their vehicles. Tuesday night was cruise night in town. Kids would drive around all night in their cars, yet very few owned the older models that were typical of traditional cruise nights back in the 1950s. The teenagers tended to "peel out" or burn rubber at intersections. Gooden knew that that was not a major issue, but he and his staff had apprehended many of the teenagers in the past. The police often let them go with a warning. Repeat offenders were cited with tickets and had to pay small fines. That embarrassed the board members. One of the committee members had his son "tagged" by the police the previous week. Those children often thought they could get away with anything, since their parents were prominent members of the board of selectmen in town. Gooden viewed the kids' infractions as a safety issue and hazardous to their own health and well-being. He was protecting the community and them by apprehending the repeat violators.

He knew his budget reduction was a reflection of the selectmen's disdain for the police force. But, Gooden was only doing what was correct for all residents—enforcing the local laws. He was convinced that the teenager incidents often kept the police from responding to more serious emergencies.

✠✠✠

Sixteen-year-old Leah Bailey sat at the kitchen table. Depressed, she hung her head low and moved her fork around her plate in a figure-eight fashion. She held one hand to her cheek, as if to prop her head up. Her father, sitting across from her, took a long sip from his bottle of Budweiser. He finally spoke with his voice raised, "Take your damn hand off your cheek, will ya? Eat what's in front of you!" His fist hit the table, causing the dishes to move.

Startled, Leah jumped at her father's angry words. Her mother, afraid of her old man, was equally on edge. His temper was quick and he had used his beefy hands to slap Leah around on more than one occasion, and belittled and taunted her. More than once she had gone to school with bruises. Her mother had a history of black eyes. Both of them tried to use makeup to cover up the effects of frequent battery. Although Leah's mother hated to see her daughter abused, she was too afraid of Clement to try to escape him. Mother and daughter knew he would find them, and they would pay the consequences.

Tears rolled down Leah's cheeks. She said quietly, "I'm not hungry, Daddy. I'm really not."

"Eat, dammit!" he shouted. The kitchen windows were open and his voice could be heard out in the street. More than once the neighbors had complained to the police about his hollering and officers responded to the Bailey home.

While Leah and her mother, Elizabeth, kept their problems to themselves, many people in town knew that Clement Bailey had a history of getting liquored up and taking it out on his family. In fact, he had lost a number of jobs because of his drinking problem. Employed in construction, he operated heavy machinery and, therefore, was a liability to himself and to others when he abused alcohol and then went to work. Today was no different—it was a common occurrence. He had just been let go from the Smythe's Sawmill that afternoon, and had been drinking from the moment that he arrived home.

He had not told his wife or daughter that he had been canned. They just knew that he was drunk again.

"Eat!" he repeated.

Leah sat quietly and then spoke, with pain in her voice. "Daddy, I can't eat . . . I need to say something that you will not like."

Swallowing hard and sobbing, she whispered softly, "I' . . . m pregnant . . . I' . . . m pregnant with Tommy's baby."

"What?" Clement shouted with fury. "What the hell did you say? You're . . . what?" He slammed down his knife and fork onto the table and stood up.

"Mom knows," she said louder, looking directly at the three-hundred-pound man towering over her.

Clement stood still, his large gut bumping the edge of the table. Then, before she could move, like lightning, the back of his hand hit the side of her face and knocked her to the floor. The young woman bled profusely from her lips and blood spattered the gray tile floor. Elizabeth screamed and went to the defense of her daughter. "Clement! Stop! . . . Stop right now! Please!" she pleaded in vain. Clement, by Leah's side, kicked her. The girl screamed in pain as she covered her face, leaving her torso vulnerable. She curled into a fetal position.

"You fucking whore!" he yelled. "Get out of your grandfather's house and my house! You tramp!"

He kicked her in the lower back with his heavy work shoe, as she screamed, trying to escape his blows. Calmly, the small-framed Elizabeth Bailey turned to the nearby drawer and removed a nine-inch knife from the plastic divider tray for utensils. She turned, and with all her might planted the sharp serrated bread knife between the broad shoulder blades of Clement's back. It glided between his ribs, propelled by her adrenaline and terror. As if nothing had happened, he turned slowly and stared at her with an enraged, reddened face, wide-eyed and oddly expressionless. Then, grimacing from pain, and blinking repeatedly, he raised his hand as if to hit Elizabeth, only to have his face pale and his eyes roll back. His massive body, and sweat-infused muscle shirt, drenched with bright crimson, crashed against the table, knocking the dinner plates and glassware onto the floor. Clement fell forward as he rolled off the broken table and onto the floor. The faded wooden knife handle prevented him from lying directly on his back. He was dead from the puncture of his aorta and left lung. He was dead before his enormous body hit the kitchen floor.

"Mother! Daddy!" Leah screamed. "Mother! . . . Mommy!"

Elizabeth stood silently, covering her face with her hands. Her head was bowed, eyes closed, and her housedress, feet, and open-toed sandals, stained with Clement's blood. Realizing what she had done in defense of her daughter, she slowly knelt beside Leah, her only child, hugging her tenderly.

"You will no longer have pain," she whispered into sweet Leah's ear, pushing back the girl's silken blonde hair. She cradled her daughter as they sobbed together. "We will never have his hand on our bodies again—yours or mine," said Elizabeth. It was beginning to dawn on her that seventeen years of abuse had ended. Clement had never wanted children and had started the mental and physical cruelty of Elizabeth after hearing that she was pregnant with his child. One episode threatened the pregnancy with baby Leah. His response to the news of Leah's pregnancy was a reminder of that fact. Elizabeth realized that she had reacted, not only to her daughter's beating but as if she were once again being attacked years earlier.

Elizabeth knew she had to call 911. In the distance, a siren was soon heard. She knew the consequences, but she had to tell what had happened. The police would need to know it was self-defense and not murder.

In shock and pain, Leah waited for the police in a faded wing chair. She could see her father's feet through the doorway. One shoe had fallen off. She grabbed her stomach tightly with both hands and wept. She had always tried to please her father, even though he had been unresponsive to her loving gestures. Now he was dead in the kitchen and her mother was sitting silently in a straight-back chair next to his still body.

Chief Gooden arrived at the Bailey home at the same time as did the rescue squad. He had received the message by page, while attending the evening's selectmen's meeting. His night of extensive interrogation and paperwork relevant to the death was just beginning and the coroner would be summoned. He knew Elizabeth and Leah well and was very familiar with the family situation. His first duty now was to help and console the two frightened woman.

Chief Gooden had responded previously to five other incidents in the home and knew that, with Clement's death, the brutality was finally over. He told Elizabeth that she would need legal counsel to represent and defend herself, because there would likely be a trial or court hearing. She knew it would be a long and painful process. She worried about the lasting effects on her daughter.

Once the coroner arrived, Gooden took the women to the police station to secure more details of the event. He also wanted to remove them from the scene and the gawking congregation of neighbors outside. Many had heard of the event over their personal home scanners. The electronic monitors of fire and rescue events were their apparent entertainment. Not surprisingly, the town had its ambulance chasers.

An hour after the coroner arrived, the body bag was removed. An autopsy by the state medical examiner confirmed the cause of death—a severed aorta, resulting in immediate shock and a massive loss of blood. Clement would be buried in the local cemetery where fifteen or twenty of his coworkers and drinking buddies would attend his funeral and mourn his loss. Elizabeth, whose action had been ruled self-defense, and Leah eventually moved from Harvest. The Bailey home was listed for sale and was unoccupied for a while. No one wanted to own the house of death. Later it was purchased by an unknown, wealthy, and local man. He ended up razing the building because he didn't want "the history" of the home near the town to be a focal point for tourists. The land, near the center of town, was more valuable as an investment.

Six

On Wednesday nights, the Harvest town hall was abuzz with residents who bitched about everything and every expenditure during the weekly town meeting. They wanted services, but without tax increases. This night they were particularity riled up about skyrocketing taxes to pay for roads, parks, sidewalks, and sewers, thanks to an influx of families with young children.

"Order in this room!" demanded the chairperson of the board of selectmen. "We will have parliamentary procedures in this room. You residents are invited to these meetings with the understanding that there is an agenda. The agenda allows for your comments during specific times, and not at random."

Catcalls were heard in the back of the room but the chairperson continued.

"This kind of behavior will not be tolerated," said Thomas Shaw, the town manager. The recent town budget discussions had been filled with dissention, and he'd been asked to help quiet things down.

"You need to wait for the specific agenda item before you can comment," he said sternly. "Keep it down or you'll be asked to leave."

"We are only on agenda item one," added the chairperson from the center seat at the head table. "We are discussing the repainting of the town hall by a restoration company at present. The bond issue is a separate item—number three."

The folding chairs, where the town residents were seated, faced the head table and were set up as three rows of ten. Many of the locals who attended the weekly meetings were regulars. Depending on the issues, their numbers ranged from four to twenty. Tonight, there were at least fifteen people sitting in the gallery.

"Then, change the agenda," yelled a resident from the back of the room. "We can't afford all this new stuff. Our taxes are already too high. In fact, my own property taxes have nearly doubled in four years, and we don't use the sidewalks, or parks, or new roads. Make the newcomers pay for their own growth. Tax them special!"

"Yeah," piped up another.

"If you continue to interrupt like this," the chairperson said, "you'll have to go."

"Horseshit," someone said in a sneeze-like fashion. The fake sneeze was easily heard over and above the snickers in the back row.

The meeting was attended by a mix of blue-collar and white-collar residents. Their dress varied from suits to jeans, as some people came directly from their jobs. Most of the shouted comments and cat-calls came from two men in the back row. They had come directly from their employment at Timber New Hampshire—a local professional tree and landscape service.

The town meeting had only been in session fifteen minutes when the loud foghorn sound of the fire department whistle summoned the volunteer fire force. It repeated itself with three quick, long bursts. Two of the four windows had been opened for ventilation and the echo of the horn reverberated off the interior walls. The fire station's close proximity to the town hall made the blasts seem like it was in the selectmen's meeting room. The same two men who had been disruptive ran for the door, and a member of the selectmen also joined them. They were members of the fire squad.

The first of the fire trucks, led by a police car with flashing blue lights, left the firehouse and headed down South Main Street. Two more fire trucks were quick to follow as volunteer firefighters arrived at the fire station. Their cars and pickups were outfitted with portable red flashing lights, powered by the electrical jacks of their cigarette lighters. The strobe flashes of brilliant red light reflected off the white Victorian and Cape Cod-style homes and picket fences across from the town hall.

"What's happened?" asked a selectman, who stood by the window of the meeting room. "All the trucks are out. Must be a large fire, for sure."

A resident in the back had a handheld scanner. "It's the Thornton homestead on South Main," he advised with concern. "Appears that the barn and house are ablaze. Looks like old man Thornton was able to get out. He's reportedly safe and sound."

"That's good," remarked another selectman. "He's my neighbor. I suggest we table the agenda until next week, adjourn, and see if we can be of assistance."

As the meeting was quickly adjourned, the selectmen grabbed their documents and briefcases, and headed out of the hall. Additional fire trucks from surrounding towns arrived to provide mutual aid to the Harvest Fire Department. Mack and American-LaFrance pumpers and a ladder truck from nearby villages and towns screamed by.

The Thornton homestead was one of the few older homes in the town center. Old man Thornton, eighty-one, was a widower. His home was his life. The fire in the central structure and attached barn raged out of control. Old beams and years of paint on the clapboards fueled the inferno. Nothing could be saved, and by morning, the historic homestead was reduced to rubble.

Mr. Thornton would have no desire to see the building renovated or restored. He stood in the reflection of the flames with a blanket over his shoulders. He held in his wrinkled hands, that shook from Parkinson's disease, the photo of his wife on their wedding day, some six decades earlier. His tears of despair were dried quickly by the heat of the fire. Local residents tried to console him as best they could and one elderly neighbor put her arm around his shoulder. He was offered refuge with another neighbor until his daughter could be contacted to assist him. She lived in Missouri and she would need to come quickly to New Hampshire to help her ailing father.

Above the town and Thornton house inferno stood the church and cemetery that Nelson Palmer would purchase. From that vantage point, one could see the flickering orange light of the blaze in the night as flames reached the sky and the center of town was illuminated by firelight.

The surrounding neighborhood was a mixture of Victorians, Cape Cods and split-level homes. In time, the charred remains would be leveled and removed. The land would be sold at auction to a local man and Mr. Thornton would eventually move to Missouri. Paint thinner and rags were thought to have been in a corner of the barn, and adjacent to the main house. Spontaneous combustion of the solvent in the barn would be cited as the cause of the fire.

✠✠✠

It didn't take Lydia Palmer very long to agree with Nelson about his plans for the church once she saw it. As she had done throughout their marriage, she continually supported his dreams, and remained the woman of his dreams. Like Nelson, she dressed "smart casual," except when gardening, when she preferred her faded, worn-in-the-knees jeans. She had watched her weight, remaining, at five-feet-ten, willowy like her daughters. Her skin, without Botox or surgery, was creamy and without signs of wrinkles, except for the crinkles at the corners of her green eyes. Nelson loved to photograph her in color and even black and white as light played on her luxurious hair pulled up in a twist when she took off her straw gardening hat. She adored him, and always smiled when she saw the way other women looked at him. Nelson had never given her cause to doubt his faithfulness, despite his travels.

Betty Morrissey, the Realtor, had indicated that the owners of the church had accepted Nelson's offer for a lower price. It was far less than the owners had wanted, but they were glad to have the albatross off their backs. The taxes had made the sale virtually worthless to them and they lost money on the deal. It was the lesser of two evils to unload it. The real estate agent would get a commission and was happy. The closing on the home was in a week and Nelson and his wife moved quietly into the structure two weeks later. They lived there in a simple fashion and planned to renovate as needed. Functional basic services were their priority. Studded walls and finish carpentry would come later.

Nelson kept his promise to Susan, the bartender and her boyfriend. They did not move to Boston and Susan quit her bartending and restaurant job. Nelson hired both Susan and her friend to assist in the renovation, which included cleaning and landscaping. He and his wife practically adopted the two young assistants.

✠✠✠

Diagonally across from the Harvest town hall, and about three hundred yards east, was the Harvest Village Store. Clement Bailey had often picked up his beer there. The discussion of his death filled the store the next morning, and continued to be the topic of the month.

The village store, especially busy before and after work, was considered the center of town. People often stopped by to get coffee and donuts in the morning, ice cream for their children after school, or bread or milk for the week. Local industrial workers bought beer and snacks during lunch and after work. The small deli in the back of the building was part of the store and sold pre-made submarine sandwiches and salads. Cigarettes were a popular item as well. Like any small New England store, it carried the various staples of a household. One aisle displayed dog food, motor oil, and shoe polish, while the adjoining aisles offered ketchup, mustard, and other condiments. One could have keys made there as well, or buy batteries, garden gloves, or wine and champagne. There was no organization to where the items were placed.

Alvin Parker owned the establishment; it had been in his family for decades. He hired local high school students for summer help and they stocked the shelves and ran the cash register. Today, Parker seemed nervous and was busy occupying his time with nonsensical chores while pacing up and down the aisles. He checked and rechecked items on the shelves. His heart was racing. He was seventy-five, and stress and excitement was not something he was used to at his age or in his type of work. He reminded the new stock boy of chores. "Stock the soup please, son. Here's the box. Please put the cans in aisle one . . . over there. If you finish with the Campbell's, I need you to load soda in the cooler. The Coke man just left and most of the cases are still on the loading ramp. Bring 'em in. OK?"

The kid said politely, "Yes, sir, Mr. Parker. I'll get right to it." He went about the task of loading the shelves when two regular customers entered the store for cigarettes and snacks. Parker said little to the men. They noticed that he wasn't his usual self.

"Marlboro, please . . . soft pack," one said. The other man ordered three lottery tickets. Mr. Parker rang up the sale and the men left. One had purchased a deli sandwich, a soft drink, and beef jerky.

From behind the aisle came the young boy's voice. "Mr. Parker. Did you see the news? This morning's news? Someone won the Lotto game last night. Somebody in New Hampshire won the $175,000,000 big game! They were the sole winners. Can you imagine? All that money? Holy crap!"

"I heard about it, son," Alvin Parker said nervously and with some interest, trying not to show emotion. He was well aware of the winner because the ticket had been purchased in his store. He was still shaking from the phone call that he had received earlier, but he was not ready to tell the kid about it. He wanted to be sure that the lottery commission confirmed the sale of the ticket in *his* little store, before he broadcast the news. Parker was ecstatic that he would get a percentage of the "take," if it were true. The commission representative was on his way to validate the store's machine. He would arrive from the New Hampshire capital of Concord within the hour. Then Alvin Parker could tell the stock boy, and the entire town. He and his store would surely be featured in the area newspapers and on TV.

"You done over there yet?" Parker asked. The boy nodded yes and proceeded to move the cases of Coca-Cola into the store.

✠✠✠

Nelson's friend, Dr. Ed Hammond, lived in the northern part of the state. Ed was a chemist at AgriChem, Inc., a northern New Hampshire company that manufactured and distributed pesticides, herbicides, and rodenticides. Ed was the founder and production supervisor for the company's organophosphate division. The organophosphates were active ingredients in insecticides marketed by major players in the industry. Ed knew the chemical industry well and had worked for a North Carolina agrichemical company for many years. In recent years, he established a smaller New Hampshire company and the stress level of working for big business was subsequently reduced in his life. His job allowed him to be active in environmental issues, and he was called to be an expert witness in many litigation cases involving industrial pesticides and their residual contamination in water and soil.

Ed and Nelson shared a love of fishing. Ed had vacationed in New Hampshire before changing jobs, so he was aware of the best fishing spots in the state.

Nelson called his former colleague. "Hey, Ed, how are you? Looks like I may be your neighbor now. We've just moved to southern New Hampshire. I bought a church."

"What? Good to hear from you, Nel," replied Ed. "You're here in the Granite State? Awesome! We can finally do some serious fishin', my friend. But what's with the church? Are you takin' up religion in your retired life?"

"Hell no, man," Nelson replied. "We decided to restore a church into a home . . . sort of a retirement project. You know, fun stuff!"

"What town did you decide on?" asked Ed.

"We wanted to have close proximity to Boston, yet still be in this no-tax state. So we are south of you and not too far from Nashua. My aunt Bess said I have 'roots' in this state. Thought it would be fun to find them."

"So, what town do you have your roots in?" Ed asked again. "Do you live down there in one of those snotty little towns with all the white picket fences? You know, the perfect little communities that even tell you what color lights you can put in your window at Christmastime?"

"Nah, hardly, Ed," replied Nelson. "They probably don't celebrate Christmas in this town. They gave up on that tradition years ago," he joked. "It's called Harvest. Heard of it?"

Ed said, "Heard of it! Hell! That's a happenin' town. They're in the paper weekly. They always have some political issue in town. At least, I think that's the town."

"Could be," said Nelson. "The townsfolk scrap a lot. Kind of feisty politics, I hear, from some of the locals. I'm too new here to know the ropes yet."

"I think they have had many issues there, as I recall. Should make for interestin' livin' there," said Ed.

"Look. I just wanted to say hi for now. Much to do, but wanted to touch base. I need to get settled into the new digs, and once I do, we can hook up. By the way, there's a lake in town here and we can do some serious fishin'," added Nelson.

"Yes, that would be great, my friend. What lake is that? Moosehead, Silver Lake or Massapot?"

"Massapot—it's right here, and three minutes away. It's loaded with bass they say," Nelson bragged.

"Hell, that lake has *the* record for largemouth bass. Think it was in the 1960s that someone caught a largemouth, about ten pounds. Still the state record, I think."

Really?" asked Nelson.

Ed said, "Think it was a ten-pound, eight-ounce fish. Some guy named Bullpitt caught it in 1967 . . . Yeah, that's right . . . 1967. I'm sure!"

"Don't know, Ed. Could be, but that's small compared to what we two might catch!" Nelson joked.

"Call me after you and the wife are settled," Ed said with a laugh. "How is the little lady? Lydia still puttin' up with the cranky old man?"

"She's well, Ed. No more episodes for her lately. Heart seems stronger than ever. She sure is a trooper, puttin' up with this guy for all those years," Nelson said lovingly.

"Good to hear . . . please say hello to her, and hope to see you soon. Good luck in that feisty little town. Can't wait to have a beer in your new home. We'll celebrate your retirement and the new abode, my friend."

"Thanks," Nelson said with appreciation. "We'll be in touch soon."

Why would Ed Hammond know so much about Harvest? Nelson later wondered. He was perplexed. *Ed lived far to the north in the White Mountains. One would think that news of a southern New Hampshire town's activities was rare for those northern residents.*

Ed was pleased that Nelson had touched base with him. He had heard nasty things about the town of Harvest, but was not going to burst Nelson's bubble. After all, the guy had just moved there and was hardly settled in. Ed had "read" the town of Harvest accurately. All that he had read of the infamous community in the past was, in fact, real. It was a town loaded with turmoil and rapid growth, and change that it didn't know how to handle.

Seven

The countryside of southern New Hampshire offered many recreational activities and scenic, panoramic views. Tourists flocked to the area in the summer and winter. The entire state was riddled with lakes and ponds. Some ponds were actually spring-fed, defunct granite quarries that remained cold during the hottest summer days. Children often swam in the dangerous pools. Diving was even more risky, since granite walls of old mines concealed jagged formations in the deep, dark water. Swimmers could conceivably dive too deep and hit their heads.

Nelson read voraciously about the state of New Hampshire in general. He was well aware of the beautiful White Mountains to the north, with much of that land protected as national forest, but accessible to hikers and skiers and summer vacationers.

"Honey," he said, soon after they purchased the church, "we'll have to check out the north country. There are many inns and B&Bs there. These tourists' pamphlets I've collected show gorgeous waterfalls and flumes we can hike to. New Hampshire is basically uninhabited above the middle of the state—only 1.1 million people total, in the entire state! Imagine that!"

Lydia was cordially responsive, but her interest was in getting their new home functional and operational as a "home." She wanted him to focus on the essential renovations needed before winter, not spend his time touring.

The Monadnock range of the White Mountains, located in the southern portion of New Hampshire, offered smaller peaks that were well-known to hikers. The range was south of the Appalachian Trail and hikers from all over the east and south incurred and experienced much of the famous range during their hikes. The Monadnock range averaged peaks of a few hundred feet or higher. Additionally, Mt. Monadnock was renowned as one of the most-climbed mountains in the United States, although other climbers, who were serious hikers on the East Coast, sometimes argued that point. The mountain was a half hour west of Harvest, yet Harvest had its own smaller peak, the mountain overlooking Lake Massapot. Now overgrown from years of neglect, the town of Harvest considered allowing the land to be parceled off so that condos could be built. The granite rock base of the mountain prevented expansion into multiple homes or condos—the land would not perk for a septic system.

The tall pines at the base of the mountain had been there for seventy-five to one hundred years. It was a pristine foothill and contained the only views in southern New Hampshire. Access to the mountaintop was by two fire roads or the old ski trails.

In winter, when snowmobiles took over, the mountain suffered from abuse on the other side in the vicinity of the former ski area. The owner of much of the mountain land was not interested in environmental concerns. He wanted land deals to go through so he could make a handsome return on his investment. He and the town even allowed the installation of a cell phone tower at the peak.

Nelson Palmer noted the unsightly tower during one of his first visits to the area. He asked Susan, "How did they allow the cell tower on top of the beautiful mountain. Who permitted that?"

She quickly informed him that the local owner appealed to the selectmen and planning board for a variance. She indicated that the town stood a chance of receiving revenue from the collaboration.

"Stupid bastards," said Nelson. "How could they allow that to happen? There are so few pristine hills and views here in Harvest. Does everything have a price?"

"Sure," she said. "Very few people care about the history, the views, or the land around here. Not everyone has your good intentions. I mean, for you to save the old church is really a rarity," Susan said. Nelson remembered the conversation clearly. His hope was to start a trend. If people saw what he could do, the town might find pride in itself again.

Susan cautioned him that the town was not that way. "No one gives a shit here 'bout stuff like that," she replied.

"Maybe we can rejuvenate this town," he commented at the bar.

"Doubt it! This is friggin' Harvest, not some prima donna town like north of here."

Nelson had showed Lydia the tower from afar. They could also see a portion of it from the church and the main road—Route 10. She was dismayed that the town was so uncaring about the fate of the mountain and its natural topography. They both envisioned Native Americans standing on that mountaintop before white settlers arrived. They may have even scouted for promising hunting grounds from that same vantage point.

The only shopping for major household staples and services was ten to fifteen miles east or north of Harvest, so Lydia had some distance to travel to reach a mall or store of any value. "Nelson," she once said, "If we are going to reside here for good, I hope you will be driving me to those shops north of here. I have no desire to be dealing with this traffic on Route 10—it's too narrow and congested."

"I'll take you anywhere you want to go, hon," he said. "I'm not workin' anymore so you just say 'when,' " he told her with tenderness. He had come to realize that this woman in his life had to be something special to agree to be uprooted at such a late stage in her life, and follow his whims for his "roots." She was a handsome, flexible woman and they loved each other deeply. Every Friday, he bought her a fresh red rose, missing only those days when he was on the road traveling for business. She was now guaranteed to have a rose in the church house each week, because he no longer traveled.

The post office near the center of town was antiquated and plans were devised to move it where it was more accessible to the general public. The new, modern facility was constructed north of town on Route 10. While it was efficient and had good parking, the charm and smallness of the centralized post office was lost. Residents no longer had a place to drop in to have casual conversations, catch up on the news, or dispose of junk mail stuffed in boxes with their bills.

Nelson suggested that the old post office potentially could be renovated like the church, but Lydia put her foot down quickly. "One project was enough at the moment," she said, reminding him that he didn't even own the old post office building.

"Don't you have enough to do, dear? You have this church to fix. Just how long do you expect to live, anyway?"

He laughed and said sweetly, "My love, maybe it could be a historical site and candy store. If I ever get rich, I hope to buy the property and put the old post office sign back up above the doorway. The town needs that kind of nostalgia. This town has died a slow death in many ways and someone with energy needs to revitalize it. I have that energy and . . . "

Lydia cut him off. "Never you mind, Nelson Palmer. You have much to do right here in this old building. You can't go changin' things here. We just got here and hardly know this town," she advised him, like she were his mother, not his wife.

Nelson's wife knew that the town's establishment was inbred. Like Nelson, she had heard rumors from locals that the old names in town vehemently disliked new blood, especially people from Massachusetts and beyond. The school committees, historical groups, and ladies clubs were composed of old names as well. Very few outsiders had the opportunity to participate in town events and functions. The community affairs excluded newer residents. It seemed like the children of the old names only associated with each other. They even dated one another. The backwoods mentality merely lacked the "woods." Newer residents joked that the locals had probably sniffed too much chain-saw oil. The derogatory comments increased the division.

Eight

Nelson Palmer enjoyed putting his considerable construction skills, including carpentry, basic plumbing, and certain electrical tasks, to good use during the church renovation. He could frame walls where needed, but hated the drywall and taping portions of the wall building. Slopping "mud" on the seams was not his favorite task either. Susan's boyfriend, young and healthy, would come in handy with the foundation repairs and wallboard construction and other heavy work. Nelson used a few outside contractors, but they were often costly. Nelson tried to use old name workers as much as possible to help with the local economy. He found out in time, however, that those local contractors were often too busy on other jobs or would not return his phone calls. He was unsuccessful in his efforts to bridge the gap of old and newer residents' issues. Young Susan had little influence on the locals as well. They felt she was siding with the new blood, not their heritage.

"Susan, what's with the finish carpenter that you suggested recently?" Nelson asked. "The little shit never returned my call."

"Not surprising. Many of these clowns have their own agenda. It didn't help the cause when you beat one of them at pool and took his 'Ben Franklins' and beer money for the week."

"Oh . . . that little turd? *He's* the one you recommended to me? Hell, if he couldn't hit the ball with a cue, what would he do with finishing nails and a hammer on my fragile interior woodwork? There would surely be 'dimples' from the hammer everywhere."

Susan roared at Nelson's comment. She just loved the man and his interpretation of life. He was frightfully honest and fun. "Nelson, with that sense of humor—if you were younger, I could go for you. Does your wife know what she has? My ol' man, Doug, isn't nearly as funny as you."

Nelson smiled back and shrugged his shoulders. "Susie, if you were older, I could go for you, too. The problem is, my wife wouldn't approve. When she turned forty, I told her I was trading her in for two, twenty-year-olds. She just laughed at me!"

"Well, she caught a good one!" Susan said with a smile. "You're somethin' else, Nelson."

"You couldn't live with me," he continued. "Just ask the sweet wife what I'm like. It isn't always pleasant. I'm pretty damned ornery sometimes," he said with a poker face.

"So . . . who isn't? I get PMS!"

"Well in that case, you ain't no good then," he said. "My wife never got that. It's all in your mind, anyway! PMS is crap. . . . Get over it," he joked.

"You wanna see PMS?" she said, throwing a dirty, wet sponge at him. He ducked in time for the sponge to hit the wall behind him.

Susan and Doug were like family now, but Nelson still knew when to kid around and when to be in charge.

"How's that cellar comin' along, dear? Makin' any progress cleanin' up that stuff they used to store down there?"

"Yep," Susan said. " I'm almost done with the back wall of old chairs and equipment. Just need to move one more table out of there. By Saturday afternoon we can hit the dump and get rid of this crap. By the way, Nelson, my man, . . . ya been to the dump yet? It's a real 'trip'."

"Really? How so?" he asked, placing his hands on his hips.

"Catch this. . . . The place has a woodpile . . . a metal pile and a compactor. Everything that isn't wood and metal, except asbestos, shingles and hazardous, flammable stuff, goes in the compactor to be hauled away. The rest of the shit sits in piles for the locals to 'pick.' The dump pickers bring home more than they leave behind, most of the time. It's like a social club of sorts on Saturdays. You can repair your sink, lawnmower, snowmobile, gas grill, or build a shed from the materials people toss out," she said.

"Really? You can still 'pick' in this town? With all the damn regulations and constraints, you can dump pick?" he asked again, with amazement.

"Sure . . . you can bring home the whole pile, if you want," she said with a laugh.

"Good! Let's go Saturday. I'm an ol' dump picker from the past! Love that stuff. Treasures everywhere."

"Yee . . . gad," she replied in disgust. "Not *another* one? My Doug does that, too. He brings home shit we end up selling later in garage sales."

"Good! We'll make a family thing of it—this Saturday. OK?"

"Sure, Nelson. Whatever you say . . . you're the boss!" said Susan, rolling her eyes as she headed back to the basement of the church.

Nelson was pleased to have Susan and Doug involved in the renovation. They were young and energetic. Susan kept Nelson abreast of the town gossip, adversarial relationships, and the issues of the old name residents. She put local politics in perspective for him, especially when he had to deal with the town officials who sanctioned or denied renovations and issued permits for construction and easements.

Nelson also learned from Susan that the local dump was overseen by two or three locals that needed part-time jobs. One of them, Emmett, was a really nice person who did not fit into the political game in town, even though he was a born-and-bred Harvest resident. For some reason, he had a different perspective and was often a liaison between rival factions. Emmett really enjoyed seeing people on junk day and kept the best of the throwaway items in a special place so that people who needed something of value could find it easily. In his spare time, he would repair items that never should have been tossed out. *People are so wasteful*, he thought.

Emmett befriended Nelson because he knew he was doing something positive for the town—restoring the old church into a useful and attractive building.

"Check this out, Nelson," he said, pointing to a cherry table with three legs. "This piece would look good in your new abode. Nothin' wrong with it . . . nice piece of furniture," Emmett added. "Ya wanna lawnmower? This one had a broken wheel. That's all."

"Not today, Emmett, but that stuff looks good," Nelson smiled.

Nelson often took what he needed or wanted, but declined what his wife would find inappropriate. After all, she and Susan were eliminating clutter almost as fast as Nelson brought it home. Saturday morning became a fun event at the dump and Nelson and Emmett would often have a cup of coffee and chat for a while.

Emmett also knew the history and every nook and cranny of the town and landscape. He would become invaluable to Nelson's quest of finding his roots. He showed Nelson historic areas of the town that most people in Harvest had never known about. Some contained remote, private family graves that would help elucidate the town's history, two hundred years earlier.

Nelson selected his friends carefully, since he was on two specific missions. One was to find his roots; the other was his massive church renovation project. Only four or five close friends would be important players in each of the quests.

✠✠✠

The sign, written in black marking pen, in the window of the local Harvest Village Store read:

RECORD-WINNING LOTTO TICKET PURCHASED HERE!
DO YOU HAVE IT?

Balloons of various colors surrounded the sign. It was Sunday morning and Nelson had stopped by the store to get the *Boston Sunday Globe* and a gallon of milk. The huge newspaper hardly fit under his arm. It was mostly composed of Filene's department store advertisements and classified ads for jobs, automobiles, and personal items. Only one-fourth of it seemed like news.

Looking over his reading glasses at the sign, Nelson said, "Do you think someone local won? Great news for you folks at the store. Congrats!"

"Don't know, sir," replied the young clerk. "Hope they come forward soon. Mr. Parker is anxious to know who it is. The trouble is—there's lots of out-of-staters who pass through here and buy lottery tickets. Could be one of them, I suppose! They probably don't even know the results of this month's drawing yet. Many people check the lottery Internet site to see what happened the night before. Hope someone comes forward soon. Don't blame them if they don't. They have a year to claim the big prize. If they want to keep their anonymity, they'll wait before admitting to being the ticket holder."

Nelson said, "Heck, son, it could be anyone. I bought some tickets myself a few weeks ago, and could be the person you're lookin' for. I've got eight or ten of those Quik Picks at home. Need to check them." He joked, "Write down the winnin' numbers—will ya, son? I need to see if I won all those millions and millions of dollars."

"Here ya go, sir. Check 'em out. Call me if you have that winnin' stub! Ya never know!"

"I'll be sure to call ya," said Nelson. "Why not give me five more of those tickets for next month's drawing, while I'm here. That way, if I didn't win, I'll have a shot at next month's winning numbers. . . . See ya, son," Nelson said, reading the numbers that were printed on his tickets for the next one.

As he drove away from the store, he toured the historic streets of Harvest. He loved the architecture of the Victorian homes and appreciated the style that was uniquely New England.

Nelson returned from the store and put the gallon of milk in the refrigerator. Lydia was downstairs doing laundry and did not hear his footsteps in the kitchen over the sound of the dryer. The new walls were yet to be painted and the plaster or "mud" was odoriferous as it cured. The taping of the wall board seams by the contractor was smooth behind the bedroom dresser. He would have one more sanding and coat of the white mud to apply.

Nelson flipped through the pile of ten Lotto stubs that he found buried under the stack of socks in his top drawer. Lydia knew they were there, because she put clean socks and underwear in the drawer a couple of times a week.

Sitting alone on the edge of his bed, he crossed his legs and sifted through the computer-printed random numbers. There were ten printed stubs, each dated at the top of the slip. The store number and ID were printed beneath the Lotto header.

Nelson carefully opened his wallet's photo section and searched for the folded piece of yellow paper that the young cashier had given him with the winning numbers written on it.

He whistled an unknown tune as he flipped lottery stubs like a deck of cards, dealt deliberately from a dealer in a casino. The yellow paper of numbers blew off the edge of the bed in a light breeze, and onto the floor, landing face up. He had just flipped his fourth lottery ticket only to have it match three of the six winning numbers. *That's good for seven bucks,* he thought. Nelson flipped the ninth lottery ticket. He had remembered only three of the numbers on the slip of paper. "Shit," he said. "The ol' memory stinks. What are the other three numbers?" he murmured to himself.

Lifting the yellow slip of paper, he strained to read the faint numbers.

"Is that an 8 or a 3?" he mumbled in disgust. "Where are those damn glasses?" he said out loud in frustration, failing to notice them hanging around his neck and on his chest. "What did that kid write?"

He just knew it was an 8. Scanning the ninth set of six numbers it was clear that he had an 8 on the Lotto stub. The number on the yellow paper looked like an 8 as well. As a matter of fact, he was flabbergasted! He had all six numbers! The winning numbers!

Nelson dropped to his knees and his heart pounded wildly. He had palpitations and shortness of breath bordering on clinical tachycardia. His glasses flipped in front of his face. Grabbing them, he lay on his back on the floor and held the yellow slip of paper and the Lotto stub side by side. The numbers did not change with glasses on. He had won! He had actually won millions and millions of dollars. He scanned the two pieces of papers, back and forth and back and forth again. He held the two up to a table lamp. Nothing changed! The numbers never changed. He closed his eyes and held his breath. He checked once more, revisiting the date on the slip. It was the real thing. Same date, same numbers, same Lotto game.

"A dream? Is this a dream?" he repeated to himself. He could not move. At that moment, he heard his wife outside the bedroom.

"Nelson . . . are you home?"

"Honey," he called softly.

"Nelson? Nelson? . . . Where are you?"

"Come here!" he said. "In the bedroom."

"Darn you, Nelson Palmer, what the . . . ? " she asked abruptly. Just then she saw him on the bedroom floor, lying on his back.

"Nelson!" she screamed, dropping an armful of laundry. "Are you OK? What happened? Should I call an ambulance?" she cried out.

"I'm fine, woman! Sit down by me . . . hurry . . . sit down. . . . Here!" he pointed to the area on the floor beside him. "Dammit! Sit down . . . please."

"What is wrong?" she said, fearing the worst. "Is it your heart? You are beet red!"

"No, woman, I'm fine. . . . please sit . . . right here."

Lydia lowered herself and heard her knee crack as she descended to the uncomfortable position next to her husband.

"Hold this paper," he said slowly. "Hold it!"

"What is this yellow paper?" she asked, becoming more per- turbed.

"Read a number," he ordered her. "Then I'll read a number from the stub in my hand."

Curious, Nelson's wife complied and read the number 3. Nelson said, "3."

She said, "A 10."

He responded with "a 10." She then rolled her eyes with frustra- tion.

"Read the next one! Read the darn number!" he ordered again.

"It's 15!" she said loudly.

Hesitating, he responded with "1, 5?"

"Yes, 1, 5 . . .15!"

"Next one!" said Nelson. "Read the next one."

"It's a 24!" she said. "Then, 35!"

I didn't ask for two numbers," he said, then he repeated the two numbers. "A 24 and a 35! OK, the last number. What is it? Tell me, lovey."

"3!" she said emphatically and smiling. "3!"

"3? Dammit, no! Read it again."

She looked hard at the blur and said, "OK . . . it's 3 or . . . 8!"

Nelson jumped to his feet as she sat stupefied on the floor.

"It's 8! . . . the number 8! We won Lotto! . . . the whole thing . . . $175,000,000 . . . six zeros after the 175." He was now jumping like a kid and waving the stub. His voice resonated off the cathedral ceiling.

"What?" she exclaimed. "The Lotto? The big one? You kidding?" she stammered, visibly moved.

"Think so . . . think so. . . . ," he said slowly and breathing deeply. "Computer? Is it on? Need to go on line."

"Why?" she asked.

"The lottery has a Web page. They list the winning numbers . . . 8 or 3, that's the question. Can't read what the kid printed on the slip. Our lottery ticket says 8. If the number on the Web site says 8, we won . . . the whole shebang!" he shouted.

Nelson knocked over a chair on his way to the computer. It was turned on in the next room, but he needed to connect to the Internet. It was slow to log on and dial. He didn't yet have DSL and the telephone lines were slow. He blew entering his password three times just logging on. Finally he was connected, and typed in the words, "LOTTO results" in the search engine at the top.

The Web site appeared and the latest four digit daily number appeared: 9-0-2-5. The three-digit daily winning number then popped up and appeared: 6-2-9.

"Where the hell is the big game—the Lotto numbers?" he stammered in frustration. His wife watched as he typed in the word—Lotto, monthly, with the date.

The Web site was slow to "think" and then the numbers appeared in tiny red balls . . . slowly and one by one. It was grueling for him and his wife. First it was 3, then 10. Then it showed 15, then 24. Next came the number 35. The last number to show was the "super ball." It could be any number between 1 and 42. Nelson held his breath. His wife did the same.

The number 8 popped up as a white "super ball" on the screen.

Beside the number 8 were the words: ONE WINNER—NEW HAMPSHIRE.

They had won! Lydia hugged her husband and both were silent, each overcome with emotion. They rocked each other for a minute or two, each gently patting one another on the back. Nelson found some wine in a nearby Waterford decanter. He poured two glasses of red, and then toasted his wife. They sat in two wing chairs facing one another. Neither one spoke as they sipped their wine and smiled, occasionally shaking their heads in amazement. The moment was literally breathtaking. They decided not to tell anyone.

The phone rang.

No one moved, and no one answered.

Nine

Scott Bonner, whose deceased grandfather and father had been builders before him, owned five or six properties near the Harvest town center. The old names knew each other and were expected to date and marry each other.

If young Bonner had children, the Bonner name, which had been well established in the community for more than one hundred years, would continue. He was engaged at the present time, but he changed girlfriends like the wind, so there was little chance he would soon marry Lisa Halliwell. Children weren't even in his thoughts.

"Can't be bothered with the marriage thing. So many women and so little time," he joked with those closest to him.

"When ya gonna marry Lisa?" his friends asked. "You been seein' her for almost a year now."

"No plans to do that. Why buy the cow when ya get the milk for free," was his standard response.

The local Harvest names dated one another. The Bonners dated the Halliwells and vice versa. Kids who went to school together ended up dating one another, out of convenience. Generally, their parents knew each other or worked nearby. Since there was little to do in town as teenagers, the adolescents smoked cigarettes and told dirty stories under the small bridge in town. The local brook and bridge was their hangout and each week a different kid stole their parent's cigarettes from the ten-pack carton and brought them to the "bridge party." Occasionally, the party-goers acquired booze or beer. The six-packs were purchased with fake IDs. Beer cans littered the banks under the Swift River Bridge in town. The occasional loss of virginity was apparent from the remnants of used condoms on the riverbank. Being so close to town, the kids often took great chances with sexual encounters. Occasionally, the police patrolled the bridge area, especially from 10:00 to midnight on weekend nights. More kids got caught and scolded on Friday and Saturday nights. The police found their hormonal escapades humorous and entertaining, in a town that was boring from the start.

Although the townsfolk were aware of the acquisition of the church by the Palmers, few people cared enough to compliment them on the renovation task at hand. The church's history meant nothing to them since it was some distance from the town center and had been empty for some time.

"Let him have the old place," locals said. "It's been the home of a groundhog and hundreds of ladybugs for years."

The cemetery was of minor interest to the selectmen, since few old name families had cemetery plots there. The other, newer cemetery had been used more frequently because it was closer to town. The tombstones reflected the names that mattered to the town council and local politicians. On Memorial Day and July Fourth, officials placed military flags at the newer cemetery. Tourists seemed impressed by the display of patriotism. It was more of a front for the locals whose homes were near the burial ground of their ancestors. They tended to place flags on all the graves, not just the stones of the military veterans. The town road manager, Morris Halliwell, was in charge of the graveyard maintenance, at least the cemetery in the town center. Sympathetic volunteers maintained the other remote graveyards located in the more rural areas of town.

Nelson had made one close friend, Jason Birch, a longtime resident of Harvest, who was a decade or more older than Nelson and very astute. He often walked by the Palmer's property during his daily exercise routine and he loved to chat—talk about anything. He watched the daily progress of the church renovation and was one to appreciate the fact that it was showing progress each week.

"Mornin', Jason. How are you this fine day?"

"Great progress on the old house of God, my friend. Look at the way the soffits look now that they are painted. They don't make them like that anymore. They look like new! Great job, Nel."

"I don't like being up that high on the ladder at my age, but the moldings are lookin' pretty nice, I must agree. You strollin' down to the lake again today?"

"Yes, sir. Love that lake in the early mornin'. She's very placid at this hour and you can see the fish surfacin' for bugs. Lots of rings in the water."

"Reminds me," replied Nelson with interest. "When we goin' for the record bass in the lake?"

"Anytime you are bored with your paintin' and all," came the reply from the avid walker. "I got these new lures that are supposed to work," continued the old man. "They say the fish love this lure . . . simple as it is."

"That won't help you, Jason," laughed Nelson. "It's the motion and the hands that makes the lure work. I've got that touch and you probably don't."

Jason was quick to respond. "You think you got the touch, eh? Do I sense a challenge or wager here?" Jason replied. He needed the inspiration from Nelson to spur on the "bet."

"I think we could have a 'little wager' here," Nelson replied, climbing down the last few rungs of the aluminum ladder. "I could use a break anyway."

"Well. You gonna go for it tomorrow? I think the mornin' will be nice, they say. Care to fish tomorra'?" asked Jason, with a slight smile.

"Sure. . . . You're on for 5:00 A.M. I'll pick you up at your place. OK?"

"Better get some early rest tonight. I'll be workin' on my gear today and gettin' it all ready for the big derby between us."

"AOK, my friend. I'll bring coffee," he said, with a laugh, knowing he just made his friend's day.

Jason continued his walk down the road and Nelson painted the remaining boards on the trim in the front of the church. He had much to do before he could justify taking the next morning off. His schedule was self-inflicted and he wanted the outside of the building to look nice to the people who might pass by. The internal renovations could be delayed until winter, when the inside jobs were more appealing on cold, New England days.

Jason's work pants and black-and-red checked shirt could be seen off in the distance. He was now a quarter-mile from the church and walking north. He walked slowly because of a hip problem from an injury during WWII when he had stormed the beaches of Normandy. The pain of his injury flared up frequently. Jason's modest home was near the church and the long walk to the lake was far enough to irritate the hip.

Nelson enjoyed the conversations with Jason. He was a friendly sort and often brought the Palmers vegetables from his enormous garden. If he wasn't fishing, he relaxed by tending his garden in his backyard. Jason found the garden to be a lifelong hobby of sorts. It kept him busy and he loved being outdoors. Nelson took to Jason quickly because of his friendly nature, general interest in the church project, and his thoughtfulness. He seemed to be different from the other residents of Harvest. There wasn't a mean streak in the man. He was merely a nice neighbor who kept to himself, most of the time.

Nelson felt that Jason Birch was a wealth of free information about the town. Nelson relied on young Susan for the scuttlebutt about the younger residents of the hostile town, but Jason provided him with a historical perspective that included renditions of town history and the burials of the older residents—in particular, those of prominence. Jason knew the older residents because he had worked many different jobs. He once pumped gas, logged the local forests, labored in the old ice company of yesteryear, and even dug a grave or two in his day. He watched the railroad come and go, witnessing the transition from steam engines to the electric trolley. Nelson took the time to tap Jason's brain, especially with respect to the history of the town during the turn of the century.

"Yes, sir. I worked that icehouse many a winter when I was young. Hard work, my friend," Jason said with pride. "The icehouse was near the peninsula, over there. If you take the boat over there, there are remnants of the ice piers still under the water. The piers supported the ice blocks after they were cut with handsaws. It was like a conveyor belt, which sent the huge blocks of ice into the storage room." Jason gestured to the area where the old building once stood.

"There?" replied Nelson. "Yep," said Jason, "let's have a look."

"Think I see the beams sticking out of the water," said Nelson. "Yipes! There's one near the bow of the boat." He shut off the motor; he didn't want to lose the propeller or a sheer pin.

"Drop anchor here," Jason said, leaning over to watch the remnant of the pier support pass under the boat. There was a clunk on the boat bottom as they passed over the huge 8' x 8" beam of the old pier. "The damn bass love to hide right here and over there. See the ripples in the water? They love this place. Those beams are good protection for the largemouth bass. Many a lure has been snagged on those beams. Must be a hundred lures down there," Jason added from experience.

"I've seen people snorkel here to retrieve lost lures and hand-tied flies. Sort of like lookin' for balls in a golf course pond," he said with a chuckle.

Jason held his pole with both hands. He spoke quietly on occasion as not to disturb the fishing. That day, the men caught many fish.

"That icehouse was the largest in New England, storing ice blocks that were not only used locally, but also shipped by train to Boston and Somerville. Those were the days of ice chests and the original refrigerator. There was no electricity or compressors to those coolers back then—just ice."

Nelson interceded, "I have one of those antiques in the cellar. Bought it at a flea market for four hundred bucks. We'll use it for a bar or stereo cabinet," he said. "Need to move it upstairs when the renovation is done."

Jason smiled as he recast his line. "That's about all they're good for today," he said. "Decorations as antique furniture and memories." Nelson nodded in agreement.

Jason returned to the icehouse story. He mentioned that draft horses were used to haul the ice out of the lake. They were large horses that loved to work hard and haul heavy loads.

"One fell in the water one day. Damn near drowned—the stupid equine," said Jason with outstretched arms. "We had all we could do to save the horse that day. Managed to get him out with a winch and rope. The horse was nearly frozen, and so were we. He survived the shock pretty good," Jason laughed.

"That had to be a close one for you folks and the horse," Nelson said, sympathetically.

"Almost died of fright, the darn beast. Weighed a good 2,000 pounds," Jason continued, nodding his head sideways once or twice. Nelson was engrossed with the story. Their bobbers and fishing lines were motionless near the side of the closest beam. Nelson and Jason used worms for bait, instead of lures.

Nelson was about to pull his line in and move the boat with the electric motor when Jason's red-and-white bobber disappeared beneath the surface. Concentric rings of water broke around the site of the submerged plastic float.

"Jesus! Ya got one, Jason!" shouted Nelson. His voice rang out and echoed off the surrounding mountain and hills.

"Holy crap! Look at the pole. It's totally bent over—almost in two!" responded Jason with surprise and childlike excitement.

"What pound test do ya have?" Nelson asked, referring to the line and reaching for a net to help his friend bring the fish onboard.

"Ten! May not be enough," Jason said with concern. "Feels pretty damn big."

"Bring it in slow . . . very slow," said Nelson while leaning overboard. "I'll get the net under it . . . alongside the boat." The boat listed precariously to starboard. Both men were now on the same side.

With that, the fish broke water and its large mouth widened in the air. It twisted and turned midair while trying to shake the hook loose, but it had swallowed the hook deep within its throat. A splash ensued as the bass tried to swim deep again. Jason's pole bent almost 180 degrees from the weight of the fish. He laughed as the monofilament line began to spin off the reel. His drag adjustment was set to allow the fish to run and tire. Patience was needed by both men to land a fish of that size.

"Tighten the drag," Nelson shouted. "He's takin' the line out too far."

Jason clamped down on the outgoing line. He managed to get the fish back to the surface and adjacent to the boat. Nelson was quick to place the net a few inches behind the fish and under the waterline. His net lengthened from the weight of the massive bass that Jason had caught. The fish fought within the net and broke the line. It didn't matter since the net was now in the center of the boat and the fish well contained.

"You old salt," Nelson said to his friend. "Will ya look at that. It's huge!" Jason grinned from ear to ear. He had never caught one that large.

"That's a keeper!" Jason exclaimed. "Damn near approaches the record, I'm sure."

"What is the record?" asked Nelson, hoping to confirm Ed's recollection on the phone.

"Over ten pounds," shouted Jason. "Happened back in the sixties, I think. It was not just a record for the lake . . . but a record for the state of New Hampshire. It was a huge fish for this size lake. Must have lived here for years before bein' caught." The bass, which now lay in the net on the boat bottom, began to flip-flop. The mouth and gills of the fish opened and closed repeatedly. It sought the necessary oxygen to live.

"Well . . . this one is close to that record. Just look at the girth on that mother," he said, holding it up for his friend to see. His fingers were buried underneath the gills and the tail hung down and touched the boat floor. The fish was now lethargic from the fight and from the fact that it had been out of the water for a couple of minutes. The mouth gasped for breath or oxygenated water. Nelson placed the fish in a cooler of crushed ice. Jason's hands shook from the fight with the enormous catch. His biceps twitched from the strain of landing the largemouth bass. The handheld spring scale had registered eight pounds. *It isn't a record catch, but damn close,* he thought. Nelson congratulated him on the fine achievement and gave Jason a beer from the cooler.

"Cheers, mate! Nice catch, my friend!" Nelson said, "Time to head in. We won't beat *that* one. . . . Are you stuffin' it for on the wall or eatin' it?"

"We're eatin' it! Right after I take a picture of it. Tonight, perhaps! On the grill. Sound good to you?" asked Jason.

"Sure does! I'll share it with you. Sure you don't want to stuff the thing? Would look awesome over your fireplace," Nelson said.

"Nah," said Jason. "Let's eat the sucker. Tonight!"

"Yer on!" added Nelson. He was happy for Jason Birch. After all those years of fishing the local lake, this was a once-in-a-lifetime catch. It would be days before Jason would come down from his high. He would be bragging about the feat for weeks.

On the ride home, Jason was quick to comment on the town in which he had grown up.

"Ya know, Nelson, we used to catch a lot of fish in that lake," Jason said. "So much has changed in this little town . . . the lake . . . the people . . . the youngsters. . . ."

"Why do you say that?" asked Nelson.

"Can't put my finger on it. Just isn't the same. People seem disinterested in the town these days and there isn't much goin' on from a social point of view," he added. "In the old days, there were fishin' derbies and more parades on holidays. The town basically has shut down except for the school functions and plays. People just don't care much about community activities anymore."

Nelson had noticed a similar atmosphere for weeks now and attributed it the fact that there were internal rifts among the residents and the political figures who were running the town. He listened to Jason vent his dismay over the demise of the town's once friendly atmosphere so many years ago. Nelson would learn much from his angler friend over the coming months.

"Hey, Jason—did ya ever want to move onto the lake? Ya know, live on the lake?" asked Nelson. "You'd be able to fish all day long if you lived there."

"Not a chance! Can't get the property there," he replied. "Too much politics. I'm not one of *the names* that owns the existing land there. They pass the property on to their kids, and 'Birch' is not one of those names that own lakefront property," he said while rolling his eyes.

"So . . . maybe there is some land left there for sale and undeveloped to date," suggested Nelson. "Must be some property on the backside or somethin'."

"Not really," Jason said. "The land was scooped up ages ago. There is maybe one lot left and the price would be exorbitant."

Nelson was nearing Jason's home with his boat still in tow. He would help him bring the cooler into the house. The fish was long dead but still fresh and chilled by the crushed ice. It retained the deep green color of its old age. They decided to freeze it for another time; Jason was too tired to do dinner.

"Let me look into the property that I saw for sale," remarked Nelson. "The sign on the lake road said there was one lot for sale. Think maybe my Realtor would know about the land. She's not the listing agent, but may have info on the land."

"I have no money for that kind of real estate," said Jason. "That land is prime and the price would be high. I still have my own house to pay off—two more years."

Nelson acknowledged his friend's comment, and was silent for the moment. He was deep in thought. *A place on the lake would be awesome for his elder friend. The man had paid his dues over the years and deserved to spend his remaining years doing what made him happy—that was fishing.*

All of a sudden, money seemed not to be an issue for Nelson. He would call his broker to inquire about the land. The parcel would surely be listed in the real estate magazine that came out weekly. There were always copies at the village store.

After dropping Jason off, Nelson headed for his church home. Along the ride, he rethought the conversation with his friend. Nelson made detailed mental notes of Jason's rendition of life in the old days and found his input fascinating. He yearned for the old days as well— a sense of community with no infighting. Nelson thought of how he could help his friend financially. Jason's home was worth little; however, the land was extensive and had much value, especially if it were subdivided and sold off. Nelson had become interested in all real estate in the surrounding area. It was not just lakefront property he had interest in; he looked at all listings near the town's center and outside the concentrated community. The renovation of the church took a momentary backseat to his new interest in real estate. When Lydia commented on the renovation slowdown, Nelson was quick to tell her that Susan and her boyfriend, Doug, still had much to do while he perused the papers and real estate listings. He spent so much time reviewing listings of property that his wife suggested that he become a real estate broker. He laughed at the thought. He had no intention of doing that. His objective was to acquire additional property that was significant in value. He became increasingly conscious of the surrounding geography and real estate offerings.

Ten

Mr. Parker entered the village store on a Tuesday morning, three weeks after the winning super ball lottery number had been announced. No one had stepped forward to claim the prize money or to seek their notoriety. He was frustrated.

"Damn winner," he grumbled to the teenager behind the cash register. "You'd think that we would know by now, who this person was." Parker accidentally knocked over a beef jerky display, which was next to a promotional Marlboro cigarette advertisement.

"Sir, the winner may not come forward for months. They may even claim the prize anonymously in Concord. Other winners of big prizes have done that, so they remain unknown. That way people won't beg them for money," the young lad said.

"Damn well spoiled my store's exposure, son," the old man said with annoyance. Mr. Parker then adjusted the suspenders on his baggy pants.

"We could have been in all the nation's newspapers and magazines. See those *Time* and *Newsweek* magazines over there on the rack? We would be in those issues. Perhaps on the front cover. It would have made us famous."

The clerk returned to his chores replacing cigarette packs stacked behind the counter and relocating them to where the young kids could not reach them and steal them. He was surrounded by large boxes of Salems, Marlboros and Winstons, loaded with ten-pack cartons of the toxic weed.

"Sir, look at it this way," the boy added. "You got your name and picture in the local papers. You won the money for having sold the winning ticket at this store. You were also kind to share some of the money with me because I worked the day the ticket was sold. I appreciate your generosity."

"Yeah, I suppose you are right, son, but I still want to know who won. It matters to me if it's a local yokel or some "outta-stater.""

By now, the handwritten sign in the front window announcing the store as the place that sold the winning number was faded—a result of the direct morning sun each day. People in town went about their business as usual. Locals checked with store personnel each day to see if anyone showed up to claim the prize. Lotto tickets still sold like crazy because people thought the store was lucky. With time, town folk would forget that there was still a major winner to be found.

✠✠✠

The lottery commission office in Concord, New Hampshire, was located in a state office building just east of the capital city's center. It was situated sixty miles north of Harvest near the geographical center of the state. Nelson and his wife entered the building on a Thursday morning at nine. He quietly asked to confirm his meeting with the commissioner of the state's gaming division. He had arranged for the appointment the day before and had asked that the appointment be confidential.

Accompanying the Palmers was the Harvest police chief, who had volunteered to drive them in an unmarked car as a security measure. He was one of three people who were aware that the Palmers held the winning ticket, and Nelson, fearful that his ticket might be lost or stolen, wanted protection for himself, Lydia, and the winning lottery stub. Nelson had a small, locked, metal security box in his lap. Inside the box, and protected from fire, rain, car crashes, and other potential disasters was the winning stub, sealed in a Ziploc bag. Nelson took no chances and his wife laughed at his precautions. His friend, Police Chief Darren Gooden went along with Nelson's concerns.

Nelson had spent the prior three weeks meeting with his lawyer and a local financial advisor of some notoriety for his creative accounting. He needed to sort out the legal and financial details and regulations that affected his unanticipated massive income from the winnings. He also wanted to maintain anonymity until the financial ramifications and strategies were in place. He knew that every Tom, Dick and Harry, as well as many religious organizations and charities would be after his winnings if his name were divulged. He wanted no part of *that* scene. More importantly, he needed the three weeks time to sort out the IRS's concerns. The IRS representative would surely be at the commissioner's meeting to be assured Uncle Sam received his cut. Nelson's lawyer and financial advisor were making sure that the IRS got the minimum amount of the windfall taxable income. Nelson paid both men handsomely to sort out those details.

He opted for the annuity payoff, rather than cash, to increase the purse and stretch the payments out over two decades. He and Lydia had joked that they hoped they lived long enough to spend it all. It didn't matter. They would be debt-free forever.

After welcoming the Palmers, the lottery commissioner asked to see the winning ticket. Chief Gooden, who remained in the lobby, smiled pleasantly at the receptionist. She knew why they were there, but neither would admit it.

"Nice day, sir," she said pleasantly.

"Yes. It is a beauty out there today," he replied.

"For some people, it is a glorious day, as well," she added with a huge smile.

"Yer right," he said. "Some people's lives just changed forever."

The receptionist continued to type a document. Gooden leafed through a three-month-old copy of *Sports Illustrated*.

The following day, the New Hampshire newspapers announced that the winner had come forward to claim the big prize at the lottery commission office—the largest prize ever in the Granite State. It mentioned further that the winner was a New Hampshire resident who did not want to have his name disclosed. The local article was picked up by the AP newswire and became public in all major papers and nationally.

The next day, Nelson drove to the village store for coffee and a donut. He bought the three local and national newspapers that were in stock at the store. The young clerk commented while pointing to the cover story, "Mr. Palmer, did you see that the winner of the huge Lotto has come forward—yesterday? The winner of the massive Lotto was from New Hampshire—the ticket that *we* sold here three weeks ago." The clerk was exuberant.

"Yes, son," he replied looking at the front page. "I heard that he or she was a New Hampshire resident! Any idea of who it was? The winner?"

"Nah," the kid added. "The big winners don't tell their names. They know their phones will ring off the hook if people find out who they are. They're probably right, I guess," the boy said. "I wouldn't want people to know it if I had won. Imagine the hassle of people tryin' to scam your cash . . . fake charities and all."

Nelson agreed, saying, "Yeah, I sure would keep it quiet if I won." Nelson could hardly contain himself. He wanted to tell the lad but couldn't bring himself to do it.

The clerk rang up the purchase. "That will be three-fifty, sir."

Nelson reached into his shorts pocket and pulled out some one-dollar bills and some change.

"Darn," he said, "I've got three twenty-four . . . must have more change in the cup holder in the truck . . . hold on . . . here's some more," he said reaching deeper in the folds of the pocket. "I owe ya five cents, son," he added.

The kid told him to forget it. He could spot him five cents until the next time.

"Thanks kid, that's nice of you," said Nelson. "Catch you next time."

Once he returned to his vehicle, Nelson held one of the newspapers in front of his face and was pretending to read. He smiled and chuckled at his conversation with the kid. He had pretended not to have enough money but his left pocket had ten, crisp one hundred dollar bills in it. He just didn't have any change.

Nelson would always have that much money at hand and in his left pocket. He wasn't just a millionaire . . . but a multimillionaire!

Eleven

Nelson Palmer took it upon himself to look at the daily local newspapers. All of them were now being delivered to the church house. People were still unaware of his newfound wealth, and it would stay that way. The local papers contained the real estate section, which listed all area homes of significance. There were pages of ads with pictures and elaborate descriptions to entice buyers. Nelson was hell-bent on getting a home on the lake for his friend Jason. He did not care that Jason had to sell his place first. If it didn't sell, he would buy his friend a lake house anyway, and let him move in without the precondition of waiting for the other one to sell.

Nelson began to clip out real estate advertisements, many of which showed new listings that were in the Harvest town center. Prime listings were infrequent, but he was interested in the potential acquisition of more homes as an investment and for possible restoration. He did not limit his investment interest to Harvest. There were interesting properties east and west of town. Some of those towns had a role in Harvest's early history during colonial times. Surrounding towns offered excellent opportunities for land and historic homes as well.

"Nelson Palmer, just what are you doing with all those papers?" Lydia asked. "They are everywhere and I wish you would get rid of those piles." She was perturbed by the mess.

"Hon, I'm savin' the best listings that I see. Look! Here's that old home that you passed a month ago and commented on. Remember it?"

"That is a beauty," she said. "I believe that Robert Frost once stayed there during his writing days. I imagine a poem or two was conceived there."

"Really? He stayed there and composed poetry?" he asked.

"Heard that he did during the critical writing years," she added.

"Want it? You want that home?" he said. "If you do, just say— yes! I'll buy it for you."

"Oh, Nelson, not really. I just think it is beautiful and very historic."

"It's yours, honey," he remarked. "I'll get my new holding company to buy it."

"They can do that?" she asked. "Just like that?"

"Sure, honeybun. That's real easy to do. No one will know you own it. It will look like some real estate broker firm bought it. I have our money invested in five holding companies now . . . all different names."

Nelson hugged her and told her to look through the papers in front of her. All of a sudden she had renewed and positive interest in those stacks of papers. They were no longer an eyesore. In the course of an hour, she had noticed and pointed out six other homes that were noteworthy and of local interest or notoriety. Nelson laughed at her change in attitude. She was obviously hooked on his quest to salvage old homes.

"Here's a cottage, hon," she pointed out. It's on the lake— Massapot. I know this property. It's on the point at the eastern end of the lake. You've seen it, Nel. It's hidden in some pines. Lots of property to it. Look!"

"You're right. I passed that property many times while Jason and I were trollin' last week. Jason knew the owner. What's the price? Who has it listed?"

His wife quickly told him the agent and the asking price of $440,000. *Peanuts,* he thought. He could buy what he wanted and at any time. He was a millionaire many times over and these listings were small change. He was pleased that Lydia was getting interested in his ideas beyond the church. They had shared so many good years together.

✠✠✠

Nelson could imagine Lydia puttering around the church home and its gardens, sadly in need of care. He could envision her tucking a flower into her favorite tortoise shell comb in her sweeping twist, as she tended the zinnias. She was five years younger than Nelson and rather quiet. At a young age, she was full-figured and the type of shy beauty that made men fumble for words, and the later years had been kind to her as well. She was born and bred in the north country of New Hampshire, but had spent much of her younger years in Pennsylvania. Because of that, she was familiar with where Ed Hammond and his wife lived. She felt spiritually close to New Hampshire towns near the Canadian border because her parents, of French descent, had come from Montreal.

Nelson met Lydia in Pennsylvania, where he had been schooled and built his career. They met because Nelson was an avid outdoorsman, who hunted and fished in New Jersey and Pennsylvania. Lydia's father ran a bait-and-tackle shop in Pennsylvania, therefore they had much in common. Well educated and conscientious, she often worked in the fishing store during her high school and college years.

As a young adult, Lydia met many men, but she never fell in love until she met Nelson Palmer. She thought him quite dapper and very strong. At twenty-six, he was everything that a woman of twenty-one looked for in a man. They courted for a few years and then married. Two years later, they had their first daughter—the beginning of their family. Each of their four daughters was the apple of their father's eye. Everyone who knew her spoke of how she was aging well, despite some health problems, and it was clear she loved every year with her husband.

Although she had some reservations about renovating the church at their age because of the amount of work, she realized that he needed the project to feel young and useful. Neither one paid much attention to television and had done plenty of traveling in the past—Europe, the islands, the cruises, and the national parks, including Alaska. Lydia was content to spend time gardening, reading, and decorating their new home.

By late summer the house had become a *home*. That alone was an accomplishment. Often houses were nothing more than that, just houses. To make them *a home* required much warmth and character. This new endeavor certainly allowed for creativity and a feeling of hominess. To foster that atmosphere, she baked often. The smells of cinnamon and chocolate permeated the kitchen and extended into the other rooms. Their new oven was constantly in use. The Palmers just knew that their first holidays there, including Christmas, would be wonderful. They looked forward to sharing their good fortune with family and friends.

None of Nelson and Lydia's four married daughters had kept their maiden names. Because their married names meant nothing to Harvest locals, Nelson bought houses for each of the daughters through his holding companies. At Lydia's request, he had told the girls of his winnings, because of the trusts he had set up for them and their families in his estate. The elaborate vacation homes for each daughter had seven to fifteen rooms and each was unusual in its own way. Nelson also acquired all available land around the lake—a lake that he had grown to love. Again, the holding companies bought the properties on his behalf. His name never appeared on any real estate documents.

A cottage on the lake was listed in the paper that very week. It was unusual because it belonged to an old-name resident. The owner was a Halliwell, and Nelson despised the family's attitude. He had seen other Halliwells' behavior at town meetings and had also had a confrontation with yet another Halliwell who was the tax assessor. The argument was over the status of the church, and the present Palmer home. How would it be taxed if at all? *Were churches taxed?* Nelson wondered. *If it were a house of God, why would his new home be taxed?* Nelson felt that "once a church . . . always a church." He stubbornly felt that it should be taxed at a much lower rate, if at all.

The assessor had rated the structure as a home and therefore taxable. The argument continued in front of some of the town selectmen. Nelson would lose temporarily, but now he had the financial resources to challenge the decision—legally. He would hire William C. Mosley, Esq. a noted local lawyer of impeccable credibility and persuasive courtroom techniques. He never lost cases and he would represent Nelson Palmer regarding the case. The town counselor was no match for the prominent lawyer, and in the end, Nelson would pay very few property taxes. He agreed to let a local pastor conduct church sermons every six months in his new home—it was more like a coffee hour than a church service. Attendance was limited to family and friends.

The selectmen now had it in for Nelson Palmer. He had pissed them off to no end. Any further renovations would be scrutinized by the planning board *and* the selectmen.

Jason Birch agreed to look at the cottage that the Palmer's had found. It was small, but neat, as he performed a "walk through" the following week. Nelson encouraged Jason to buy the cottage. It was perfect for one person.

"It's exactly what you were looking for, Jason. It has a dock and a cove where the bass are often hiding under the water lilies. Look at those water lilies, Jason. That's where the little buggers are hiding. Right there!" Nelson said, pointing.

"Nelson, how can I buy this? I still have the other home and land."

"Not to worry, my friend. Do you like it? The cottage, that is?" he asked.

"Yes, Nelson. It's perfect. I really, really like the smallness of it. Not much to maintain. It's mostly wooded. No grass to cut . . . and its . . . solitude," he exhaled slowly. Jason was enamored with the view.

"It's gonna be yours. Let me work on it. I have friends. We'll get it for you. We can sit on that deck over there and drink beer, Jason," Nelson said, smiling. "We'll clean the fish on that old table over there. OK?"

Jason nodded. He was both confused and happy all at once. He knew that Nelson was a bright man and that he could help him acquire his dream home on the lake. Nelson assured him that his old place would sell. It would not be a burden to him.

Nelson called one of the holding company representatives. The deal was done in a day. Nelson was there only to help with the details. No one in town associated Nelson with any of it. In the end, Jason's land and other home were sold off to a developer. He didn't know it, but it was another Palmer holding company that purchased the land. Their future plans were to subdivide the original property and build fifteen more homes on the large acreage. The field would become a small community with premium homes, which was to attract new out-of-state, white-collar residents, who were professionals. Nelson secretly termed the development "Palmerville." Only he and his wife joked around the house about the name.

Jason had Nelson keep his boat at the new cottage. It was docked twenty feet from the home. Together they could fish when they wanted to. Both Jason and Nelson were happy to have actual property on the lake. They would no longer need to trailer the boat to the public launch to go fishing. Jason Birch felt at home in no time.

✠✠✠

The selectmen not only argued over many of Nelson's requests for easements in his church home, they also frequently badgered the police chief and rescue squad over routine budget requests. Nelson was infuriated with their attitude after he attended yet another town meeting at which Chief Gooden presented what seemed to be very reasonable requests—again. The selectmen obviously cared little of the DARE antidrug program, the request for another full-time police officer, or the defibrillator that the EMTs, needed. A second request for a new police car was flatly rejected. The town was too small for more cars and police staffing," they said. Chief Gooden insisted that the requests were justified, since the town had grown and patrolling the outskirts of town took his staff far from the town's center. The selectmen asked him to reduce the surveillance of town land on the outskirts and to focus on where the populous was the largest.

"I can't disregard the folks on the outside edge of town. They are the most vulnerable to break-ins and robberies. There are fire and emergency responses there as well," he said firmly. "They have children who get injured, or the elderly who need protection. They don't just live around the corner and near the town hall." The chief was adamant about the needs of the public.

"Chief, we told you previously that you will have to do what you can within the existing budget," said one selectman. "The town won't allow for a budget increase and the town hall needs painting. It's unsightly."

The chief raised his voice, "You would consider the town hall repainting over personal protection of the community residents? I don't think the residents consider *that* a priority over personal safety."

"You have mutual aid, right? You can rely on other towns for help, especially on the borders of our town. The borders abut other towns with emergency staff and police. Can't we call on them?" asked another.

"There is mutual aid in an *emergency* situation. Those chiefs of those towns have their own needs. We do not use them as if they were our ancillary salaried employees. It's for special situations where we can't respond to all calls . . . ya know . . . multiple 911s, all at the same time. It's for multi-alarmed fire calls. That is what mutual aid is . . . covering one another. It is a *courtesy*," explained the chief.

"We can't help you this year. I'm sorry. Live with the budget you have. Perhaps next year."

The police chief liked Nelson long before he knew of his lottery win. He never asked Nelson for anything but his friendship. Nelson, in the chief's mind, was "normal" and genuine. Nelson was outraged that the selectmen were not sensitive to the chief's requests.

Nelson decided that when he could help the chief financially, he would do so. The time was not quite right, but the chief and his staff would have what they needed. Gooden would get what he needed anonymously. In the meantime, the selectmen would begin receiving small, helpful checks for the Little League and teen community functions. The anonymous notes that accompanied the checks were typed and read: "For the teen center at the old community building" or "For the Little League uniforms." There was never a return address. They were postmarked from a town seven miles from Harvest. The gracious gesture baffled the town selectmen. The town treasurer accepted the gifts without question. Anonymously inspired public announcements of the monetary gifts assured that the revenue was applied to the proper allocation and was not misdirected to some other town fund.

Twelve

Ed Hammond's company, which manufactured and distributed agricultural chemical products for farmers and homeowners, was a minor competitor of larger players like Monsanto, Scotts, Novartis, and Chevron. AgriChem did however have proprietary chemical compounds that the large agricultural chemical companies utilized in their formulations of insecticides and herbicides. The company's "active ingredients" were unique chemical structures that shortened the duration of the application of the major industry's product lines. The quick, efficacious technology was novel and in high market demand. Ed sold the usage rights to many of the major corporations that needed his technology, but he maintained the patent rights to all product lines. His company was a target for corporate takeover.

As founder and production supervisor for the organophosphate division of the company, Ed wore many hats. His knowledge of organic chemistry, toxicology, and risk assessment aided the bench-level scientists in devising new insecticide formulations that were shorter in duration, biodegradable, and efficacious in reducing insect infestations. His role was to help find new chemical entities that would not remain residual in the environment. The metabolites of those chemicals were synthesized to disappear in a short time and be more environmentally friendly. Ed Hammond offered suggestions on chemical structures related to the pyrethrins; agents that were effective but disappeared shortly after their application. They were considered "green" or environmentally acceptable.

Ed had stayed in touch with Nelson Palmer and they each had promised to fish one another's lakes. Nelson had been so busy with renovations and his recent windfall, that he figured he owed his friend another call.

Nelson's call finally caught Ed in his office, after playing phone tag for a few days.

"Hey, Ed. Long time no talk to, friend. How's life in the north country?" asked Nelson.

"Life's great, my friend. How's the renovation goin'? Livin' there yet? How's the lovely wife?" Ed retorted.

"We're fine and in," Nelson replied. "When we gettin' together?"

Ed replied, "Soon. . . . I've got a new lure for you to try. It's a Mepps 3. Ever heard of it? Works great on large and smallmouth bass."

"Lure sounds interesting. Never had one. By the way, the wife still loves me, Ed. Puts up with my antics. She's a fool, I guess, to love this old coot. She's busy with the inside of the house. We moved in a while back. Hey, that lure you mentioned? Bring it down here," Nelson said. "Me and a local friend caught an eight-pounder a couple of weeks ago. I've got a great spot here for bass—a secret hiding place of sorts."

"Sounds like you are settled in now. That's great," said Ed. "When did you become an old coot? You aren't that old. You must think you are Henry Fonda or something."

Nelson laughed and changed the subject. "Ed, I need to see you and chat about some of the products you have. Come on down and bring some of those chemicals you sell to the big boys. The lawn looks terrible and I think we have grubs, ants, and other beasts eatin' the roots. Damn gypsy moths are back as well. Raisin' havoc with the maples and the oaks."

"No problem, Nel," Ed said. "We have stuff for all that, and by the gallon. Got some great new products. They disappear in a week in the soil or water. Break down to next to nothin'."

"Save the chemistry conversation for our fishin' derby down here," Nelson replied. He wanted him to come down to Harvest and see the old icehouse piers and try his new lure. "We can chat in my boat while you wait for your line to get tugged."

"What's up for Saturday then?" Ed asked. "Got time to get together?"

"Sure," Nelson replied. "Bring the wife, and the two gals can chat while we look for 'the big one' in my pond. Time for a new record. Surely there must be a relative of that 1967 fish, that we've talked about before, still in this lake. It weighed ten pounds, eight ounces and was twenty-five and a half inches long." Nelson continued, "We'll grill the stuff that we catch. I'll have the wife go to the fish market, just in case. We'll boil lobsters if you fail with the new lure," he said with a laugh.

"We'll be there, friend. Start diggin' the worms. You probably use worms, right?"

"Matter of fact . . . I do. They work just fine, and the graveyard is right next door," he joked.

"You . . . my friend, are a sick man," replied Ed.

Nelson added that he had relatives in that graveyard. "I'll introduce you to my Uncle Erza and family as well," he said.

"Ezra?" asked Hammond. "Who the hell is Ezra?"

"I'll tell you on Saturday. Better than that . . . come on down Friday night and stay over. We'll fish early Saturday mornin'," suggested Nelson.

"Fax me the directions. Nel. Gotta go now—they paged me."

"See you Friday night. 'We'll keep the light on for ya'!" Nelson added.

Nelson was pleased that Ed would be coming down that weekend. In preparation for the day and "fishing derby," he went to the sporting goods store to seek out the state records for fish. The New Hampshire Fish and Game booklet listed the records for all freshwater species. Nelson was amazed at the records to date:

Smallmouth bass—7 pounds, 14 ½ oz., 1970

Bluegill—2 pounds, 1992

Carp—30 pounds, 8 oz., 1985

Lake trout—28 pounds, 8 oz., 1958

Yellow perch—2 pounds, 6 oz., 1969

All those species existed in Nelson's local lake. There were eighteen other records in the state, but many of those fish were in the larger lakes up north. Nelson would brag about the records to impress Ed once he arrived. He didn't want to be outdone by his friend from the North Country.

Nelson even knew the New Hampshire brown trout record, which was from a river near Ed's local lake. It was 16 pounds, 6 oz. and caught by Ken Reed in 1975. He would test Ed on that bit of information if he got a bit cocky on Saturday.

While he was at the store, he bought the lure that Ed had mentioned on the telephone. The Mepps 3 was surely something that Jason had heard of as well. He would buy Jason a couple of them.

✠✠✠

As a former environmental engineer, Nelson Palmer took note and interest of the mountain that partially framed Massapot Lake. He and his wife often walked the fire trails to the top and noted the frequent abuse by the ignorant town folk and their young offspring. The Palmers picnicked on the grass at the top until he finally built a pine picnic table. They enjoyed the panoramic views of the town and scenic beauty.

"Look! How awful!" his wife cried out during a recent climb to the top.

"Shit!" Nelson exclaimed. "The little bastards destroyed the table . . . they used it for firewood . . . the nasty bastards!"

Nelson was aghast as he picked through the charred remains of the table, a table he had carefully built. The seats had been ripped off and broken into splinters to fuel the adjacent campfire. What remained of his creation was the tabletop and framing, which had yet to be destroyed by the teens. Beer cans littered the site near the table.

"What *is* their problem?" Nelson asked Lydia angrily. He threw a stone at the campfire. "Does no one in this town see what *we see* from here? Do they not appreciate what they have in this fuckin' little harlot of a town?" he fumed. "Just look at this crap on the ground! They can't even clean up for themselves. Who do they think will clean this up . . . a forest ranger?"

"Honey. . . let me get a trash bag from the backpack," she replied. "I'll work on the cans and bottles and you can see what you can do about the table."

"Screw the table!" he replied angrily. "Let the nasty little bastards burn the rest," he said, with absolute venom. His face was red and his blood pressure was off the scale.

"Come over here, honey," she said tenderly. "I've got some tuna sandwiches and some veggies. Here's the blanket you can spread out for us. We'll have our picnic anyway. Just look at the views, hon, Don't look at the ground."

"I'm sorry, love," he said. Nelson looked at her and his anger subsided. As the flush left his face, he smiled and kissed her forehead. She was his granite rock in times of duress. He loved her so much that he followed her lead in moments like this. They found a quiet spot to the left of the broken, charred remains of the picnic table. After the meal, they lay back and stared at the sky. The cumulus clouds passed overhead. There was a flash of red as a cardinal flew between the pines. An occasional single engine airplane flew high above them. A commercial jet silently left perfectly formed, white contrail behind each engine and dissipated after a few miles. The Palmers soon forgot about the charred scene around them on the ground.

"Honey," he said calmly, "this is why we are living here now. Look up . . . and then look down at the valley below. It's the view, and the sky, and you and me. We've been together for some forty odd years. Seems like yesterday."

"You old coot," she said, mimicking Katharine Hepburn in the movie, *On Golden Pond.* You are a sentimental old fool, after all."

"Yep," he said, almost dozing off in the soft, warm breeze from the west. "But watch what you say about 'old' coot. I'm not quite there yet."

His wife kissed his forehead and whispered, "I still love you, Nelson Palmer."

"I love you, too," he whispered back and kissed her, softly and tenderly. "Ya know . . . we used to '*do it*' on mountains. . . ."

She cut him off from his fantasy of yesteryear. "Nelson Palmer! . . . Don't you get any ideas up here!"

"Oh, " he said with a laugh, "it was just a thought . . . a memory."

They both rested for awhile, then finished her attractively arranged fruit plate and basket of picnic treats before they strolled back down the mountain in the early afternoon. He eventually replaced the picnic table with a bigger one. This time he called the local lumberyard and had them fabricate one of oak. He also had them deliver it to the top of the hill. Accompanying the table was a note to the kids in town, and a Rubbermaid plastic trash can. The note Nelson composed merely read:

> PLEASE USE THIS TABLE AS YOU SEE FIT.——IT IS NOT FOR
> FIREWOOD. THE TRASH CAN IS FOR TRASH.——PLEASE USE IT.
> ENJOY THE VIEWS.

The note was signed: CHIEF, HARVEST POLICE DEPARTMENT

On the next trip to the mountain, Nelson found that the picnic area was clean and the new table remained in one piece. All that was indicative of others being there were the initials or names of lovers carved in the tabletop. Most initials were encircled by penknife-carved hearts. One set of names read: JAMIE LOVES TAMMY.

Nelson could live with the graffiti. After all he thought, *Love makes the world go round*. And Nelson knew love required an occasional billboard for its expression, and for all of posterity to see.

Thirteen

Nelson Palmer and Ed Hammond went fishing as scheduled. They each caught two bass, and Ed was impressed with Nelson's knowledge of the state's sport fishing records. Lydia and Muriel were content to chat and discuss the future décor of the church house. They took time to shop locally for accent pieces that would enhance the new home.

"Nelson," Ed said with appreciation. "Many thanks for inviting us. I love the little lake. Can't imagine that the record largemouth bass came from the little pond."

"It did, Ed. It's right in the Fish and Game booklet. I'll show you," Nelson said.

"Well, the little guys we caught today were not indicative of the old days in the 1960s then," Ed said, holding his fingers inches apart to indicate the size of the small fish they had caught.

"Must have been that Mepps 3 lure, Ed. Probably not as good as you claimed."

"It works up north, my friend. I think your pond is all fished out or polluted," he joked.

"Speaking of pollution. How's your business?" Nelson asked. "It's probably your products that make the fish bigger in the north and smaller in the south."

"Not a chance, you old fart. We did all the toxicology and mutagenicity testing on each product. The EPA found our products to be clean toxicologically. Our chemicals are very effective and biodegradable. Your lake has just been fished out!"

"Tell me, then," replied Nelson. "What do you have in your product line for the problems that I described on the phone—ya know, gypsy moths, ants, and stuff? How long does the stuff last in the soil? The wife worries I'll kill her famed poppies and bulbs."

"I brought you what you need," Ed replied. "They work well and won't even be there a few weeks from now. They're harmless to fish and waterfowl, so leaching of the active ingredients or their metabolites are no problem. We'll take care of you. Besides, you'd have to eat or drink the stuff to get ill."

Nelson grilled some steak, ate fresh bass, and boiled lobster for a relaxing dinner that evening. It was an opportunity to reminisce about college days and their respective careers. Ed left Nelson with his product line of agricultural chemicals meant to alleviate his pest problems. There were samples for every rodent, flying pest, and insect known to bother the avid gardener. Ed explained their application and personal protection. "Use the pyrethrin-like product for the insects and flying things. Use the other stuff for the grubs in your lawn; it may take longer for the second product to break down. Use it sparingly. What with pesticides being under close scrutiny for potential illness or toxicity, you'll want to use as little as you need. Use our biodegradable products first. The are 'green friendly' to environmentalists and pretty damn effective."

"Thanks for the advice, friend," said Nelson. "We've enjoyed the visit and hope to see you folks again soon. We'll come up your way next time. I'll get the photos developed of your two *enormous* bass that you caught this weekend. Maybe you can crop the pictures or enlarge the photos. They do wonders with digital photography now. They can make you look smaller . . . and the fish bigger!" he laughed. Ed roared at the idea.

Nelson and Lydia went back inside, still talking about their wonderful weekend with old friends. Nelson later stored Ed's products in the tool shed.

✠✠✠

Without much fanfare at its next meeting, the Harvest selectmen formally approved the application for a second cell tower on the top of pristine Massapot Mountain. They made their decision in closed session, returning from chambers to vote without allowing public input or any discussion of their own. The cell phone carrier had petitioned the town to install a more powerful tower for its southern New Hampshire customers, and made the deal palatable to the board because it would increase revenue. The cell phone company would pay a yearly fee for the right to install and utilize the tower. It was the highest point in southern New Hampshire and its placement would benefit their customer's phone quality and clarity in the general area. Rumor had it that the selectmen themselves secretly received payoff from the telephone carrier to swing their votes. No selectman admitted to the bribe, but the supposition was there, and the issue was pursued by some residents who questioned the committee's approval of the monstrosity. The vote passed far too rapidly for most folks. To mollify the residents, the cell phone company agreed to paint the new tower green or modify the exterior to look like a pine tree to make it appear less conspicuous.

Nelson Palmer read of the new tower's approval in the local paper. He was irate that the selectmen had sold out to big industry for monetary reasons. The mountain would now be marred by two steel structures at its highest point. And worse, the new tower would be in the middle of his favorite view from his community picnic table. He and Lydia were annoyed beyond belief.

Nelson decided to sue the town over its decision to install the technological wonder without resident input and detailed environmental impact studies. The suit would throw him into weeks of meetings and confrontations. He began to attend the weekly selectmen's meetings so he could badger them at every opportunity, even though he still had projects at home that needed town approval. He was well aware that his adversarial relationship would mean difficulty getting permits he needed. But one thing that the selectmen did not realize was that when Nelson Palmer became riled up, he was like a bulldog. They would not be able to shake him. His legal bill mattered not to him; he now could afford any level of representation. In the end, the tower would be removed and the contract canceled, as lack of public testimony would weigh heavily in the court. The issue thrust Nelson into the forefront and local news, and he was recognized now and began attracting a noticeable following.

Meeting privately at the town manager's home, the selectmen agreed that they had a common mission—to get rid of this *outsider,* this *man from hell.* They had no idea what they were in for and Nelson was smiling all the while.

✠✠✠

Susan and Doug, still very much involved in the renovation of the church house, enjoyed helping Nelson challenge the selectmen on his renovation issues. Young and energetic, they also encouraged their young friends in town to become more involved in the business and politics of the town. They saw Nelson's impact as a positive influence on the town's atmosphere. They were energized by his commitment to change the town's attitude.

"Nelson, you sure do stir up the pot," Susan said. "It is refreshing to see someone take on those assholes. I've wanted to see them squirm for years, and now they are."

"Susan, dear, my agenda is simple. They do not own the town of Harvest. The residents do. For years, the impression has been that the old-school network has dominated the area. They are myopic and restrictive to the community. They stifle creativity and excitement and they hinder the interaction and energy of young people who are the future of Harvest. This town will grow with or without them in office. They can't stop free thinking, especially when newer residents come forth with positive ideas. Elected officials are supposed to represent the people, and their ideas. That is why they are elected," he said.

"I admire your courage, Mr. Nelson Palmer. You are a breath of fresh air, especially in this town. It has been stagnant for years. But you have balls, as they say. We are very impressed with your drive and fortitude. My honey and me really love you and the missus," Susan said, teary-eyed. "You have taken us under your wing and made us productive. We really appreciate that. Our parents didn't devote that much attention to us, but somehow you have, by fate," she said.

"We love you guys, too," he said. "Look how you have changed this place here. It's almost a home and you have made it all happen. I only 'directed' the concert here, so to speak. You are the players and I want to repay you for your efforts."

"You already give us an income," she said. "How could you re-pay us? There is no need for anything else. We are happy just to be part of it."

"Well . . . there is one thing," he said. "You and Doug are made for each other and we were hoping that you will eventually formalize your relationship further. You may just do that and we have watched you grow closer together. You're in love!"

"Yes, that is true, but . . . ."

He cut her off. "Listen. You two have been livin' in an apartment and getting nothin' in return for your rent payment. I think you should be in a house. Ya know . . . building equity. There's a nice one in town—near the village store. You can walk there for milk and bread."

Susan said with a laugh, "You think we are in a position to buy a house? . . . In this town? The prices are out of sight! You pay us well but we have nothing saved between the two of us. I was your friendly bartender and go-go dancer—remember? Doug is a laborer . . . a good one."

"Not to worry, dear. I will buy you the house. It will be in your name," he said with a slight smile and raised eyebrows. "I will take care of it."

"Is this a joke? Have you been drinkin' or takin' Viagra, Nelson? Drugs?" she asked with surprise.

"Nah . . . wife won't let me take Viagra!" he said with a laugh. "I have a deal in the works. You want a house there? I can work the deal. Besides dear, you are like my fifth daughter and I want you in a house . . . one that you can renovate yourself and be proud of. This town needs some pride—some caring individuals. You folks have proven your worth . . . both to me and the missus."

Susan gave Nelson a hug, than sat down. "What do you expect from us in return?" she asked. "We don't deserve this."

"Nothing," he whispered. "Nothing, except that you stay 'nor-mal' and be a responsible citizen in the community. Take an active part for positive change. Your heritage demands it. You are a relative of the founders of this town, you said. Right? Prove it! Be as proud as they once were when they lived here," he said. "When you get married and have children, raise them here and be a significant part of their lives here. Change something in this current 'town from hell.' Wake people up if you have to. Run for office . . . Jesus! . . . Do something positive!" he said.

Susan sat back, listened intently, and thought for a moment. She was silent. This man was so inspiring that she couldn't resist asking him if he was going to become involved in the politics of the town.

"You runnin' in the next election?" she asked abruptly. "You gonna run?"

"Maybe, hon, just maybe," he said. She grinned and gave him a hug.

Their conversation shifted to the church house and its problematic septic system, which needed to be replaced or fixed. That meant that the town would need to be involved in the approval of the new system. Nelson needed to rectify the problem as soon as possible since the leach field for the septic tank appeared to be "dead." *It probably was never adequate to begin with,* he thought. *It may have been too small for the congregation way back when, or may never have been up to code. It was probably installed long before local regulations existed anyway.* There were no records or plans for the old septic system that accompanied the purchase and sales agreement of the church.

Nelson and Doug had found the holding tank quite by accident with a metal detector. They were trying to locate the rebar in the cement tank with the useful tool. The leach field had already been located in an area behind the church because of a slight surface odor. If the leach field was clogged or saturated, the watery effluent from the tank appeared in a grassy area. There was a problem about twenty feet from the tank. Nelson called a local contractor and requested an estimate to fix the problem. In the end, the field would need replacing. Normally, a costly endeavor of about $7,000 to repair, the price was not an issue. The septic problem was more of a nuisance to him, and he knew that town officials would want him to replace the entire system, which wasn't necessary.

Fourteen

The board of selectmen met at 7:00 P.M. once a week to review budgets, plot plans, requests for variances, residential issues, and complaints. Nelson had appeared before the group on many occasions during the church renovation process. Because of his lawsuit regarding the cell phone tower, he had become a thorn in their side and a threat to their control of the town. They responded by making his life miserable when they could through bureaucratic paperwork and superfluous regulations. He played their game but despised appearing before them. *They are such idiots,* he thought.

The building inspector was in the hip pocket of the board. The incestuous little group protected one another on all decisions regarding home modifications. Nelson was rapidly getting tired of the politics and arbitrary regulations. *Improvements to dwellings meant that the town would look better,* he thought. *Why would the present town fathers not want to see dwellings improved upon?* He was particularly annoyed because he knew more about construction and environmental concerns than any of them did anyway.

The septic issue began to take on a life of its own. Over the years, standard plumbing was added to the lower level of the old church. It was unclear as to whether it was functional or not. Some copper pipes were "married" to PVC plastic and certainly were not orthodox connections. Local regulations for leach field square footage had changed, increasing the square area needed per family. Since the church was not a standard dwelling, the town selectmen requested that Nelson provide documentation of what currently existed for a septic system. There was next to nothing for historical paperwork provided in the purchase and sales agreement. The original commodes were obviously outhouses. As the congregation grew, modifications for modern plumbing were added to accommodate the masses. The specifics of those changes were not detailed in any plans that could be readily located. They most likely occurred haphazardly and as needed in the early 1900s. Local codes for waste disposal were unheard of in those days. More than likely, waste went into a tank and the liquid spilled over into a bed of crushed stone, a wash-well of sorts. There was no clear evidence that a leach field ever formally existed.

Nelson came to the meeting about the septic system early. The selectmen were prepared for him. The building inspector, who had been talking with the chairman, was seated with sheaves of papers at a table in the front of the room. Nelson defended the old system by saying that "if it worked for an entire congregation each Sunday, what else is required when only *two* of us reside there?" He merely wanted to replace the existing failed system and add a new leach field to the current holding tank. Nothing else indicated that the present tank itself was malfunctioning. Reconnecting it to a functional leach field would be simple and effective for a two-member household.

The board did not see it that way and desired documentation and a perk test of the soil where the new leach field would be added. Perk tests were actually percolation assessments of liquids in a pre-dug hole. The timed tests determined if water dissipated into the subterranean ground at a specific rate of dissolution. If the area of the proposed leach field were shale or other rock, the perk test would be slow and fail. If it were sand or porous, water would dissipate quickly. In failed tests, the board would require an above ground, costly system requiring a specialized pump and sand mound leaching system. A simple leach field of a few thousand dollars could easily escalate to costs in the tens of thousands of dollars for Nelson. As expected, he found the selectmen's demands to be an annoyance.

There was one civil engineer on the board, who also happened to work for a local septic company. He was most interested in Nelson Palmer's issue of the leach field. He was very aware of what the geological landscape of the church property might be. He had recently surveyed a property in the general area and was aware of the granite veins that ran near Nelson's property. It was unlikely that Nelson's land was any different from his neighbor's terrain and subsoil. The geological landscape of the church property was assumed to be similar, at least in the minds of the building inspector and selectmen. That meant that it probably would not perk well for a standard system. The costly elevated leach field and pump system had been recommended to Nelson's neighbor just two weeks earlier.

"Sir, you may have to have some backhoe work done to assess the land on which you reside," the town inspector said to Nelson. "A perk test will be required to see if the land can handle the drainage of the septic effluent. In my opinion, it is unlikely that it will pass. The land up there is loaded with rock. We've seen it before."

"Why is that necessary?" asked Nelson. "This church has had hundreds of people in its congregation in the past. The old system operated without a pump and extensive leach field. It was a simple system in the past and was efficacious—so it worked. As a former environmental engineer, I suspect that soap or grease clogged the leach field pipes and now they merely needed replacement. It perked properly for decades."

"I don't agree Mr. Palmer. You may have a bad tank and distribution box there. The whole system may need replacing. The new codes are strict," said another selectman, clearing his throat.

"That's a bunch of hooey, sir," Nelson shouted. "The surface effluent in the one small spot on the grass suggests that replacing the existing leach field with new pipes and proper sand and stone will probably accommodate a two-person dwelling. We can even redirect the washing machine effluent to a separate wash well, if you wish. That way, the leach field will not be saturated with additional soap or greasy discharge—a potential complication for the future."

"Sir," replied the arrogant inspector, "my recommendation to the selectmen is to have you dig a test pit or two to evaluate the land and perk capabilities." He looked to the board for approval.

Nelson was beyond irate. He had attended the meeting to propose a simpler solution that would work and still be cost effective. It was not the cost that bothered him. He had the money to do anything that they suggested, but disagreed with their assessment. It was the principal of the thing, and he was being badgered by the council because of the lawsuit. Payback time. He knew that they would take every opportunity to harass him over future renovation efforts. Since the purchase and sales agreement had indicated that the system was in working order, Nelson felt that it alone proved it was a decent functioning system in the recent past. Replacing and expanding the square footage of whatever leach area remained there would work according to Nelson's educated thinking. The cost difference was tremendous between what Nelson wanted to do, when compared to what the selectmen were recommending.

"This is overkill," he shouted. "There is no real reason to jump through hoops here to get the problem solved. I don't wish to evaluate the whole existing system for replacement—it is not needed. I merely think that the leach field needs replacement. If it drained perfectly fine in the past, the new one should do the same, and would be less expensive," said Nelson, picking up his folding chair and slamming it against the wooden floor.

The selectmen did not budge. They told him that an entire new system might be needed to meet existing regulations. At a minimum, the soil tests would be needed to see if the land would percolate.

Furious, Nelson left the room. His face was red with anger and his footsteps were loud on the wooden floor. He would certainly have a few beers when he got home. Lydia found him in a foul mood. She let him stew a while and then commented softly, "Nelson, dear. Why not do what they want? We have the money."

"Dammit, Lydia," he said. "They're hosin' me here . . . Makin' my life miserable because of the lawsuit—the sorry bastards. The money is not the issue. It's the principal of the whole thing. They control the whole damn town with their stupid regs. Now they are telling me how to go to the bathroom—literally!" He paced back and forth in the living room, stopping to stare at Aunt Bess's picture of bucolic Vermont.

Lydia hated to see him so stressed. She knew this anger was not directed toward her, but toward the town officials. "Nelson. It is not worth the hassle. They are like little kids with power. They think their decisions are meaningful. They *have* no lives, except to make people scared and irritated with them. They find it humorous and dominating." Lydia was right, and he knew it.

"You're right, dear. They are little trolls, of sorts, with elected insignificant power. Who the hell do they think they are, anyway?"

"Nelson, you're in a tizzy over these fools. Don't let them get your dander up. That is what they want you to do—get ticked and have a coronary," she said. "Come sit by me. Let's think this one out."

"Probably right hon, those dirty little bas . . . "

Lydia cut him off. "Nelson, it's late. Let's go to bed and deal with this in the mornin' . . . OK?"

"Sure, that's enough for tonight, but I'll tell ya . . . I ain't doin' what they want. I'll repair the system myself and forget about their approval forms and crap." Nelson cursed under his breath as they headed off to bed. He had decided he would do what *he* wanted, with or without *their* approval.

Letters from the town officials arrived almost daily ordering him to cease and desist. He ignored all town-related mail. The selectmen of Harvest threatened to have him vacate the property, citing improper and unsanitary living conditions. Nelson put his legal team in motion to "stay" the town selectmen. His attorney had ways to stall the town's order for two solid years. Meanwhile, Nelson finished his repairs to the leach field and doubled its capacity. He and his workers had discovered that the required pumping of the main tank had not been performed often enough so that the overflow of sewage, rather than fluid, extended into the leach field, plugging most distribution piping. In the end, the job cost him $4,000, not $12,000, to repair. He was more pleased that he had defied the town fathers and fixed the problem at low cost.

☩☩☩

Lydia Palmer felt that their new home had *waited* for them for many years. In summer and now fall, she planted flowers in areas that Nelson had rototilled. In the yard and landscaped area around the church she had planted peonies, petunias, daffodils, roses, and a multitude of bulbs. Each garden was carefully arranged to bloom from spring to fall; most flora were perennials. Morning glories and ivy climbed the stone walls and gates. She felt at peace, even if Nelson was at war with the selectmen. The crisp, autumn air was refreshing as she cut fresh flowers for her table.

It bothered her that the town did very little to maintain the old cemetery plot, but she was happy that since they had established their residency, vandalism had all but disappeared. Perhaps the kids were respectfully afraid of Nelson. He was growing in popularity with the residents of the town—that is, everyone except the old names and selectmen. People felt that he had clout, and welcomed his austere presence. He was called "Nelson" by some residents, or Mr. Palmer, by others that knew him less well. Either way, he was admired for his challenge of the town officials and their local ordinances.

The maintenance of the graveyards was also aided by volunteers who took care of family plots and other personal memorials nearby. They mowed and trimmed the grass without town sanction or reward. On Veterans Day and Memorial Day, volunteers placed American flags on the graves of each military person's grave site. Lydia Palmer tended flowers that she planted on the graves of Nelson's relatives. She made sure that the Ezra Raby family gravestones were always clean, free of parasitic moss and lichen, and the grass around them mowed.

As he helped her prune and weed and prepare the garden for winter, Nelson said to Lydia, "I've got to get to the library and re-search this family. The name has been here for so long. It must have been one of the earliest families to arrive and reside here."

"I agree," Lydia added. "After all, this is *your* history. Why don't you go to the library this week? I'm sure it would be fun to start your formal genealogy quest."

"Maybe I will, dear . . . maybe I will," he said, while pruning a rose bush. "Look at those beetles. Eatin' every darn leaf of those roses. I need to use some of those chemicals that Ed Hammond left here. That should do it." He settled into a white slatted summer chair.

"Here's the paper, hon," Lydia said, passing the local rag to him. "Looks like the library hours are limited. Tonight it will be open. Perhaps you should check it out."

"Think I will. I could at least get oriented there. It doesn't seem to be a very big building. Maybe I should show them Aunt Bess's book. They may never have seen it," he said with a laugh.

✠✠✠

The original library was contained in a small alcove of the Harvest town hall, but the weight of the books had caused the floor to sag over the years. As the library aged without proper ventilation, it became dank. The books picked up the musty odor and many residents felt that they were in jeopardy of becoming moldy and full of silverfish.

In time, the library was moved into a building that had been built as a community center, after the townspeople stopped having dances, potlucks, and rummage sales there. The selectmen decided that portions of the historic building could be used as a small library. The number of volumes had grown substantially and space was at a premium. Most of the old books and newer volumes were moved to the new building shortly after the renovation of the community center.

The Harvest town library had one librarian and a few volunteers who were avid readers. They encouraged the library to acquire the latest novels, documentaries, and videos for its collection. The library, located diagonally across from the town hall, was an historic landmark.

"Wow," Nelson said to himself, as he approached the building in the early evening. "This place is gorgeous." He stared at the white clapboards and was impressed that there wasn't dry-rot anywhere. The roof edging and soffits were structurally sound. The belfry had once contained a bell that summoned the townsfolk to the functions. *It may have been a church as well,* he thought. He held the door open for an older woman who was leaving; her arms were full of old books.

"Good evening," he said to the woman, who was short and dressed in black. She nodded pleasantly, walked down the steps, and turned onto the sidewalk. She was Mrs. Perry, a long-term resident and self-appointed town historian, well into her eighties. Occasionally, she wrote an article for local newspapers. A kind person, she cared little about the town politics and infighting. As she walked away from the building, she turned her head and smiled. She was aware of who Nelson was and appreciated the fact that he was renovating the church on the hill. She knew the history of the town and of the church.

Mrs. Perry stopped suddenly, and spoke to Nelson, who was watching her walk away. "Sir, do you have a moment?"

"Yes ma'am. Is there something I can help you with?" he replied. "Need help with those books? They look heavy."

"No, thank you. You're the Palmer man, aren't you? The one who owns the church on the hill?" she asked.

"Yes, ma'am. I'm Nelson . . . Nelson Palmer. My wife, Lydia, and I live there now."

He hesitated, then asked her name.

"Perry . . . Mrs. Perry . . . pleasure to meet you. I've heard of you and suspected that you owned the church," she responded. "Nice job." She then turned and began to walk away. "I have something for you, Mr. Palmer," she said from afar. "I will bring it by for you and the missus to see."

"Yes, ma'am, thank you," said Nelson, perplexed. He decided that he needed to consult the librarian on duty to find out who "Mrs. Perry" really was. Nelson entered the library and approached the oak desk. The librarian was happy to oblige, but was equally as mystified by what the old woman had said. *What could she have that would be of interest to this man?* the librarian wondered.

"I am curious about her. I'm Nelson . . . Nelson Palmer," he said with a smile.

"I'm Libby Bishop, but people just call me 'Ms. Libby.' I think that I have seen you in town on occasion. Perhaps at the village store."

"Perhaps. I am often there to get bread and milk and the newspaper."

"She's a wealth of information," the librarian added. "She was a Parker before she was a Perry. That was her maiden name—Parker. Her father was *the Parker* who wrote some town history, way back when. Her second cousin is Alvin, who owns the Parker store."

"Interesting," replied Nelson. "Might you be able to direct me to that book, or others like it? I have a keen interest in this town and the old days."

"Sure, there are some volumes in that stack over there. Most are on reserve, but I have been known to loan them out. Few people have interest in the reserved-book section. No one cares about the town history all that much," she said with raised eyebrows.

Nelson sat at an oak desk and spent time researching the Harvest town history. A green glass and bronze lamp illuminated the pages in front of him. There were many other lesser-known historic documents in the library as well. Many were unbound and early accounts of the past centennial or bicentennial celebrations. There was a pictorial history of the railroad, especially the Boston & Maine Railway line that once passed through the area. Trains brought granite and ice to Boston from southern New Hampshire. Historic photos of the once popular Harvest railway depot were strewn among the other town photos. He knew that the depot was long gone but the rail beds remained as trails for walking and for riding snowmobiles. He himself had walked some of the rail beds as he searched for old grave sites after his friend Jason Birch had shown him isolated family graves in remote areas.

Nelson was fascinated by the older library volumes of history relevant to the town of Harvest on the reference shelf. He recognized his new home in many photos from days of the town's beginnings. The pictures showed only a few cemetery plots in a field behind the church. A book of old postcards also contained a photo of the church. The front of the card had the words: GREETINGS FROM HARVEST, NH and the back contained a handwritten message and note from an Isabelle LeGrand, on vacation, to her friend in Pennsylvania. She wrote: *Dear neighbor: Having a wonderful time here in NH. Attended a service at this church on Sunday. We picnicked by a nearby lake that afternoon. It had a funny Indian name. Aunt Nellie is fine. See you soon. Yours truly, Isabelle*

The card had a one-cent stamp, and unfortunately, the date was missing from the hand-cancelled blue ink postmark. Nelson loved reading the cards as he looked for them in antique consignment shops in the area. Five or six such stores were on a major thoroughfare north of Harvest. He would search for postcards of his church home, especially ones that were from Harvest's early days. His intention was to matte and frame them as a collage by the years of their postmark. The framed, collage of scenic cards was to hang in their den, once the renovation was completed.

"You OK over there, Mr. Palmer? . . . Find what you need?" she asked. "I'm about to close for the evening. Do you wish to check out some books before I lock up? We have no overdue policy here, and you can keep the books for as long as you like. In fact, not many people check out books here. Just parents, who get their children books for the week. Children love to read."

"I like these two here. One is Parker's. They have loose bindings. May I check them out?"

"Sure. Just let me record the library number. Look! They were last checked out eons ago. Oddly enough, it was Mrs. Perry who last took them home for awhile. She spends her whole day reading about the town . . . has done so for years," Ms. Libby added.

"Has she ever written her own book?" Nelson asked. "If she has researched the town all these years, she must know more than anyone here . . . ya know . . . about its history."

"Don't know, Mr. Palmer . . . really don't know. She just takes books out and comes and goes. She doesn't say much other than hello and good-bye," Libby said, shrugging her shoulders. "There you go. You're all set now. Plenty of reading for you. Also, let me know if there is any information that we can access for you on the Internet. I have a working knowledge of the Web and have often searched for additional information on local history."

"Thanks. That would be helpful. And thanks for the library orientation. I should be back next Saturday to research a bit more," he said. "Please call me Nelson."

"I'll be here from nine to twelve, Nelson," Ms. Libby said with a smile. "By the way, what are you searching for? Maybe I can help. Are you writing a book?" she asked, as she shut down her computer.

"No . . . no book, but I have family here . . . roots . . . relatives tell me. Kind of fun tryin' to figure out where I came from . . . in terms of genealogy."

"We can help you with that. There are a number of genealogy-based Web sites and some will surely include the Palmer name in New Hampshire."

"As the Bard would say, 'Ay . . . there's the rub.' It's not Palmer that I'm interested in at present. It's the name Raby I'm researchin'. There was a relative of mine named Raby. He was a pastor in town. I need to look for the Raby name history. Uncle Ezra, I think," he laughed.

"Odd that you should bring that up," Libby stated. "Mrs. Perry was interested in that Raby name last week. She asked me if I knew of documents that went back a couple of centuries. I think she said her mother's name was Raby. We found some information on the Internet and in old boxes here at the library. I'm not sure if she ever found what she was looking for. You best check with her and see what she might have located. She's a whiz at sourcing the town history. Do you need her number?" asked Libby. "Don't think she would mind."

"I don't wish to hold you up at closing," Nelson said, "but I would love the phone number of Mrs. Perry. I could also save you the effort and look it up in the book."

Mrs. Perry, a Raby? he wondered.

Libby wrote the number down, noting that it was unlisted.

"Thank you," he said as he left the building. "I'm sure I will see you again soon."

"Hope so," Libby replied, while turning out the library lights. The only illumination remaining was over the doorway. The library had not yet replaced the yellow bulb used during the summer to dissuade insects from flying around the door.

✠✠✠

Mrs. Perry sat in her dimly lit den and wrote slowly on a lined pad of yellow paper. She was sipping on chamomile tea and noting the documents in front of her. An old volume with a cracked spine, that had been penned by Col. A. D. Hunter in the 1800s, lay on one side. She had found it in the annals of the reserved section, tucked back in the archives. The volume was titled: *The History of Raby.*

She was making notes on references to the 1700s—it was a gold mine of information. She spent the evening skimming each chapter. She was drawn to sections that featured the Raby family tree. Her pen marked the events of significance on the yellow pad. Her notes had become a manuscript, and this recent reference volume filled in much of the needed historical blanks and cleared up discrepancies.

"Oh my," she mumbled to herself. "I never realized the role Ezra had in this town." She continued to record each noteworthy observation of history.

Nelson would follow up and call her as promised, and visit her old home. Mrs. Perry later visited the church house and was pleased with the renovations. She had stories to tell Nelson, from her life residency in Harvest, as she sat in Lydia's favorite wing chair.

"Nelson," Mrs. Perry said, fishing for a hanky in her bag. She wiped the corner of one eye. "You remember that I had mentioned that I had something for you . . . when we met at the library that evening—before they closed?"

"Yes," he responded. "You didn't say what it was, but I remember you mentioning something." He leaned closer.

"Well . . . here it is," she said, handing him a box of papers and handwritten notes. "It is really two things," she teased. "I'm an old lady and have compiled a manuscript over the years. It is not typed and I don't have a computer. Those newfangled things just confuse me. My eyes are bad . . . glaucoma they say. I want you to have my manuscript and a reference book."

"Oh, my God," he said with surprise. "Why me?" He held his breath as he flipped through her notes. There was a sigh that followed, and then a smile.

"Nelson Palmer . . . I've been watchin' you closely. You are good for the town. Those other hoodlums don't care nothin' 'bout this town. We older folks do! How old are you?"

"Sixty-six—soon to be sixty-seven," he replied.

She sat back and stared straight ahead. "I've compiled information over fifty or more years on this town. Some observations have never been known or read about. It's all in there," she said, pointing to the manuscript in the very large box. "Perhaps someday it will be published . . . maybe you can arrange for that . . . after I'm gone."

She looked at the cathedral ceiling. "I'm almost dead, my eyes are bad and my health is deteriorating each month," she whispered to Nelson and Lydia. "Not much time left here." Nelson and Lydia tried to console her as she slipped into what appeared to be a moment of depression.

"Oh, by the way . . . here's something else . . . another piece of reading," she added, passing the book to him. "It has even more information on this town. Stuff no one has seen, I'm quite sure."

Nelson and Lydia were amazed at what the old woman was doing. She was sharing her entire life's observations in a journal, and with the Palmers—who were basically strangers to her.

"In case you are wondering why I'm doing this," Mrs. Perry said, "it's my legacy to the town. I have no one left for relatives and surely didn't want to pass this information on to the locals . . . those miserable bas . . . ," she said without finishing her sentence.

"This is phenomenal," Nelson said, with amazement. "I will read all of this as soon as I physically can. I am amazed at what you have done here. It is so valuable to history, and to this tiny town," he said.

Mrs. Perry sat back and looked at both of her new friends.

"I was married in this church. Me and the mister. I've always loved this building and ceiling. You have maintained its beauty and classic architecture." She then looked at the Palmers and indicated that she had to leave. There were pills that she needed to take for hip pain and her stomach ailment. She winced in pain. Nelson looked at Lydia with concern—she returned the look with a frowned expression.

Nelson held her hand for a moment. She felt his warmth.

"I'm fine, dear . . . I'm fine . . . but I must go. These old bones can't sit for long. They cramp up my legs and my feet swell up."

Nelson was concerned. "Can I drive you home?"

"Can I get you water or iced tea?" Lydia interjected. "A drink of something, perhaps?"

"No thank you, dear. I really must go. I have a doctor's appointment tomorrow. Let him figure out this old broad's problems," she said, standing slowly.

As she headed for the door, Mrs. Perry said, "Enjoy the knowledge, Nelson Palmer. . . . You deserve to know the truth. You seem to care."

He could not wait to read what she had left behind.

He walked Mrs. Perry to her 1982 faded blue Chevy. She settled into her seat and closed the door.

"I've enjoyed this afternoon," she said out the car window. "I've not had many friends over the years, but you seem so good for this town. Take care of this town. And one more thing!" she added emphatically. Nelson listened intently. "Straighten out the history . . . I mean, get the damn history straight . . . please. Those nitwits don't know nothin'."

Nelson, puzzled by her comments, agreed to do what she asked. Mrs. Perry cranked up the window, then drove off, slowly.

Lydia stood by her husband's side and looked up sadly at his furrowed brow. "Honey, what does she mean?"

"Don't know, dear . . . but assume she's referring to something in the manuscript. Need to read that soon," he said, almost nervously. Returning to the house, Nelson sat near the manuscript box and the older reference volume that was partially broken apart from age. The title page of the handwritten manuscript read *Return to Raby.* Nelson found that most interesting. He was compelled to delve into it.

In addition to the manuscript there was a cover letter addressed to the Palmers. It was signed by Mrs. Perry who bequeathed the entire compilation to them. It was a legally binding transfer as far as Mrs. Perry could make it legal without professional counsel. She apparently hated lawyers and legal mumbo jumbo. She had given Nelson and Lydia her life story and her dedicated perspective on the history of the town of Harvest. The additional historical book supplemented her written manuscript. It contained voluminous information about a town . . . a town she referred to as *Raby.*

✠✠✠

The 911 call came into the local Harvest town dispatcher at midnight. It was an emergency call from the Perry homestead . . . one that suggested that she was having difficulty breathing. The EMTs never had a chance to revive her. She sat dead in her parlor chair, the phone next to her side and "The Late Show" still on TV. At 1:30 A.M. the coroner released her body to the local funeral home seven miles north of town. The coroner's report would be "death by natural causes." He did not deem her demise the result of foul play, so no autopsy was needed. The coroner merely concluded that she died from old age—cessation of the heart. Her personal physician was contacted and shared her medical history with the coroner. He confirmed to the coroner that she had been failing during the previous four months.

Nelson heard of Mrs. Perry's passing when he stopped by the store to get the morning paper. Lydia was visibly moved by the news. It was almost fate that their meeting and significant discussions occurred the previous day.

Nelson was surprised that the Perry family plot was next to the church home. Her husband was buried there. They attended her funeral, remaining in the back of the group of friends who attended.

Lydia decided to take care of their graves by planting bulbs and raking the heavy layer of fallen leaves. In time, Nelson paid for a larger and more contemporary stone for the Perrys. It would be an anonymous donation. The memorial would be engraved with Mrs. Perry's full name—*Abigail (Raby) Parker-Perry*. She was a Raby after all, he found through his research. She was related to him and Aunt Bess. Nelson would have the stone engraved with the accolade: *Harvest, N.H., historian, respected citizen and author of Return to Raby.*

Nelson Palmer would make sure that the Abigail Raby Perry manuscript was published in due time. He and Lydia would edit the book themselves and then seek a publisher. If there was no interest by a major house, he planned to self-publish the volume. In time, the volume would shatter the myths and inaccurate history of the town. Through his quest for his roots and with the aid of the Perry document, the Palmers would be thrust into the "infrastructure" of Harvest, New Hampshire. Life for them would change dramatically following the Perry death.

⊞⊞⊞

The Palmers decided to share with Susan and Doug what Mrs. Perry had told them. They were increasingly interested in town history. The Palmers also brought them into their confidence about their lottery winnings, and swore them to secrecy, just as they had done with the rest of their family—their four daughters.

Susan, in turn, encouraged Nelson to donate money to short-funded community activities, and he often did so—anonymously. Some parents and their children noted that town activities were becoming more formalized and more embellished. Local fund-raisers often exceeded their goals in revenue—this was never achieved before. Autumn fairs and fall barbecues seemed to realize more donations than in previous years. The prosperity of the town looked more promising. Much of the change was due to Nelson's investments through his holding companies, as well as his subtle but large contributions to worthwhile functions in town. In time, more team sports were added to the local schools. Donations for band equipment and sports equipment made a huge difference in the attitudes of the children and their parents.

With the Nelson Palmer investments in real estate and his numerous secret donations, came the renewed attentiveness of the newer residents. They became more visible at football games and town functions. Some assumed that the town had a new and more active interest in its youth. Activities for kids became more prevalent and the crime rate of teenagers decreased proportionally. Harvest was changing quickly and teenagers were involved in productive after-school activities.

There were fewer altercations and more interest in creative endeavors. In reality, it was Susan's influence on Nelson and his generosity that was subtly changing the locals' attitude.

✠✠✠

Massapot Lake, which Jason Birch and Nelson Palmer often fished, was naturally spring-fed from the bottom and also stream-fed from the north. Jason's new home had been built on the shores of that pristine lake. The lake's egress was a river that flowed from the south side, then meandered through the town of Harvest. Surrounding Jason Birch's new home were old-name neighbors, who passed their homes to their offspring. Generation to generation of ownership of those cottages and homes maintained their family control and heritage. Outsiders had a limited chance of acquiring the cottages, which became available for sale from time to time. They rarely were listed with Realtors.

Relatives grabbed all available property to keep the land within the family.

Oddly enough, two of the cottages caught fire and burned in October. They each were a total loss and the state fire marshal attributed both of the fires to improperly installed woodstoves and creosote-coated chimney flues. The thick, tar composite was the result of infrequent cleaning or the improper use of softer firewood. Pine wood was burned by the owners because it was cheaper and more readily available from nearby woods than hardwood—it saved on annual fuel bills, but was risky because of the residual creosote. Arson was never suspected in either case.

The cottages were never rebuilt; the insurance policies were inadequate to cover the cost of rebuilding. Nelson had his holding company purchase both lots, even though the prices were extravagant; the old-name families were testing the market and did not want to really sell them. They were shocked when the holding companies paid the asking price. With their acquisition, Nelson owned five pieces of land around the lake. Two were undeveloped pieces of land previously purchased through his holding companies. One he had purchased for Jason, and the two recent acquisitions. A pattern was occurring around the lake. Old names were no longer in control of the best property. People began to realize that Harvest was changing and that the homes in the center of the town and the lakefront properties were no longer owned by the old-timers. What people did not realize was that Nelson Palmer had a hidden agenda; a mission that was masked by holding companies and an incessant desire for change.

"Honey, how many properties do we own now?" Lydia asked.

"A few honey, some here and some there. Why, doll?"

"I was just curious. You seem to be becoming *the* town father. All these prime properties come up and you grab them," she said. "The lakefront ones, the ones for our girls, and Jason's, just may make people curious. It's all happening so fast."

"Uncle Ezra inspired me, dear. Uncle Ezra," he repeated, with a grin.

"How's that?" she asked. "What's Uncle Ezra got to do with this?"

"Well, I've been studyin' the ol' reverend at the library. Mrs. Perry's manuscript is full of information on his life. He was extremely prominent at one time and owned some of the land by the lake. I'm just slowly collectin' his old land back."

Lydia just smirked. "How much of Ezra's land do you want dear?" she retorted. "All of it?"

"Maybe . . . just maybe. Actually, it would be nice to reclaim what he used to own. He lost much of it in bad land deals and through corruption and false promises. Turns out he was conned quite often by the locals. Mrs. Perry's notes suggest that Ezra Raby was a significant landowner within various parts of this town."

"Really?" she added. "Like what did he control?"

"Turns out that he was in politics and contributed much to the town in general. He was very unusual in that he mixed church and state by becoming both pastor and a local representative. He was very influential and creative. He practically raised all the money to build this church . . . solo."

"Really? He did both jobs—religious leader and statesman?"

"I think he did a lot of things besides raise a large family. He was an icon in the early days. I haven't read all that much yet, but he was a man of action and community. He obviously wanted the town to be the embodiment of God-fearing people, who were also productive, communal citizens."

Nelson told Lydia all that he had learned about the good reverend. Nelson had became a voracious reader of the town's history and of Ezra. The problem was that most town biographers and historians had written little of Ezra Raby's influence. Some books didn't even mention him or his contributions, much less the impact that he had on the town. Mrs. Perry's lifelong history of her family, and the town, was as in-depth a review of the town's beginnings as existed anywhere. Her Raby family name was her inspiration for documenting her own mother's roots and the town's accurate, hidden history. It was probably the only factual account of who had settled there and fostered the growth and prosperity of the original town. Nelson considered that his roots depended on knowing the role of the Rabys in Harvest's history. He would become possessed by the challenge and seek all historical accounts that Mrs. Perry had pursued. He would go beyond her knowledge and energy—using her manuscript as the baseline and then stepping stone for seeking the truth. Her ground-work over decades facilitated his quest, and without her research, he would be at a loss as to where his relatives actually came from, or settled.

Fifteen

It was a cool Saturday night in early October. In a field at the base of Mt. Massaspot, a young woman's legs were widespread and her feet sticking out the back window of the car, and a boy was experiencing his loss of virginity. The girl, who was on her back and had braced her feet on the car windowsill, was writhing in ecstasy underneath him. She was none other than the notorious Tammy Prescott, affectionately recognized by the locals as the "town pump." Her promiscuity and apparent nymphomania were well known, especially by young men. Budweiser cans and stale cigarette butts surrounded the outside of the car. The couple had been there a while and Jamie, aged seventeen, was pumping his way to heaven. He and Tammy were so into the event, that they never noticed the passing cars.

The police, attending to an accident, had no time that evening to be looking for anyone "parking." Tammy and Jamie were safe from being caught. They ended up smoking a joint and making love again. Tammy would get home at 3:00 A.M. Jamie would not go home and would crash at a friend's house shortly thereafter. He ended up telling his friend all about his evening with Tammy Prescott. Jamie now had something to brag about for the first time in his life.

✠ ✠ ✠

In November, Tammy Prescott, inebriated from five beers, sat on the edge of her bed and picked up the telephone. She dialed Jamie's number, the boy who had been her latest love conquest. She missed few of the local boys who found her attractive and sensual. She had been promiscuous throughout high school and into her twenties. She was somewhat distraught over the fact that her period was five days late. It had always been very predictable. Young Jamie, whose virginity she had claimed, was her target of responsibility for the delayed menses.

"Jamie . . . this is Tammy. I have a problem—a big problem."

Jamie, who was a few years younger and infatuated with her sexual prowess, was not prepared to hear of her physical dilemma.

"Jamie . . . I think I'm pregnant," she whispered. She sighed deeply. He was silent for a few seconds. "Actually, I am pregnant!" she said emphatically.

"What? What the hell are you talking about? You can't be!" he responded, shaking. "You just can't be."

"My period is late. I think I am," she said. "It's never this late."

His parents, watching TV across the room, caught snatches of his desperate conversation.

"What's wrong, dear?' said his mother. "Is there something wrong?"

"Nothin'," he responded in a cold sweat. He spoke quietly to Tammy and then stood up and hung up the extension phone. He ran to the bedroom, slammed his door, and sat on the edge of his bed. He picked up the receiver on the nightstand, knocking a picture frame to the floor and shattering the glass.

"Tammy," he said slowly. "You . . . you . . . said you were on the pill. You said . . . "

Tammy cut him off. "Dammit, Jamie! . . . I'm pregnant. I guess I missed a pill or somethin'. It . . . it happens. I probably missed one or two."

Jamie was shocked with her lack of concern. He became irate. "Jesus, Tammy! People don't just forget pills like that!"

"Shut up, you twerp," she said with venom in her voice. "This happened once before. It just happens."

"You mean you've been pregnant before?" he said with surprise.

"Yes! Why?" she asked, as if it were a routine for her. "You aren't the first one to have had me in a backseat. What's the big deal

121

anyway? If I don't bleed soon, I can have the 'coat-hanger' deal," she continued, coldly.

" 'Coat-hanger deal'?" he asked naïvely. "What's that?"

"You stupid kid . . . an abortion! You know . . . I can have one done for a couple hundred bucks in Concord. Not an actual coat hanger like people use in poorer parts of the world. A professional abortion."

He was shocked.

"I'll need some money. Can you steal some from your parents?"

"Ah . . . for the abortion? You mean . . . money to kick the kid?" he said with sadness. He was mortified by her attitude over the value of human life. He was brought up Catholic and never envisioned himself in this quandary.

"I'm not gonna stay pregnant, if that's what you mean," she added spitefully.

"But maybe we could stay together and raise the baby," he suggested. "I don't want to kill the thing."

Tammy laughed. "You can't be serious," she said. "I'm not ready for kids and you are kind of young. Besides, I don't love you. This was just fun, right? Ya know . . . fun sex," she exclaimed.

"Well . . . well," he stammered. "It meant more to me—the sex and love. I kind of . . . love you. You are the best," he said, trembling.

But she was merciless to the young man with inexperience in relationships. "Jamie, I don't want kids. I'm only 'the best' to you because you never had sex with anyone. I wanted you to have an awesome experience the first time. I enjoyed making you feel special . . . but I don't want kids with you."

"Jesus, Tammy!" he said. "Don't I mean anything to you? I was just a lay to you?"

"Jamie. . . Look!" she confided, "I have been with many men. You are not the only one recently. I dated Bob for a while . . . he knocked me up last time, claimin' that the rubber failed. He just wasn't careful when we were done. I've been with him in the last month."

"What?" he cried out. "You were seein' someone else too, while I was with you?"

"Jamie. It doesn't matter. It's your kid. I need help now. Please help me get some money together. If you love me, you will help. I can get my friend Lisa to go with me to Concord. She's been through this problem before, herself.

"I've gotta go," he said. "I really feel ill right now. I think I'm going to puke."

The phone went dead for Tammy. Jamie ran to the bathroom and vomited. He was pale and sweaty as he bent over the toilet. His mother thought that he was sick with something he had eaten. She questioned him about the phone call, but he did not say much. He could not sleep that night. *He was about to be responsible for the loss of a baby if she was truly pregnant*, he thought. He was too naïve to realize that it might not even be his child. And he didn't know how to dispute her claim that he was the father. All he knew was that he loved her and that her love was unrequited. He was sweet, young, and foolish. She was older, manipulative, and controlling—a side of her he had not known until that phone call.

✠✠✠

Life in Harvest was that of a small town that never changed. It consistently had situations where young folks were in trouble. Chief Darren Gooden and his staff were often distracted by young persons whose escapades were foolish and time-consuming for the police force. There were teenage parties—kids drinking booze in the woods and stealing beer and cigarettes from their parents. Gooden often thought that it was merely the lack of things to do in the community, and he was partially right. The part that could elucidate the issue was the "parent factor" or the lack thereof, in the local teens' lives. Few old-name residents really cared about what their kids were doing or where they were late at night. That was because they themselves acted that way when they were young and figured their kids should be able to do the same. Each week, the police dealt with the same old issues. They knew where the kids hung out when they were getting in trouble. Bringing the delinquent children home to their parents was a common occurrence. The chief was often chastised by irate parents who claimed that his staff was profiling their kids, and ruining their reputations. A recent episode in town resulted in an harassment lawsuit against the police by a family that had children who were frequent violators of the law. They claimed that the police officers singled out their children and their family. When the family did not win the suit, which was deemed irrelevant, they became even more abrasive and outspoken of the "new" police chief. Old names banded together against the police, citing that the town had become a police state with a gestapo attitude since he came to town. Nothing was further from the truth, but the old names sought local support to fight the town's law enforcement procedures and their standard operating methods.

What the parents of the delinquent kids didn't understand was that the police were distracted from more serious business because of *their* children's misbehavior. Emergency response and mutual aid calls from surrounding towns were hampered by the Harvest teenagers' behavior. The youngsters were jeopardizing the safety of normal, law-abiding citizens, but parents didn't understand the chief's concerns.

Chief Darren Gooden made it a point to drop by occasionally to visit with Nelson, urging him stop at the station when he was in town. But, one day, when Nelson took him up on an offer of a cup of coffee at the police department, their conversation was shorter than intended.

"Crap! Oh no! Gotta go! Emergency! Just got paged!"

"What's wrong? What is it, Darren?" Nelson asked with concern. The chief was obviously distressed as he stared in silence at the message on the pager.

"Shit . . . Jamie . . . that young Jamie in town. . . just hung himself . . . the little shit just did himself in. . . . Oh God . . . he was so young."

Jamie's mother had found him when she went out to dry some sheets from the laundry. Gooden ran to his police car. His blue lights were flashing before he left the parking lot. There was no siren as he responded to the "silent alarm." An ambulance pulled out from the rescue squad and followed the police chief.

Nelson, left standing alone in the parking area, was stunned by the news of the event. Even though he had only met Jamie in passing, he wondered why a young person would find something so distressing in town that he would take his own life.

Across town, Tammy Prescott was not aware of the suicide. It had been four weeks since she had asked him for money. She had talked to him two hours earlier, after she had returned from an abortion clinic in Concord, and she was drunk. Budweiser cans accumulated in the trash can of her parent's home. She decided to call Jamie. She thanked him for a portion of the money he had stolen from his parents. His stress and grief over her phone call, and his role in taking cash from his parents for an abortion was contrary to his Catholic upbringing, plunging him into immediate depression.

The rescue squad and Chief Gooden lowered his limp torso from the backyard willow tree. They began resuscitation as fast as it was humanly possible, but there was no response.

Jamie's mother knew that money was missing from the drawer, but never told her husband about it. She surmised that Jamie had taken it and used it for drugs, booze, or some other thing related to teenage entertainment. Jamie's infatuation for Tammy had caused much anxiety and depression, and his mother was aware of his feelings for the slightly older woman. But Jamie's mother, who was always attentive to his needs, had no idea Tammy was pregnant or the extent of her son's psychological state of mind, or she would have had him seek professional counseling or medical attention.

The event had an impact on Nelson's way of thinking toward the young folks in town. After he found out the details of the tragedy from the chief, he utilized Jamie's demise as fodder against the selectmen for their neglect of the young people of the community.

What could have been done to improve the environment for young residents? he wondered. *Perhaps constructive nurturing through community activities would have given Jamie something more to hold on to than Tammy Prescott.*

Sixteen

The early winter snow blew across the windswept graveyard next to the church home, catching in the dried, brown flower stalks in Lydia's garden.

The snow drifted against gravestones, partially obscuring the names and dates. But the howling winds were rarely heard inside the well-constructed and well-insulated church house. Nelson had installed a woodstove that could accommodate three-foot logs, and the cathedral ceilings trapped the hot air that rose from the heating system. Nelson turned on fans located at the peak of the ceiling to blow the warm air back down to room level. The system worked perfectly.

During the day, even in winter, the stained-glass windows cast beautiful visions of art onto the interior walls and floors. The cascade of colors moved with the low position of the winter sun, and the pastel hues from the framed stained glass augmented the warm feeling of each room. The Palmers were enjoying their first winter.

Nelson was still tangling with the selectmen over renovation issues. They blocked many of his proposed changes to the house and property. He bypassed their authority to get his projects done, regardless of how it annoyed them. Most of the litigation between Nelson and the town was tied up in motions and delayed hearings. He had heard that the selectmen were digging deeply into town reserves to fight him, wondering where his money to continue expensive legal battles came from. They even speculated that he was a drug dealer. "Who is this man?" they asked. They looked for ways to annoy him so that he might even go back to wherever he had come from. Good riddance.

The town was supposed to maintain and plow the paved road to the church. The Palmers, like many of their neighbors, knew they were responsible for digging out their own driveways and parking areas. Road manager Morris Halliwell, from an old name family, was well aware that the Palmers were residing in an unapproved dwelling with an unpermitted septic system. He decided to give them a dose of their own medicine. If they weren't going to play by town rules, why should he? He decided to have the road plowed last in the rotation, or perhaps not at all. The road to the church was not heavily used, especially in winter. Inadequate plowing would inconvenience these nasty newcomers and restrict them to their houses, Halliwell decided.

"Damn," Nelson said, looking out one of the clear glass windows. "I pay these asswipes and this town my taxes, and on time. They can't even plow this simple road. I wanted to go to the store today. I can't get beyond the driveway. Look at all that stuff." Lydia said nothing; she was used to his tirades.

Nelson called the road manager's number. He got the answering machine.

"Hey, you turkeys, this is Palmer. We haven't seen a plow since this snow started. We need to get to the store before dark. What the hell is the matter with you guys?" he fumed after the beep.

When Halliwell listened to it, he laughed and played it for his cronies. "Let them shovel!"

As the snow deepened, Nelson became concerned about being without access to the highway. He did not like the fact that there was no way for the fire department to reach his property, if needed.

"Bastards. They are going to have another lawsuit if they don't get here soon," he said to Lydia, as he paced back and forth, watching the road.

The heavy, wet snow continued steadily through the night. It was stunningly beautiful all around the property. Nelson had used his snowblower in the area where the car was parked and shoveled the walkway three times during the storm. He expected to see a plow at least by daybreak so he could make a run to the store.

As the skies began to clear the next morning, Lydia awoke with severe chest pains.

"Love, I think I have heartburn. It was probably that silly pizza from the freezer last night," she said, wincing, when Nelson brought her antacid tablets. Pains were not that uncommon from angina and heartburn, but her mother had a history of heart disease and had died at a young age. Lydia and Nelson had annual physicals and she never missed an appointment. Her high cholesterol and high blood pressure were controlled by medication. Atherosclerosis was prevalent in her family on both sides, but she was reluctant to change her dietary habits. She ate what she cooked for Nelson and that wasn't always heart friendly, and she was used to having heartburn and indigestion from her excesses. Her recipes were not low-fat by any stretch of the imagination. Her file of recipes was a series of volumes. She was a culinary expert with subscriptions to many cooking magazines. She knew she shouldn't have had that pizza but, without being able to get to the store, dinner options had been limited.

Her pain did not dissipate with an antacid tablet or Pepcid AC.

"Nelson," she cried out again. "Come help, please," she said, grimacing. She grabbed her chest and lowered herself into an easy chair. Her hand covered her heart and breasts as she held tightly the pearls around her neck—the same pearls he had given her on their recent wedding anniversary.

"Honey . . . what's wrong?" he asked tenderly. "Not another episode . . . is it?"

"'Fraid so, hon. Can you get me a nitroglycerin tablet from the cupboard, please?" she asked, struggling to find a comfortable position in the soft chair. "I think it's my angina, again."

As Nelson raced to the kitchen for the pills, he heard her scream, "NELSON!"

He dropped the pill and ran back to his wife. She had fallen to the floor and was struggling for breath. Nelson cried out, "Lydia . . . oh, my sweet Lydia . . ." She was breathing heavily and clutching her throat. She was pale and becoming cyanotic. Nelson grabbed the phone nearby and dialed 911 as fast as he could locate the buttons. He missed a number and redialed.

"Jesus," he said, looking down at her. He knelt beside her and grasped her hand tenderly.

"Emergency!" replied the voice on the other end of the phone. "Is this a medical, fire, or police emergency?"

"Medical! Help, please. Need ambulance . . . heart attack, I think. Please, help!" Nelson stammered.

"Sir . . . where are you? Location, please!" responded the dispatcher.

"Church home on the hill . . . the old church in Harvest . . . the Palmers . . . my wife . . . she's on the floor . . . heart I think . . . hurry! Please!" he added in tears.

"Mr. Palmer, is she breathing?"

"Yes," he responded, checking her mouth and nose. "Yes . . . she's breathing . . . it's shallow and fast . . . please hurry!"

"Sir, we are on our way . . . *they* are on their way . . . stay on the phone with me . . . stay with me. I need to know her condition constantly so you and I can help her," she said reassuringly. "OK?"

"Yes," he responded softly. "Lydia . . . they are coming to help . . . stay with me girl." He sobbed as he cradled her head in his lap, his tears falling on her forehead.

Lydia looked up at him and managed a smile. "Not my time yet, Nel," she mumbled softly. He smiled back at his wife of decades. Her eyes drifted and refocused. Her eye muscles oscillated her eyes repetitively, a medical condition called nystagmus, often seen in anesthesia.

Outside, the skies were overcast, and the snow had started again. It was even more intense. The drifts became enormous due to the northeasterly wind. The storm was recirculating the area—a common effect of a counterclockwise "nor'easter."

The damn road was still not plowed. Nelson had forgotten that when he called 911. Lydia was sweating profusely and her breathing was becoming labored. She became ashen. Nelson was scared. *Is she having an actual heart attack?* he wondered. *The visual signs were there.* He knew CPR from his training at work, but that was on Resusci-Annie, a CPR training doll. Lydia moaned and the dispatcher was still trying to garner information from him . . . her age, weight, family doctor, medical history, and vital signs. Nelson knew most of the answers. He had no way to monitor her blood pressure. Her heart rate and pulse were rapid. He counted her wrist pulse for fifteen seconds and multiplied it by four. Normally sixty to seventy beats per minute, it now seemed extremely rapid to him.

The EMT response team in Harvest had a standard four-wheel drive ambulance—a truck-like rescue vehicle, equipped with the latest diagnostic instrumentation, a defibrillator, and multiple cardiac drugs. It responded to the vicinity of the Palmer's road within two minutes. The siren could be heard from the rescue squad building as it traveled to the church house. The ambulance turned and slid onto the Palmer's road, but could not proceed farther. The road was impassable. A police cruiser arrived. Chief Gooden jumped out. He had heard the distress call on the emergency frequency. Nelson was his friend and supporter and he needed to help as best he could.

"Damn road!" he shouted. "Where's the fuckin' plow? This snow cannot be negotiated," he radioed back to the police station. "Get me a plow, now! Stat!" he screamed to the dispatcher. His face was red with rage.

The EMTs', heads and shoulders now snow covered, were aghast. They could see the church in the distance, but could not get there. The dispatcher reiterated that Lydia's condition was dire. They needed all the equipment in the vehicle for maximum cardiac response, but had to leave the vehicle behind, in a snowbank. Instead, they took off on foot, jumping through the snow like they were traversing waves at a beach. It was extremely slow going, but still forward progress. Time was of the essence. They carried their red emergency cases containing essential cardiac equipment, and emergency drug therapy. They surmised that she was experiencing a heart attack. One EMT carried a portable green oxygen bottle. It was heavy and cumbersome.

Nelson left Lydia's side just long enough to peer out the front door. He could see the flashing lights in the distance and saw two men wading toward him in knee-deep snowbanks. When he returned, Lydia was having difficulty breathing. A gurgling sound came from her throat, and she twitched and jerked, gasping for air. She stopped breathing. Her eyes were wide and rolled backwards. The whites of her eyeballs became more prominent. She was dying and Nelson was panicked. The automated external defibrillator (AED) was in the hands of an EMT and he was still seventy-five feet from the home. He was exhausted from running through the deep snow. Nelson started CPR on Lydia. He tilted her head back, pinched her nose, and covered her mouth with his lips. He attempted to breathe for Lydia and then positioned his crossed hands over her chest as he had been taught. He compressed her chest and counted . . . one, two, three, four, five, six. He would then breath in her mouth again. Lydia did not respond; she had ceased breathing on her own. He was her breath and heartbeat. He frantically tried to revive her.

The snowplow arrived just as the EMTs entered the Nelson Palmer home. It was of no immediate help. It didn't matter now. Nelson was holding Lydia in his arms, as he bawled like a child. His tears fell on her now pale, beautiful face. Her face was still, her eyes closed, her mouth slightly open. The EMTs politely asked Nelson to step aside. They began formal CPR and requested input from the local hospital ER doctor. But their attempt to defibrillate her was in vain. They resorted to intracardiac epinephrine, as a last resort. There was no ECG. A clot-busting drug, TPA, was without response as well. There was no pulse and no ECG. After a few minutes they sat back and hung their heads. Five minutes had made all the difference in their potential ability to bring her back. All it took was a single pass by the plow. A third ambulance attendant was finally able to drive the emergency van to the front of the house. It was of no help at this point.

Chief Gooden stopped the plow driver on his way out and lambasted him. "You fuckin' asshole! Where the hell were you? Do you know that a woman died because you didn't the run the plow as scheduled? Why was this road in this condition? All other roads in the area had been plowed at least once. Why not this one?"

The driver shrugged his shoulders and lowered his head.

"I'm telling you, I'm going to be a witness in the mess. I'll see you and your boss and the rest of the crew in court. The condition of this road is a travesty. We . . . you and me, are public servants. I could not get up the road either. Lydia Palmer is dead! Perhaps she had something that was treatable. Did you hear me? . . . You . . . you ass! I ought to have you arrested for neglect of the public thoroughfare in an emergency situation."

The snowplow driver said nothing, then drove slowly off—the yellow-flashing strobe lights atop his truck cab fading in the distance.

His shoulders covered with snow, Chief Gooden went inside, with his hat in his hands. He rotated it slowly as he saw Nelson standing to his left. Nelson looked at him and the chief hugged him. "I'm so sorry . . . I'm . . . so sorry," he said, patting Nelson on the back. Nelson looked at his wife on the floor. He looked at the chief and whispered, "Those bastards will pay for this, Darren, they will pay!"

Darren Gooden whispered, "Nelson . . . please sit down. I will stay with you . . . and wait."

"Wait?" Nelson said angrily, "Wait for what? . . . The coroner?"

"Yes, Nelson," replied the chief. "We need to follow state procedures prior to moving Lydia's body. I'm sorry. These are state laws now, not local ordinances. OK? Please sit a bit longer."

Nelson nodded and sighed deeply. He stared at his wife, and then looked to the cathedral ceiling as he sought solace from the Lord. The EMTs covered Lydia with a white sheet and Nelson knelt again to kiss her one more time. He peeled back the cover and kissed her forehead and lips, which were now closed. She was cool to the touch . . . and pale. Her face was relaxed and beautiful, her hair in place. She looked peaceful and appeared to be nothing more than sleeping. Nelson smoothed out her clothing. He patted her hand. He placed a pillow from the couch under her head. One EMT distraught that he had been unable to revive her, said, "I'm so sorry, sir," he repeated over and over again. "There was no response to our efforts. If only we could have . . . "

Nelson cut him off. "You mean . . . if only you could have gotten here faster?"

"Yes, faster would have helped, Mr. Palmer—even three minutes would have helped. We had the latest in AEDs— the best defibrillator out there. Dammit! There are 400,000 people that go through this each year. The morbidity rate is high, but at least 100,000, or one-fourth, of them are saved by this little device I have here beside me, but . . . we have to be able to *get* to the patient!"

The other emergency personnel bowed their heads in dismay and depression, then departed with their equipment. *All this unnecessary agony and a loss of life, over a snow-covered road,* they thought. It was a good thing that the plow had already gone. If the driver had gotten out of the truck, Nelson would have killed him in anger. Alone with the police chief, Nelson mentioned that as Lydia struggled for breath he had contemplated murdering the plow driver or the road manager. The chief calmed him down and said, "Nelson, for the record, I never heard that . . . I know how you feel about the loss of Lydia but I never heard what you just said . . . OK?" Nelson apologized. "Please relax. I will stay here with you. I promise."

As they waited for the county coroner, the chief rotated his white hat in his hands and smiled compassionately toward Nelson. Nelson said nothing more. He lay beside his wife on the floor, one more time, lifted the sheet and caressed her body. He wept as he touched her hair and cheeks. Chief Gooden could not bear to watch him. He looked up at the wide-blade fan in the cathedral ceiling as it circled in slow motion. The chief felt his own tears well up, and wiped them with the back of his hand. He paced once or twice and checked his watch from time to time. He turned off his two-way radio on his belt. The entire church home was silent. He had summoned a backup officer who remained outside the church door.

A local funeral home sent a hearse to the church house. Nelson was allowed a few more moments alone with Lydia. Once the coroner arrived and had completed his exam and death certificate, Lydia Palmer's body was carried out on a gurney. Alone, inside, Nelson wailed out loud. He realized that his beloved Lydia would never see the autumn bulbs, which she had planted, emerge in the springtime—hundreds of them, which she had carefully and strategically placed about the churchyard. They would no longer share a life, a love, and a retirement together.

A deeply shocked Jason Birch arrived to console Nelson shortly after the hearse left. Nelson whispered, "Jason, please stay. My beloved Lydia is gone. I need to talk to you. I will be back later on. Wait for me here, please, and watch the house. Can you do that for me? I need to arrange for Lydia's funeral."

"Nelson . . . I'm so sorry . . . I will wait for you. I'm here to help you," said Jason, with tears in his tired, old eyes. He wiped them with a cloth handkerchief.

"Thanks, my friend," replied Nelson. "Darren has offered to give me a ride to the funeral home. I will be back in a while."

"Nelson, take your time. I'll watch the house for you till you and the missus get back." He cringed, realizing his slip. "I'm sorry, Nel."

"That's OK, Jason. This mess is moments old. You are a true friend in my time of need. I will pay you back. I may need you in the days to come. I will not let this travesty go unspoken. That is when you can help me . . . OK?" Nelson patted his friend's cheek three times.

"Yes," replied Jason. "Whatever you need, I will help you with. You can count on me Nel. Just ask," he said.

"Thank you, my friend," replied Nelson, shaking Jason's hand firmly, and then met the police chief outside. He would be driven to the Johnson Brothers Funeral home, seven miles to the north. Nelson looked at the recently plowed road. It was totally clear of snow and heavily sanded. He became nauseated by the pristine condition of the road, but he did not vomit. The chief said nothing along the way to the funeral director's office. Nelson wept silently in the passenger seat of the cruiser.

The nightmare was just beginning for him. He first needed to take care of the arrangements for his deceased wife and then he could address the real issue—the irresponsible assholes in the town of Harvest. For Nelson, his grief was only surpassed by his anger—he would find a way to punish those responsible. Even if they didn't like him, they had no right to create a dangerous situation in which a beautiful, innocent life would be taken.

As Nelson and the chief were heading north on Route 10, Susan and Doug rounded the corner to the Palmers' church road. They had been shopping and were unaware of what had just occurred. Jason Birch would sadly bring them up-to-date.

Susan dropped to her knees, her head in her hands. Lydia had been her surrogate mother in many ways. Doug stood by her and touched her shoulder gently. Overcome with emotion, Susan ran into

Lydia's bedroom and shut the door. Doug and Jason Birch did not follow her. She stared at the photos on the wall, and held a piece of Lydia's clothing close to her heart. Susan then placed the blouse slowly under her nose—it had Lydia's perfume on it. She cried out in pain from the memory of her familiar scent. She saw the many smiling photographs of Nelson and Lydia about the room. There were photos of when they were young, and snapshots taken in Pennsylvania before their move to New Hampshire. An album of the recent renovations in Harvest was on her dresser—even pictures of Lydia and Susan together. Each milestone of events was recorded in pictures. There were moments captured of the changes in structure and décor.

"Dear God," she prayed as she looked at the ceiling, "please grant my beloved friend, Lydia eternal rest. Please God, do this one thing for me . . . please."

Doug opened the antique liquor chest that Nelson had refinished and poured himself a scotch. Jason declined his offer of a cocktail. The men spoke quietly, reminiscing about Lydia's life and her generosity toward the young and the old. Everyone who met her, loved her beyond compare.

"Just yesterday," Jason remarked, with fingers folded and his head bowed, "she baked me a cake for my cottage. She called to say that when the road was plowed they would bring it over and we'd have cake and coffee. She was so thoughtful and loving. I . . . I can't believe she's gone," he stammered.

Susan returned holding a photo of Lydia working in her church garden. She held the framed photo to her breast. She began to ask many questions. Jason relayed what little he knew. Doug kissed Susan on the forehead and then left to see if he could help Nelson with the funeral arrangements.

Susan was outraged as Jason told her that the EMTs' response was delayed by snow in the road.

"Are you fuckin' tellin' me that those bastards didn't plow . . . and that is the reason for Lydia's death? She actually might have been saved if they could have gotten to her?" she asked. Her profanity seemed to be the antithesis of the prayers that had been said in the former house of God, long before Nelson bought the property.

"Those bastards . . . I'll get them," she said loudly. "I know those slime dogs personally . . . the ones that plow the roads. They are all hired help, on subcontract by the town. Local yokels . . . all of them."

All Jason could do was listen to her vent.

She continued speaking, but a bit more softly and deliberately, "They will pay! They all make their money in the winter from plowing. They are under contract to do all streets . . . all of them. They have their construction trades all summer and then milk the town for plowing cash, to carry them through winter. Those bastards were drunk more than sober in my bar at the Three Pines Inn. They were always hammered! I'll fix their asses."

Jason Birch said nothing. He was too old to seek revenge for the town's actions or lack of actions. He stood up and walked around looking at the recent renovations of the house. His hands were held together behind his back as he leaned over to view some of the restoration work. He observed the many changes that Nelson and Lydia had designed and completed. Each room had a personality of its own and exuded warmth. She would be missed.

✠✠✠

Prior to the cremation, there was a wake and service at the Johnson Brothers Funeral Home. Mourners consisted of the Palmer's closest friends, their immediate family, Ed Hammond, his wife, Muriel, and some Harvest residents. The police chief and staff showed up as well. Even the EMTs stopped by. They still felt awful that they were unable to save Lydia.

"I am so sorry, Mr. Palmer," said one EMT. "If only we . . . "

Nelson hugged him. "You did what you could. . . . You and your colleagues did what you could."

Ed stood by Nelson's side at all times, especially during the afternoon and evening viewing hours.

"How are you holdin' up, my friend?" he said softly. "Can I get you anything? Coffee? A drink of water perhaps?" Nelson nodded yes, but said little else. He stared at Lydia's face and felt the warmth of their years together. He cried out loud and his daughters rushed to his side. He sat down and rested for a while. *Thank God the wake is only one day*, he thought. He could not stand to have it go longer. It would be too much for him. The daughters gave him sanity. Two of them looked like their mother. He saw Lydia in their fair complexion, and high cheekbones.

The local townies, selectmen, road officials, and other appointed officials avoided the funeral and wake and paid no respects. No one from that group wanted to admit that they caused the death of Lydia Palmer.

Two weeks after Lydia's funeral, Nelson met with his attorney, William Mosley, to assess his options in filing litigation against the town, the plowing company, and the road agent. He sought damages based on a case of neglect and irresponsibility, since the road was not maintained in a timely or reasonable fashion for emergencies, resulting in the loss of life. The town manager and selectmen were well aware of why the road was not plowed. Nelson had documented all of his calls to Halliwell and the time and date of those calls. The town anticipated a massive lawsuit, and they would get it—$2,000,000. If he won the suit, the town would go broke, but Nelson didn't care. He was ready to break the town financially and the selectmen, mentally. He didn't care if the liability insurance company dropped the town's coverage as a result.

✠✠✠

Except for his four close friends, no one saw much of Nelson Palmer during the winter and for weeks into spring. Mosley represented his interests at meetings of the selectmen and took care of new legal papers. He deposed the entire road crew, and brought Nelson copies of the transcripts.

Nelson read and raged and wept. He placed the urn with Lydia's ashes on the fireplace mantel in the living room and put tall candles on each side. He brooded about the day of her untimely demise and he still could not believe all that had happened or that she was actually gone. It was a senseless, tragic event.

The road the Palmers lived on was maintained impeccably after the emergency episode, through the winter and into spring. All it took was three snowflakes to bring out the plow.

Jason Birch spent a lot of his spare time at Nelson's home. The two men played cards and drank beer. But at night, Nelson was alone and lonely. After so many years of being inseparable, Nelson was lost without his beloved companion. He saw his Lydia everywhere and in everything in the house. He saw the results of her labor in the gardens she planted in the fall when the flowers bloomed in the late spring. Nelson dispersed a small portion of Lydia's ashes in the garden that she loved so much. The foliage and bloom from year to year would remind him of her. She remained a perpetual presence in the land about the church home.

Nelson decided to spoil himself. He bought a Mack dump truck, complete with a sander and plow attachment, which filled the new garage that he had built behind his home. Although he had never gotten a building permit for the new building, the selectmen did not challenge him, especially when they found out what was stored in it.

Nelson would never be stranded again in a snowstorm. If the town plowing contractors failed to remove snow in a reasonable amount of time, he would do it himself or have Doug assist him. Doug and Susan thought the truck was cool. It was a toy to them and they were ready for the next winter's snow.

☩☩☩

Without Lydia, Nelson lost interest in the renovations. As the snows melted, he rededicated his free time to researching the family tree. His quest for his roots had been on hold as he grieved through the bitter winter. His research, combined with his town lawsuits, occupied much of his time, even as the weather finally warmed enough for walks through the woods.

To trace his genealogy, he traveled to any library that had archives on the town of Harvest or southern New Hampshire history. Some libraries were local, but for some research he had to go to Boston to learn more about the colonists who migrated to New Hampshire, primarily from Massachusetts.

Libby sensed that Nelson's relentless endeavors were a substitute for the loss of his wife. She aided him where she could. She was no more enamored with the town selectmen and politics than he was.

She had lost many budget battles in the past and the library operation suffered from the town's lack of funding.

"Nelson," she said one day, "all I requested last week was a set of new encyclopedias for the students in town. I admit they have gotten expensive," she added, "but the kids need them for the basics on book reports. The volumes are on disk now and the kids love to use the computers to search for information."

"Libby—order them!" he said. "Just order what you need, and I will pay for them."

"Really? They are costly now . . . hundreds or thousands of dollars," she remarked while reviewing the order form.

"Ms. Libby," he said with a smile, "please order what the kids need and have the bill sent to me . . . at the church house. OK?"

"Nelson, that is too much for someone to cover the expenses. It is a *town's* responsibility, not a resident's, to acquire these items. People will wonder why you did this," she added with concern.

"OK then, I'll donate money anonymously, in Lydia's memory. I will do it tomorrow and bring you a bank check. It will not have my name on it. OK?" he said firmly. "This is not a huge expense and the children deserve updated information on the world in general."

"Nelson, that is sweet of you to remember Lydia by a donation. You are a very thoughtful man."

"My thoughts and memories are all that's left . . . thoughts of her," he said staring at the vertical shelves of books. "I will get you a check for $10,000 tomorrow."

"Ten thousand dollars? Are you serious?" she asked, flabbergasted. "Did you say $10,000?"

"Yes . . . I did," he responded, smiling. "It will be here tomorrow with a written stipulation that the librarian, that's *you*, have control over the funds and their use. It will be clear to everyone in this town, *who* gets the funds."

Libby was in shock. That was more than the town budget for library materials for the entire year. It was enormously generous of him and she was amazed by his offer—made without hesitation. The amount would clearly cover many other needs for equipment and supplies.

Nelson folded up his files of historical notes and decided to read the remainder of Mrs. Perry's manuscript at home. Before he departed, he asked Ms. Libby to search the town codes and regulations regarding his septic system battle and other environmental issues. Nelson had researched most codes but had seen references to others that were older.

Eventually Nelson became well-versed in town law, so much so that he knew more than the selectmen and the town counselor. He began attending weekly town meetings and reciting regulations that counteracted what the officials thought to be true. He became a master at belittling them; they looked foolish. He began to gain the respect of residents, which was evidenced by the increase in their attendance at the meetings. Newer residents were there to cheer him on and to witness his legal prowess regarding every town issue in question. He was considered a hero for his fight with the elected asses, and a force to be reckoned with.

His *ad hoc* supporters called Nelson at night and encouraged him to run for public office. They indicated that if he didn't run, they would write him on the ballot anyway. He decided to test the political waters by asking his friend at the town dump to start questioning people on Saturdays about what they thought of "this Nelson Palmer guy." Nelson knew that the only way the town would change was if new blood was elected. He knew that Susan, Doug, Jason, and others would be there to help him with a campaign, if he decided to run for office. Lydia would be there in spirit. Gaining the support of the police and ambulance squad personnel would be a piece of cake. They had renewed respect for him and were influential.

✠✠✠

When Nelson arrived home from the library, he called Jason and asked him to come over for a beer. After chatting for a while, Nelson handed Jason a large paper bag. Jason Birch was already aware of the secret task at hand.

"Thanks, my friend," Nelson said. "You know what to do and where. Should be easy to accomplish late at night. Pick a night when the kids aren't there by the bridge, screwin' around. You can access the backyards easily if you follow the path. No one will see you . . . no one. I walked back there last fall and saw no one. I have no doubt that a subterranean aquifer runs near the brook and beneath their land."

"I will check it out tomorrow night . . . late. OK, Nelson?" Jason responded without hesitation. "I know that area well. It was once the railbed for the old railroad. No one will see me."

"I want to acquire the rest of the Victorian houses along that strip of town. They are prime property right in the town center. Let me know how it goes."

"You bet," Jason said. "I'll keep you posted."

Nelson was tired. As had become his custom, he kissed Lydia's urn before retiring to bed. He lit a candle on his nightstand and reflected on the memory of his deceased wife. He remembered how they always kissed good night, agreeing to never to go to sleep mad or in anger, and they never did.

After a while, he blew out the candle.

Seventeen

By spring, residents of the town of Harvest began to realize Nelson Palmer's impact. Yuppies who opposed the narrow-minded thoughts of the "townies" suddenly became proponents of change. They were no longer apathetic or distant and they seemed to have an advocate in Nelson Palmer—someone with clout. Nelson's participation in town hall meetings angered the council. They had scorned him from when he first showed up, but now realized that he was a force to be reckoned with. He was more knowledgeable and intelligent than they were.

One drizzly Saturday in May, the local paper reported that tainted well water had been discovered at three homes near each other in the center of town. Some longtime residents had become ill, perhaps from drinking the water from their wells. The only common link between the homes was a subterranean aquifer and a local brook. The brook, which flowed through town and behind the homes in question, was a tributary of the stream that was the egress from Massapot Lake.

The state officials from the EPA and Board of Health analyzed the water for toxins, pesticide residues, and animal waste runoff from nearby farms with cattle. The state checked for agricultural chemicals, and bacteria, like *E. coli* and other microorganisms. Each water sample from the residents' wells seemed to harbor household pesticide or herbicide contamination. The levels were higher than the normally accepted rate established by the U.S. EPA. Minimal levels of pesticide and herbicide residue were found in the nearby brook. Officials checked local farmlands to see if these products came from pastures and/or local produce fields. The leaching of residues into water could occur during a hard rainstorm; it had rained within the last few days. But usually the pesticide runoff was diluted by rain and dissipated rapidly in fast-running streams. This brook however had been low in volume and was virtually motionless in recent weeks. Chemical analyses of the water showed higher concentrations of contaminants in the wells in each of the backyards. *Is there a common connection between the wells?* officials wondered. *Why, all of a sudden, were there moderate contamination issues and higher levels of lawn and insecticide products?* one EPA inspector asked himself. He surmised that someone had used too much product on their lawn or garden.

"This doesn't make a whole lot of sense," he commented to his colleague. "These are not deep artesian wells; they are dug wells and not that deep."

"Yeah," replied the colleague. "The residents claimed that they used very little of those products on their grass. Some weed killer and TurfBuilder perhaps. That would result in some of the chemical metabolites we've measured, but I don't know if they would have toxicological effects at these levels." They were perplexed.

The residents who were hospitalized with nausea, headaches and malaise, showed blood levels of the chemicals or metabolites in question. Their clinical signs were that of toxicity. In the interest of public safety, the EPA officials temporarily condemned the homes and the wells. Obviously the owners had used the water for cooking, drinking, cleaning, bathing and other utilities. There was no way to know the origin of the contamination or the extent to which it was in the ground water. They rechecked the wells over a period of weeks. The contamination continued to persist, but at lower levels.

Before their property value dropped to zero, some of the owners decided to sell. They took what they could get. The stipulation in each sale was that the new owners assumed the clean up and remediation of the sites. Other local neighbors in the surrounding area feared the worst and considered listing their properties before the bottom fell out. They knew that their properties would be devalued in time. None of the original owners suffered long-term medical effects once they stopped ingesting their water.

The worst of the contaminated properties were eventually auctioned. Nelson's holding companies bid and won all but one. Eventually the continued testing by the EPA showed a reduction in the contamination of the original wells. Even when they were deemed pesticide free or at acceptable limits, the wells were ordered closed permanently. The holding companies were instructed to drill artesian wells at least one hundred and fifty feet down to seek a new water supply if the property was to be reused residentially.

Residents on the outskirts of Harvest looked at the availability of other property as investments, especially after the EPA revealed that the contamination problem was resolved, at least for now. Younger residents, who weren't from old-name families, began to seek the available properties in the town center. Nelson encouraged his advocates to take advantage of the situation and move closer to town. That way they could participate much better in town activities and the quest to have the town become more receptive to transplants or younger citizens.

Nelson made sure that his Victorian properties were renovated to the highest standards and used as rentals, or sold to his closest friends in town. The face of the town center was changing, and it was for the better.

"Isn't the town a little warmer?" Nelson said, smiling, to Jason a month later. "Isn't it more pleasurable? The old farts and old names are headin' for the hills. They can't stand the change."

"Yes, Nelson," Jason responded. "I like the change. By the way, do you think I can ditch Ed Hammond's products now? He said that the stuff wouldn't last long and it didn't."

"Those chemicals were right on," Nelson added with a subtle smile. "Better than that, no one died. The safety precautions were right. Nothing caused permanent damage. The risk information was true to form. I am sure that the old wells that they filled are free of the chemicals and their by-products by now. Too bad the EPA had them fill them in. It was probably unnecessary. The stuff breaks down quickly and basically disappears."

"You did well, Nel," added Jason. "You've gotten to be pretty sneaky and payback is sweet."

"No Jason, *you* did well, you sneaky old bastard. You travel at night like a damn cat, you old coot," Nelson laughed.

✠ ✠ ✠

As his condition worsened, Mr. Parker, the elderly owner of the Harvest Village Store, had no strength left to run the business establishment. He also had no heirs to continue his lifelong business enterprise so he enlisted some temporary help until he could find a buyer for the business. Finally, as things got worse, a power of attorney was appointed to handle the store's sale.

Penelope, one of Nelson Palmer's daughters, who had moved to New Hampshire after her mother's death, had a keen interest in acquiring the quaint store. She was living in one of the Victorian homes that Nelson had purchased with his lottery winnings. She was Nelson's youngest and favorite. "Penny," as her dad called her, said, "Father, that little store is really cute. I like the atmosphere of the little building. I could turn that into a nice little business. Maybe I could turn it into a *real* village store with a twist. I was thinking that it could have gifts and a wine display as well. That would make it more of a New England general store, reminiscent of the old days. People congregated in those old stores. It became a communal affair."

"That's a great idea, hon," Nelson responded, while sipping his morning coffee. "I think this town certainly could use a store of that caliber."

"It would certainly make it more upscale, don't you think?" she added. "We could get rid of the cigarettes and crap, Daddy, and probably the riffraff as well. I was thinking of a small corner in the store with gifts—arts and crafts. Tourists would stop by and get soda and ice cream for their kids. They might buy local crafts and artwork— folk art. Creative residents in town could leave their creations on consignment. You know, those quilts and carved wooden gifts of rural New Hampshire."

"That is a great idea," Nelson said. "I think that the craft idea is great. That way, people could still get newspapers, milk, and bread and other household staples, yet they could also shop locally for greeting cards and mementos. I could help you spruce the place up."

"I'm glad that you like my dream. The floor will surely need refinishing. It's the old, wide-board pine slabs that give the place character. Can you help there?"

"No problem," he said, "Let's look into it. Ya know, see what they're askin'."

Nelson had one of his holding companies make an offer and eventually purchase the building at close to the asking price. He would have Penny shut the store down for a month and renovate it with the help of Susan and Doug. Nelson would stay in the background of the project, so that the old names would not know that he was behind the acquisition. Penny's married name, Browning, was not familiar to anyone in town and there would be few people that would know that she was related to Nelson—at least for a while. Shortly after the acquisition of the store, old man Parker became ill and died, ending the line of that old name.

Eighteen

As Nelson Palmer became an even more formidable force in town, he realized he had gathered mainstream supporters. He was growing more and more popular, and his opinions and visionary outlook were well accepted by the newer blood in town. As they listened to him, the people of Harvest were becoming more open-minded and concerned with real community issues, such as roads, education, taxes, community functions, and public services. Nelson decided that if he ran for office, it would not be for a selectmen's position—he would seek the top position, the town manager.

Pressure for his candidacy continued to build. One summer evening, a female resident cornered him in a stairwell as they left a town meeting. "Why don't you run, Nelson? We need you in this town. We need you in public office, and you've got those clowns scared."

"Thank you for the vote of confidence," he said with pride. "Maybe I will . . . just maybe I will," he said with a smile. "I need to think about it. I have lots of irons in the fire right now and running for office is a full-time job. I need to finish my church house and I also have other personal projects that are ongoing."

The woman was soon surrounded by other supportive neighbors, who also pestered Nelson in a gentle, reassuring way. They saw him as a leader, and were angry at what had happened to Lydia.

"Nel, we'll help you. You will have enormous support in your campaign—that will make your quest easy. We'll talk you up. You know, distribute literature and seek donations. All you have to do is agree to run and then go around and meet with people—you know—say hello and listen to their concerns."

Nelson was overwhelmed by their support. He could sense their passion. He had a huge decision to make. Could he tolerate politics?

"You folks make it hard for me to refuse. I will certainly give it some thought."

The position of town manager was influential, especially if the selectmen were in concert with his or her beliefs. Nelson would need to encourage newer residents to run for office as well. He would need a political party of new selectmen candidates to change the town. He didn't think there would be a problem putting together a slate; many people had expressed their desire to run for office with him, and his supporters had interest in running for other positions as well. Seats on the school board and planning board, plus the tax assessor and tax collector's offices were up for reelection.

He found it interesting that the people who wanted to run for office with a Nelson-type candidate were not political party affiliated. Many were registered Independents—freethinking individuals who voted in national elections for people whom they thought could do the job, not because of party registration. The new voices were people who cared about the school system for their children or they were environmental advocates. They sought more recreational facilities for the youth in town or wanted town functions to be more participatory for residents. Most of all, the newer residents wanted harmony and a sense of community. The only way to accomplish that was to take part in the town functions and elected offices, and to rid the town of old-name, myopic individuals through attrition.

The pressure to run for office increased until Nelson finally decided to seek the top slot in town. He decided that, although he could fund his own election, it was more important to build grassroots support. Nelson was not ready to divulge to the masses that he had won the lottery. They needed to make it happen psychologically and financially. If people were serious about change and wanted him to win, they would need to prove it by funding the campaign. He did not wish to be elected because of his financial stability and influence; with the help of his accountant he was able to hide his millionaire status.

Let them help me, he thought. *If they help me, they will also help themselves.* Nelson publicly declared his candidacy just before the filing deadline. The selectmen and town manager were clearly shocked.

Nelson was encouraged by the early efforts of his constituents to raise money. They also sought and achieved the formal list of supporters' names to file in support of his candidacy. Thousands of dollars came in the first month, mostly acquired by door-to-door campaigning by hardworking fund-raiser volunteers. The campaign was beginning to gel and the supporters of Nelson and his running mates named themselves the "Take Back Harvest Party."

Each candidate in the new party gathered the necessary signatures to be placed on the ballot. The old town name candidates and incumbents were amazed at the momentum of Nelson and his followers' campaign in such a short period. They met in their homes each week and plotted how they would strategically counteract the efforts of this threat of challengers. Their plots were simple and devious. They managed to tear down or steal the political signs of their opponents and circulated derogatory comments about the candidates from the Take Back Harvest campaign. Most of the theft and vandalism was performed late at night when people were sleeping. The old name supporters spray painted graffiti attacking Nelson and his slate of newcomers on walls and trestles around town. They sprayed highway overpasses and the sides of abandoned buildings.

Nelson countered the vandalism by printing thousands of signs for himself and the other candidates in his Take Back Harvest Party, stockpiling them in his cellar. The incumbents were unaware of the large stash of signs. The stolen political signs were easily replaced by volunteers and his visual exposure never diminished.

Fearing that someone might demand access to records, incumbents began to "cook the books" at the town offices. Any indiscretions in the budget figures, the tax assessor's office, or other offices were adjusted to look more pristine for the campaign. The property tax assessor had been padding the evaluations of town properties and his record books were erroneous and hinted of graft. The problem was exacerbated by the fact that the town auditors were on the take as well. Local residents knew that their property and land valuations were high, but did not challenge most of the town's subjective appraisals. Until now, they had no chance of winning their protests against the corrupt town officials.

The final straw was the decision of the selectmen to hold closed-door meetings in back rooms and on off-nights, as well. The general public became irate at the suspected secret sessions, but could not prove what was going on. There was no way for the locals to partici- pate and the selectmen were collaborating on issues without resident input to prevent the further erosion of their control of the town. Nel- son championed the effort to uncover the secret meetings, and it helped fuel the call for newly elected, noncorrupt officials. Protesters pick- eted the town hall and residents began a letter-to-the-editor campaign that chastised the local officials for conducting public business "in the shade." Some residents decided not to pay taxes or to seek rev- enue-producing permits for new construction or renovations. It was a calamity for local officials.

The town of Harvest was in financial chaos and the selectmen were to blame. The news media wrote articles about the feud for months. Summer in Harvest was an inferno of political heat.

✠✠✠

Signs supporting Nelson's candidacy popped up everywhere—on lawns, on the outskirts of town and in public gathering areas. They proclaimed: PALMER FOR TOWN MANAGER—HONESTY—INTEGRITY—INTEL- LIGENT POLITICS. And, TAKE BACK HARVEST!—VOTE PALMER! There were bumper stickers on vehicles and telephone poles everywhere that read VOTE SMART—VOTE PALMER!

Susan and Libby became co-chairwomen of Nelson's campaign. The women and other volunteers distributed leaflets door-to-door throughout the town. Nelson stood at the town dump entrance each Saturday morning and greeted local residents. He spoke of his vision for the community and talked about the positive changes he had in mind for the now infamous Harvest. They listened to his oration and got to know him far better.

"If you vote me in, I'll make you proud of this town of Harvest," he said. "I promise sidewalks, parks, more children's programs, and a more responsive board of selectmen. We will make it easy for people to get permits to improve their property. Our officials will respond to your needs. Those in our party running for the school board have pledged to support better schools and a better student-teacher ratio. Vote for our entire slate." His grandfatherly attitude pleased people, especially the women. They cared about their children and the community.

"I can see a local daycare facility is needed," he would add. "There are working mothers and dads that need help with that."

People gathered about him. "I like your attitude, Nel, I like your style," one woman said, as she approached the trash compactor, hands laden with garbage bags.

"Let me help you with that," he offered.

"No thanks," she said. "That was kind of you, but you need to stand there and greet people. I can handle this, Nelson." Nelson smiled and returned to his self-appointed post.

"OK, ma'am, hope you keep me in mind at election time," he said. "Tell your friends of my plans," he shouted to her over the noise of the trash equipment.

"I will . . . you can bet on that."

Nelson was pleased with the general response and obvious grass-roots support. Only seven people, who were ingrained old names, taunted him at the dump. One, driving a beat-up Ford F150 with an NRA sticker on the back window, gave him the finger. Another bumper sticker showed his support for Ducks Unlimited and yet another—a local country radio station. His truck was rusted-out over the fender wells and his red Budweiser baseball cap hid his matted long hair underneath. *The man was probably not even a registered voter,* he surmised. Nelson didn't care.

After three hours of shaking hands and conversing with concerned citizens, Nelson was hoarse. He went home to nap for a while before he did his afternoon chores. Susan took over for him at the recycling center until it closed at three. She handed out all of the literature that she brought with her. She was a trooper in her campaign efforts and intelligent in her responses to residents' queries about Nelson's agenda. She knew Nelson well and voiced his plans in detail to each potential supporter. No question went unanswered. She emphasized the integrity of the man—Nelson Palmer.

Libby was responsible for coordinating mailings of Nelson's campaign fliers. She gathered supporters together on weekends and evenings and oversaw their coordinated "mail shot" by helping address envelopes and placing stamps on them. Palmer volunteers used the previous year's voter list to enter names into the computer database. Labels were printed out for each mailing. The potential constituency in support of Nelson Palmer was astronomical. Hundreds of people became campaign supporters. Incumbent Thomas Shaw's campaign was stagnant by comparison.

"Susan," he said, one clear evening. "This is all coming together, isn't it?" As he was staring at the starlit sky, he began reminiscing about his life and marriage to his devoted wife. "Wish Lydia was here to see this! It's really working," he whispered. "She would be proud of our efforts and the winds of change."

"She *is* here, Nelson, dear . . . she *is* here," Susan interjected. "She's present in your living room, in your flower bed, and in the stars above."

The humidity of the summer night was almost overwhelming. Nelson stared out the church door and then looked up at the sky again.

"I bought her a 'star,' Susan," he said sadly. "It's in the constellation, Ursa major."

"You did? . . . You named a star after her?" she asked. "How sweet!"

"Yes," he said quietly, amid the sounds of the evening crickets. "I mail-ordered the certificate. For forty dollars, they name a star after someone. It's not an official thing . . . but a gesture of love . . . and her name gets logged in some Star Registry or somethin'," he said, his voice breaking.

"Nel, you are the most thoughtful and tender man I know. Where did you get that sensitivity and thoughtfulness?"

He was silent for a moment, and then clasped his hands to his cheek, as if in prayer. "Don't know . . . I'm a sentimental old goat, I guess . . . my mother, perhaps. Yeah . . . from Mom," he repeated with renewed conviction.

"Well, whoever gave you those genes should be complimented. They broke the mold with you . . . you old coot!" Susan said, with a tender smile. She patted his back.

"This has been a long day. Think I'll crash for the night, dear. Damn! We never got to 'dump pick,' girl!"

Susan laughed as she headed for her car.

Nelson gazed up at the moonlit sky and whispered, "Good night, sweet Lydia. I love you."

✠✠✠

When Nelson's opponent, Tom Shaw, realized that money was not an object for Nelson, he considered withdrawing his bid for reelection, but then changed his mind. Old-town names needed the incumbent to run, to solidify their efforts to hold onto their corrupt control. Town manager Shaw knew he wouldn't win this time. There was no way he could compete with Nelson's campaign efforts and dedicated volunteer support. *There are just fewer old-name supporters than before*, he thought. *How can I compete with this man?* Informed residents were disgusted by the mudslinging and dirty politics and eventually sided with Nelson and his Take Back Harvest Party candidates. The townsfolk were obviously ready for change, and Nelson Palmer was their man!

✠✠✠

Libby continued her Internet search of Nelson Palmer's heritage. She found more reference books that were directly related to his roots. Those additional volumes, when added to the manuscript of Mrs. Perry's history of the town, further showed that Harvest was a town that had its own roots in England. The revelations in the materials she discovered documented the argument that Harvest's town history was actually different from what people knew it to be. When she wasn't helping Nelson with his campaign and/or handling her responsibilities at the library, Libby researched the British influence relevant to colonial life in the emerging new America. It was clear to her that she and Nelson were about to embark on an adventure of historic proportion and ramifications—one that would bring them closer as friends and closer to seeking the roots that his Aunt Bess had shared with him back in Pennsylvania.

✠ ✠ ✠

Susan suggested that Nelson throw a campaign shindig to give himself and the candidates even greater political exposure. He decided to sponsor a family picnic for the residents who shared his beliefs and who were his most avid supporters. Although some people questioned how he could have the money to host a party of that magnitude, he led them to believe that the funding of events came from his campaign contributors. A reporter from the town paper questioned him about his finances and campaign strategies, but Nelson was cagey and revealed nothing. Even when it was time to open his campaign books and file financial disclosure statements for public view, Nelson, through his accountant, was able to hide his true holdings. His previous year's income tax was on record, but the lottery winnings would not show up until the next year's tax filing. He did not want to give any ammunition to the opposition—the very people he knew were breaking the law.

"I don't care if I have to stoop to some devious tactics to win, like a lot of politicians do," he confided in Libby. "It is the only way to deal with this bunch of corrupt idiots. We've got to get them out of office."

She nodded her support, knowing that winning now obsessed him.

But even some of his constituents wanted explanations and Susan became seriously concerned about how his lack of information might affect the outcome of the election if undecided voters thought he was less than honest.

"Nelson, we must disclose the funds and contributions. People will see that the picnic expenses exceed the income from our contributions to date," she said. After talking with his accountant, Nelson finally released a more extensive list, but it didn't tell the whole story.

"OK, then. We'll scale back the size of the picnic. Chicken instead of lobster, and encourage supporters to bring a dish to pass," said Nelson.

Through his holding companies, Nelson continued to make anonymous contributions to the town—to the schools, the police, the rescue squad, and the fire department. The middle school received a chunk of money for a badly needed new classroom wing; the rescue squad and EMTs received funds for medical equipment and a new ambulance. The police department received a four-wheel drive truck for responding to off-road emergencies, a donation toward their DARE antidrug program, and funds for a new cruiser—one that had VHS video capabilities for traffic-related stops. The video camera aided the police in court cases and was high resolution, state-of-the-art recording equipment.

"You sure are making a difference in this town," Chief Gooden said, knowing without being told that the gifts to his department were Nelson's doing. "I've wanted this technology for a long time."

"Well, Darren, you folks do good work here and you deserve the best equipment to perform your job. Since the town selectmen won't fund you, I will," Nelson said. "They are narrow-minded control freaks."

"Me and the officers support your campaign, all the way," said Gooden. "The crime rate is down and fewer teens are causin' problems . . . except for one or two old names, that is. Your financial help has really been timely."

"'Fraid that the attitude of some kids won't change," Nelson said with concern. "Part of the problem is genetics!" he exclaimed, laughing. "Apples never fall far from the tree."

"Right about that, Nel," said Gooden. "These townies will never change, especially the young ones. They are clueless."

"Ya know, Chief, I just funded the library's expanded need for books and the community center renovation, yet I rarely see these troubled kids at either place. We ought to get them there somehow. Any suggestions on how to accomplish that?"

Gooden thought for a moment and then said, "Those kids probably would like a concert, a band or somethin' like that. Perhaps we could get them involved in a small rock concert—a *small* one. One or two of the troubled kids apparently play guitar in a local band. Maybe you could hire them for one of your campaign gigs. That would satisfy their need for exposure and recognition, get them some small coin for the gig and add young supporters or converts to your cause."

"Good idea, Darren. They might even be willing to distribute campaign literature if they like the changes they see in town."

Nelson was impressed with the chief's idea. This was certainly a way to steer the younger generation toward community participation. The town youth could easily influence their peers and many adults. They yearned for someone to pay attention to them. Nelson was some-one who was doing just that.

"Awesome idea!" Nelson said, smiling and tapping his forehead with his fingertips. "What an idea! They have a young following for sure, right? Those kids would attend and support the band, and even-tually our agenda in time. I will try and book them for the next cam-paign function. Better than that, I'll establish a memorial scholarship fund for Jamie, the boy who died."

✠✠✠

Nelson was rumored to be the "landlord of Harvest." Even if people didn't know of the extent of his holding companies or possessions of land and homes, they slowly became aware that he had additional property. However, his daughter's property, or at least her relation-ship to him had become public knowledge. Some residents speculated that the holding companies and Nelson Palmer were one and the same. Betty Morrissey, his Realtor, had figured him out because she was losing listings left and right. She could not hold her own without sales, and people were selling directly to new buyers to avoid the commis-sion to brokers.

Nelson, on his own, had changed the economics of the town.

Suspecting he had enormous resources, a number of the older residents of the historic homes secretly contacted Nelson to see if he would purchase their houses. He told them he was in no position to do that, but he advised the managers of his holding companies to scoop up what he could, especially if the homes or buildings were historic or near the center of town. He envisioned a community center for kids in one building, and dreamed of activities such as dances, movies, func-tions, crafts or sports. He had already anonymously donated state-of-the-art computers to the local schools. Teenagers would finally have a place to go to in the evening, instead of under the local bridge to smoke or have sex. Nelson Palmer hadn't even won the election yet and his visionary agenda was taking the town by storm.

Nelson hired Libby, his confidant, to monitor his personal real estate transactions, and entrusted her with the story of his lottery winnings. A well-organized bookkeeper, she eventually went to work for Nelson part time, because he paid her more than she was able to earn at the library, and because she shared his vision. She reduced her library position to just one day a week, but never stopped helping him in his quest for his roots. She researched the town history constantly while handling the books for his private real estate deals, and aiding him as a volunteer in the campaign.

"Nelson," she said one day. "You own half of the darn town. Do you realize what you own? You have acquired most of the key properties—it's just that no one knows it."

"Sure," he said, cracking a smile. "And I'm not done yet." He started to walk away slowly, but then turned, hands on his hips, and asked, " Libby, why did you never marry?"

"Nelson Palmer, what kind of question is that? Why does that matter to you?" she said, startled.

"Libby, you are a smart, handsome woman. I'm shocked that you never wed, that's all!"

"Well . . . I was jilted by the bastard," she said, with an edge to her voice.

"Bastard? What bastard?" he asked with concern.

"Never you mind, Nelson Palmer, it was a hundred years ago, it seems. No matter now," she stated. "Wasn't meant to be."

"I'm sorry, Libby. Didn't mean to pry. None of my business."

"Someday I will tell you the story. Right now, we have work to do . . . the heritage roots . . . and the campaign! No time for stories," she said with a smile. She was preparing a general mailing to his constituents and had many envelopes to address with preprinted labels.

Nelson didn't bother her with any more questions about her personal life. If the situation presented itself, he might dig a little deeper into her life story. This was not the time.

Nineteen

Nelson's youngest daughter, Penny, had moved to Harvest with her husband, Ray Browning, and they had two daughters. She was tall and thin and had her mother's wheat blonde hair. While Ray spent much of his time with clients in Boston, Penny worked on renovation plans for the Harvest Village Store. He wasn't much interested in her plans to be a shopkeeper in the town where her father lived. The first floor fix-up was done, and she was ready to start cleaning the second-floor storage loft as well. It was filled with junk and old furniture, which Mr. Parker had stuffed into every crevice, nook, and cranny. There were stacks of papers and even an old desk where Parker had done his bookkeeping. Next to it was a tall, four-drawer file cabinet. Boxes and boxes of old papers took up the rest of the space.

Nelson recruited Susan and Doug to help Penny clean out the second floor so that the space could be leased. However, it was a project no one wished to tackle. Years of dust and grime covered the objects that Mr. Parker had saved. Most of the contents were useless and had withstood the change in temperatures and the humidity of many New England summers and winters. The upstairs was not heated or cooled, so anything stored there was at the mercy of the elements and rodents.

"Just look at all this stuff," said Penny. "The old man must have been a pack rat. He surely never threw anything away."

Doug said, "But look at the pile in this carton. These papers are *old* . . . very old. Hell, they must go back to the seventeen and eighteen hundreds."

"Really? They must be interesting if they are that old," she said, perusing one paper that was crumbling in her hands.

"Jeez, Penny," Susan said, "They probably should be brought downstairs where we can go through them one by one. If there are interesting headlines or bylines, you can frame them and hang them in the store. They would be great conversation pieces for the customers to see. They surely have history. It's cooler downstairs and far more comfortable if we spread the papers out on a table."

"Heck, if they are antiques, we could sell the ones we don't want in the antique and craft portion of the store. Many antiques dealers love old paper," said Penny, as they each grabbed a stack of the old newsprint and brought them down to the first floor. The summer had been unbearably hot, making the upstairs stifling during the day.

Penny and her friends spent many evenings methodically going through the newspapers of yesteryear. Even Libby was consulted and helped them sort the most historic pieces. Libby was aware of the old publications, but had not seen any authentic pieces of an original *Town Crier*.

One night, Libby took a few of the documents home. She was amazed that one or two newspapers were in excellent condition. Stacked in piles, some of the papers were protected from light and moisture. The sheer weight of the stacks compressed them and they resisted oxidation and eventual ruin.

She sat in the living room easy chair and gently turned the sometimes yellow-colored pages. A newspaper of sorts, the *Town Crier* bulletin from 1730 was adhered to the back of a news column, dated 1750. The odd piece was not similar to the others and appeared to be very old typeset—the letters of the words were uneven in their printing. She knew it was historical and extremely valuable. Libby did not contact Penny right away, but instead, immediately called Nelson to tell him of her intriguing acquisition. He happened to be sorting some newspapers himself and became even more interested in the wealth of knowledge they all had stumbled upon.

"Nelson!" she exclaimed, "I have found a document that was addressed to the British government and the king. It was a petition of sorts to the royalty for the establishment of a town that is located near what we know as Harvest. This document suggests that our town may have been split off from Homestead, the neighboring town to the east." She was stunned. "The darn description here mentions roads that I think are old dirt roads that may still exist in Harvest."

"What are you talking about, Libby? Have you had wine tonight or somethin?"

"No, dammit! Get over here!" she said. "You must see this."

"This better be good, woman! It's late and I was half asleep!"

"Trust me, Nelson Palmer. I think I have come across part of your roots."

"I'll be right over." He hung up quickly, dropping his keys in his haste, and jumped in his vehicle. It was a two-minute ride from his place to her house in town. His Jeep groaned from the speed at which he accelerated. He was due to receive the new four-wheel vehicle that he had ordered. It was on delivery to the dealership, but he still had a week to wait.

Nelson arrived at Libby's door, which was ajar in anticipation of his arrival. She guided his shoulders to the kitchen table, where there was ample light to view the paper.

"Here," she said, "Look at this . . . look at the petition!"

Nelson put on his reading glasses and read the document slowly and deliberately. Libby paced while he read—one hand was held on her chin as she moved slowly back and forth. Nelson's eyes scanned the historic request.

It read:

> To his Excellency John Wentworth Esq., Captain General, Governor and Commander in Chief in and over his Majesty's province of New Hampshire . . . .
> WE petitioners declare that the portion of the town west of the center of Homestead are destitute and are so remote that we cannot attend Town privileges and hereby pray that your Excellency and Honours will grant the formation of a new town. . . .

John Wentworth Esq., and the governor of the day would present the plea of the people to George III in England and thereby justify the reasons for the new town's formation. That was clearly stated in the historic document that Libby had found in the pile of old newsprint.

Nelson was amazed at the detailed account of the boundaries that seemed to match the location of markers and boundary descriptions for a portion of Harvest that Jason Birch had shown him. He continued to read the yellowed paper. He took off his glasses and pushed the kitchen chair back slowly.

"Damn, Libby! . . Look! The town they petitioned for, *is* Harvest; a town that separated from Homestead. Harvest was once part of Homestead! And look, they even petitioned to rename that proposed town. It was their suggestion that the town be called—Raby."

"Really?" she said growing increasingly impatient. "Read on Nelson! I hadn't gotten that far yet."

"Look . . . " he continued, "the people wanted to form a town because they were separated on the western side of Homestead by a river and bramble bushes. The roads were impassable. They paid taxes on the west side of the village and apparently got nothing for benefits in return. Says here . . . that they wanted to form their own town . . . they basically wanted to secede from Homestead . . . to represent themselves!"

Libby leaned closer to Nelson and the document. "This must have been an early rebellion," she added. "They were early renegades, but for a positive cause."

Nelson looked up at her and quietly said, "This is phenomenal. Mrs. Perry mentioned a Raby in her manuscript but did not elaborate on the connection. It's clear! The town of Harvest was once called Raby . . . . Jesus! The history books that I read did not mention that. All they mentioned was Harvest . . . the friggin' history of Harvest. This town had a *different name* at one time. What the hell happened? How did the name change, of all things, to Harvest?"

Libby shook her head slowly. She squinted and reread the document.

"Nelson, I don't know. This is the first I've seen of this notation in all the years I've researched in the library. Kids who have written term papers on the town's history never came across this fact. How strange and amazing," she added.

"Who signed the petition?" she asked quietly. "Look at the end of the paper."

He perused the last paragraph and saw four signatures. "Damn," he exclaimed. "Ezra Raby! EZRA RABY was one of the cosigners. Holy crap!" he shouted, now standing. "Ezra is *my* relative. He was a Raby. Aunt Bess was right . . . Ezra is a significant part of my roots and the surname explains the original town name."

With a bit more research on the Internet that night, it was clear to Nelson and Libby that the town, Raby, was named after a town of the same name in the northern part of England, in the county of Durham. Many early colonists came from that town in England.

Nelson stayed up for hours, continuing to read the Perry manuscript for more clues. *Did she have more information in her document that would help?* he wondered. It was his firm conclusion that Harvest, New Hampshire, *was* once called Raby, New Hampshire. *Why did it change?* he wondered. *Why did the history books not mention that fact? The damn town changed names way back when and nobody was aware of it?* He couldn't sleep. His ancestors had actually formed and settled in the town that he now lived, and few people knew that fact. He would share the news with Penny, Ray, Susan, and Doug in the morning. His "roots" were Ezra Raby, in England, and in the town of Raby. He was a direct descendant of a founding father . . . himself! Even Susan was a distant relative and would know of her roots, as well. She would be astonished by the revelation, and Nelson couldn't wait to inform her and Penny of their common heritage.

Nelson was even more gratified that the current town selectmen and their old town names were not the original founders. They were descendants of transients and carpetbaggers most probably. *Those same asses in the town hall are not descendants from the original colonists after all. They are nobody!* Nelson realized. The selectmen's relatives were probably responsible for the name change to Harvest, he surmised. He hoped that the Perry manuscript would continue to better define the history of the town. She had hinted at the mystery and, in the end, her document would support Nelson's theory.

✠✠✠

Nelson called Jason Birch as soon as he thought his friend was awake, concerning the newfound information about the town's history. Nelson needed to know where the tract of land was that was referred to as the Mile Slip. That particular tract of land was highlighted in the petition to the king of England.

Jason pointed out that, as far as he knew, there was an overgrown dirt road that was referred to as the Slip Road. He surmised that it was the area in question referred to in the document.

Nelson delved further into Mrs. Perry's manuscript. It was noted that many of the first inhabitants of the town met annually in a "meeting house." It was designated roughly as a location east of the current Harvest center, and a mile or more from the present town hall.

"Jason," he asked. "Think we can find this area of town easily?"

Jason shook his head and responded, "Nel, the only area I think it could be is rough travel . . . overgrown and very marshy. Could be hard to negotiate."

Nelson and Jason decided to search the woods in an area thought to be the Mile Slip. Ultimately they stumbled upon a stone foundation and a partial fieldstone fireplace. It was quite large and well hidden by brush and vines over the centuries. It was likely that no one knew of its existence—at least within the last one hundred years.

Nelson studied the intricate stone base and smiled. He commented upon finding the historic site—thought to be a potential piece of the historic colonial puzzle and the history of Raby.

"Jason, my friend, I can't believe this. I think that this may have been the first town meeting site for Raby. I'm sure from the territorial description in her manuscript this is where the town fathers could have met."

"I agree with you, Nel," Jason responded. "This foundation is much too large to have been a home. It must have been a large meeting house or community building of sorts." They studied the stone base and structural integrity. The foundation was basically an intricate interlocking wall of mossy stone that appeared indestructible. It was a style of construction typical of the British farmers and rigid enough to support a wooden structure of enormous proportions.

"For sure it is larger than a homestead," added Nelson. "Look here! Just look at the massive fireplace remnants. It would have heated a large building, not a home. For God's sake, this foundation is not in bad condition—considering it may be two hundred-plus years old. The wooden structure is long gone, but the stone is sound. You'd have to go well off the beaten track to find this relic." Nelson smiled at his friend. They knew they had stumbled upon something incredible. "I'm glad we decided to head left instead of right back by that old oak. We would have never happened on this site," added Nelson. "You OK to walk back, Jason? You look tired and you're limping," he stated with concern.

"Darn leg," Jason responded. "Always acts up when I stand or walk too long. I'm ready to ramble back. . . .You?" Jason asked.

"Sure. We can do that. We know this supposed Slip area pretty well now. It only took us two hours to find it," Nelson commented. "You surely must be tired from fightin' those bushes and thorny brush . . . but you did good, my friend."

"You mean . . . we did good," stated Jason. "Glad I could help you get your bearings on this site. I remember seeing it decades ago, but never associated it with anything of importance. It looked to me like some farmer's stonewall back then. Most of the stone must have been hidden in overgrown brush. Surely didn't look like four walls then—I would have remembered that, I guess."

Nelson and Jason walked to where Nelson had parked his Jeep— an area near the old railroad bed. They used the trail to access the marsh and wooded area, considered by them to be the Mile Slip. It cut short their journey.

Jason reminded Nelson of the old railroad and how it impacted the town. They conversed about the history of the trains until Nelson dropped Jason off at his lakefront home.

"Nelson, that foundation was probably the birthplace of the town of Raby. I feel it in my bones. I'll bet they held their first meetings there."

"Think you're right, my friend," responded Nelson. "The town of Harvest certainly never had its origin where the *current* town hall is. That structure in town had nothing to do with its beginning. The historical beginning was clearly in the *Raby* name, not the Harvest name. I need to get Susan and her boyfriend out there to assess the integrity of the foundation. Doug knows stone well. If it looks structurally sound, I would imagine that a new structure could be built on top of it again. I'm gonna find out who owns that land now and buy the damn thing. Don't tell anyone of the plan. Hell, they don't even know the foundation is there." Nelson hesitated and then spoke. "If we can drop a road in there, we can access the foundation and restore town history."

"Really?" asked Jason, stopping to catch his breath. "You want to do that?"

"You bet I do! The town of Raby is my roots and that foundation was a part of my original town, and ultimately . . . *my* roots. My guess is that Ezra may have preached there or helped build the original building. Back then, they were community citizens who helped one another survive the harsh new land and weather. Their lives were dependent upon helping one another," Nelson said.

"Probably right," agreed Jason. "They had no doctors back then and they had to deal with the injuns who preceded them. Those were hard times, and not always the friendliest of times, either. Imagine many of those folks in Raby died in battles with the red men."

Nelson, unaware of how ill Jason had felt that day, watched him pull the door open to his little cottage. Everything had seemed an effort during their trip to Mile Slip. Jason had stopped frequently, perspired more than usual, and seemed to walk through the tall grass with unsteadiness. He hadn't bothered to pull the burdocks off his cuffs or kick the dirt out of his boots before getting back in the Jeep. Even if he needed immediate medical attention, Jason was not one to call the doctor; he believed in home cures for ailments.

Nelson tried to reach Jason on four occasions the next day, but there was no answer. Concerned, he decided to go over to the cottage. He knew that Jason rarely went anywhere far and he was never gone for very long. He wasn't fishing, since the boat was still tied up to the dock. The front door was locked and the shades were drawn in the bedroom. After pacing around the cottage, Nelson called Chief Gooden who told the rescue squad to meet him there. Upon breaking the lock and entering the cottage, they found Jason Birch dead in his bed. Jason's skin contained blotchy areas on his back. The darker areas were locations where the blood had pooled in his body. The coroner ruled the death the result of a stroke while he slept, saying that he probably died very rapidly and painlessly.

Nelson was shocked and saddened. This was another personal loss—of his fishing buddy and a true gentleman. The man had shared Nelson's quest to find his roots and was there to find the historic stone foundation just the day before. That memory alone was a consolation. Had Nelson never met Jason, he might have concluded that the town of Harvest was his family's origin.

Nelson arranged for his friend's funeral. He paid for Jason's cherry-wood casket, the flowers, and even the granite monument. The large, precision-cut stone was sculpted from a rock he had found in the field where the original Raby community building or town hall probably existed.

Nelson had purchased the land from a money-hungry owner who thought it contained too much marshland to be of any real value. Nelson thought otherwise. He had Susan and Doug make arrangements for clearing the brush, and then, using heavy equipment, he dropped a dirt road into the area. As the road was cleared, artifacts began to emerge from the landscape clearing. The remnants of their cleanup would help substantiate the fact that the site was the true beginning of the town of Raby.

Nelson decided to continue his campaign without mentioning the cultivation of historic data on Raby.

✠✠✠

With the mountains surrounding Harvest ablaze with color, residents were already washing storm windows and putting them up. Frost had already browned the remaining gardens. As he drove through town, Nelson smiled as he watched children jumping in freshly raked piles of leaves. He wondered if mothers were baking cookies and fixing hot cider for them, just as Lydia had done for the girls when they had played and worked outside in the fall.

Nelson's campaign continued to surge. People liked his philosophy and ideas, and the current board of selectmen grew more irritated each week with the popularity of this annoying upstart. They continued to meet without public participation or opinion, even though they knew that it made residents angry. Morris Halliwell, the road manager, was badgered at every turn by Nelson's supporters for his refusal to admit responsibility in Lydia Palmer's death. The harassment finally took its toll. Morris became clinically depressed and attempted to end his life, but did not succeed. He was paralyzed for life from the failed self-inflicted gunshot wound. A replacement, one of their old-name cronies, was quickly appointed by the selectmen.

Nelson's lawyer, Mosley, called him to ask if he wanted to drop any of his lawsuits against the town.

"Hell no," he replied. "I intend to milk the bastards—right to the end."

"You realize that you are possibly bankrupting the town, Nelson," the lawyer said, "Is that what you want to do? Win at all costs? It might affect your election."

"Nah, I just want them to know what they are up against. If they admit to killin' my Lydia and messin' with my septic system plan, I may let them off and end things."

The lawyer continued, "Nelson, judges don't like people playin' games in court. I sense that they might find that you are doing this for spite or revenge."

"I am sort of playin' a bit, but this is no game. The septic problem may be, but my wife's loss was no game. I intend for them to admit their guilt in front of the town. They meet behind closed doors each week. How arrogant is that, counselor? There is no remorse from them, no apologies," Nelson exclaimed, tapping a pen on his desk.

"I know you grieve for your loss, Nelson, but you should consider diplomacy in the eyes of the court. That would be my professional recommendation. Then again, it was not my wife who was lost by their callous attitude and dereliction of duty. I can only advise you."

Nelson hesitated, then said, "Look. I don't need those bastards in this town. They are about to be voted out. Once that happens, I'll drop the suit on the septic issue. As for my wife's wrongful death suit, I will not relent. If I can cause those slime-dogs to lose their homes, their families or their personal possessions, I will go for it!"

"OK, Nelson, I hear what you want. I will go forward with the case . . . as we already discussed."

"Thanks, counselor. I appreciate you stickin' this one out. I may let up on the rope in time, but I want those bastards to squirm a while longer."

"Nelson, I wish you luck in the election—you sure have impacted the town. I hope that you win."

"We got this one sewed up, I think," Nelson said.

Twenty

At ten-thirty, after having several beers and looking at his favorite snapshots of Lydia, Nelson became melancholy and decided he needed some fresh air. He was increasingly angry at the selectmen and their families, who had altered the town's history and then had the audacity to make life difficult for everyone else. "Outrageous," he said, as he stepped on the gas. "The bastards won't get away with this forever."

He headed into the dark toward Harvest center. For awhile he drove aimlessly, then went north toward the nearest "real" town. Route 10 was quiet that evening and he passed few cars along the way.

✠✠✠

The fire horn at the Harvest fire station blasted into the stillness of the chilly, fall evening. It blasted numerous times seeking volunteers of the fire brigade. The two-alarm fire was reported by numerous residents who smelled smoke and saw the orange glow in the night. It didn't take long for an enormous fire consuming the Harvest town hall to illuminate the sky. Most of the structure had been recently renovated, including the slate roof, broken clapboards and window frames. Flames quickly towered one hundred feet above the two-story structure, swirling and dancing in the intense heat like vertical orange-red waves carrying sparkling embers and debris into the black October sky.

Residents surrounded the building, their reflections and shadows backdropped by the raging inferno. Their numbers increased one by one to view the worst disaster to hit Harvest in more than seventy years.

"How'd it start?" asked a resident of a passing firefighter. "Anyone know?"

"Not certain," he responded rapidly. "Could have been the old wiring or could have been an accident. Workers were using acetylene earlier in the day in one of the lower basement rooms."

"What about arson?" asked the resident of a fellow townsman. "We've had so many fires in this town in recent months. There must have been three in the last few weeks. Must have been arson." The man nearby offered no comment but stared at the flames while shaking his head back and forth. He felt his cheeks flush from the heat. They were standing behind the roped-off area, yet his body was hot from the radiant, intense fire.

"Coincidence," he finally murmured. "Could be a coincidence, these recent fires. These old buildings are tinderboxes and are as dry as wood can get. Even with the addition of sprinkler systems and modern fire blocks in the corridors, they spread from floor to floor through the vertical framing. Insulation was different in the old days. It settled like sand between the studs and left open pockets of air. Vermiculite just settled out and opened gaps for the fire to spread throughout the walls," he continued, in a low voice. He was knowledgeable, having worked in construction for many years.

A fireman, with suspenders draped around his waist and a white T-shirt visible, removed his black protective jacket because of the heat. Sweat poured off his face as he rushed to the nearest truck to check the water pump. Water pressure had dropped precipitously in the last few minutes and he needed to assess what had caused the problem. *It is certainly not the time for the nearest fire pond to run low*, he thought. Its level was maintained by a nearby stream, but the summer had been a dry one. If it's too low, the fire department would need to seek an alternative water supply and run the pumper trucks in tandem with long hose lines emanating from another water source. Other firemen assisted their colleague, who was baffled by the drop in pressure.

The inferno was further fueled by the multiple coats of paint that had covered the original northern, white pine clapboards. The intense heat melted nearby telephone lines and ignited a creosote-impregnated telephone pole. The protective black residue that waterproofed and prevented insect infestations, ignited easily as the flames ran the length of the pole. The vertical column of flames licked the transformer that was attached at the top of the pole. Just then, the transformer exploded in response to the intense heat. The oil-filled metal container showered the nearby area with flaming oil droplets that resembled fireworks. Two firemen scrambled from the left wall area, which collapsed nearly fifteen feet from where they were standing. They were coated by the shower of oil from the transformer and temporarily became human torches. Screaming for help, they dropped to the ground and rolled to smother the flames. Their colleagues doused them off with hoses.

The sheer weight of the slate roof exerted extreme lateral forces on the supporting ceiling beams, which were already weakened by the well-entrenched fire. There was no way that the beams could sustain themselves, or remain elevated above the eroding support of the roof rafters.

No one in Harvest had ever seen a fire of this magnitude. The fire chief and his crew were amazed at the speed of the rapidly spreading flames and the accelerated demise of the building. The town offices, which contained those rooms of the selectmen, the tax assessors, and collectors, were destroyed within minutes. Historical documents on display in oak-framed glass cases on the first floor vaporized before their eyes. The documents were irreplaceable and were important chronological accounts that contained artifacts of Harvest's history. They were on loan from the historical society, which had a building one mile down the road, and north of the center of town.

The elderly town clerk, a native of Harvest, cried at the sight of the building in flames. Many documents listing her ancestors among the town's early settlers were obviously destroyed.

How could this happen? The fire department is located close to the town hall. Why could they not contain the fire and save the building? she wondered, in tears and unable to speak. *It all went up too fast. Could there have been an accelerant involved? Arson? What about natural causes? A faulty wire from the old days, perhaps? The build-*

ing, after all, was dry from two hundred plus years of history, she wondered.

The sky above "ground zero" was illuminated by an orange glow that flickered in intensity and could be seen from twenty miles around. Within minutes, the remaining structure of the building fell and only a few supporting beams remained standing.

Steam rose from the center core of the blaze as firemen concentrated their hoses on the hottest portion of the unrecognizable pile of timbers. Many more residents arrived, now aware of the tragedy. They congregated in the town center as third- and fourth-alarm fire companies arrived and encircled the charred remains, like a wagon train. Reporters from area newspapers and TV stations pestered the residents, seeking witnesses to comment about the terrible event. One reporter was particularly persistent.

"Anyone inside the building when this happened?" he asked.

"No," was the curt reply from the irritated bystander.

"Anyone see it start? Have they determined a cause?" the reporter repeatedly asked individuals in the crowd. No one responded.

It was now 2:00 A.M. and the cast-iron bell was the last item to be seen lying horizontally in the mass of debris. The glow of its metal had whiter areas and spots of severe heat. The molten blob was the original cast bell from the town hall tower. An apprentice of Paul Revere in Boston had made the famous shell and ringer. It now appeared as a mass of molten metal that sizzled from the water being sprayed upon it. The inferno's base vaporized the metal into iron oxide, thereby reducing it to an unrecognizable object.

✠✠✠

A man in jeans slowly approached his four-wheel-drive SUV and opened the driver's side door. The courtesy roof light did not illuminate; he had purposely switched it off before climbing the small mountain. He had watched the fire from the mountaintop above the center of Harvest for more than three hours. His view from there was unobstructed; a spot near an old ski trail, unused for years, that was not yet overgrown with tall pine trees. From that vantage point, the eastern view of Harvest, and major roads to and from the village, were clearly delineated by the streetlights. The fire's glow was now diminished in the center of town, but steam and smoke continued to rise as firemen saturated the burning embers. Standing next to the SUV's open door, the man spat. "Screw the bastards," he said as he took a deep drag on his cigarette. He threw the butt on the ground and flattened it into the soft earth beneath his boot heel.

"The arrogant assholes will have to meet somewhere else from now on. It wasn't their town hall, anyway. It didn't even belong to them. It belonged to no one of prominence in this town and these pricks don't deserve a place to meet that is not authentic. What do they know of the town history, anyway?" he grumbled. "The founding fathers would roll over in their graves if they knew what had happened to their town. They wouldn't stand for these idiot selectmen, or their arrogant crap of today," he said. He inched his way onto the front seat and turned the ignition key.

The man planned on descending the mountain the same way he came up—by way of the old fire road. He drove down the winding access road, which was obviously rarely used. The fire road was designed for direct access in the event of a forest fire. His last view of the town below was a side glance from the side window. He saw a collage of fire vehicles—flashing lights and steamy smoke billowing upward into the heavens. He drove slowly down the shrub-laden fire trail. The SUV rocked back and forth in the stones and ruts, barely visible in dim yellow parking lights. He did not want to attract attention. It was designed to accommodate the unwanted slalom course of natural hazards. He negotiated the occasional boulder that protruded from the ground after years of frost heaves and ground thaws typical of New England. He smiled slightly as he studied the terrain and then negotiated the obstructions one by one. Using the parking lights made it difficult to follow the road down the mountain. As the fire road leveled off in an open stretch of field at the bottom of the hill, he wiped his brow of the sweat produced by the ordeal of the almost dark journey from the mountaintop. He turned right slowly onto a paved road that was seldom used because it was a dead end to his left. He could see an occasional broken beer bottle and litter in small piles near the intersection of the dirt and asphalt roads. An old mattress was propped up against one tree not far from the paved area. Local kids used the dead end area as a place for "parking" or they hung out there and illegally drank wine coolers and beer. Known as "The Grove," adults and kids knew of it as a place for teenagers to make out and get laid on Friday or Saturday nights.

Once the SUV was on the solid ground of a paved road, he flipped on his main headlights. Prior to that, the dashboard lights were the only illumination of his face in the cab. He noticed a stream of tail-lights from the cars ahead, as they slowed and were diverted by police on to a highway north of town. There was no access to the town center, since the streets were crowded with numerous emergency fire vehicles. The acrid smell of the fire was more prominent at ground level. It permeated the entire town and the countryside for miles.

The deed had been completed and he had witnessed the effects of the plan from the mountaintop. Except for some residual tire treads in a muddy rut, there was little evidence that anyone, or any vehicle, had traversed the mountain road that evening.

✠✠✠

As cleanup began, members of Harvest's well-trained volunteer fire department returned to the meeting room behind the station to discuss the events of the tragic fire. They talked for several hours trying to piece together what they believed was its cause. *Town halls of this size just don't ignite that fast,* they thought. The building seemed to be engulfed in flames in minutes and the points of incineration appeared to be multiple and varied in location. That was unusual. They also realized that they never had a chance to save the building. The fire got way ahead of them in intensity.

The fire department was composed of fifty-two men from many walks of life—shop owners, loggers, construction personnel, and salesmen. They were a small network of friends who acted like brothers, socially and at work.

Fire Chief Norman McKay, a construction supervisor by day, was in his thirties, married with a young family. He was the son of Melvin McKay, whose own grandfather had settled in Harvest in the 1800s. All McKay generations were dyed-in-the-wool New Englanders who hunted and fished the local area. It was in their blood to be part of the woods, and Harvest suited that need.

The discussion in the firehouse meeting room began as more members of the department arrived. They each smelled of smoke and were clearly exhausted from the lost battle at the town hall.

"Chief, what do you think about the fire's origin? Any thoughts?" asked a fire brigade member.

"Haven't a clue, just yet," he responded. "It certainly hints of arson—the fire seemed to be fueled from different corners of the building. Did any of you folks see any evidence of an accelerant?"

No one mentioned observing any.

"Guess you are right about potential arson. It moved so fast, I doubt if the construction and renovation crew could cause multiple focal points of ignition," said the questioner. Most firemen agreed that the speed of the fire's onset was faster than they had ever seen in other building fires.

"What about the original wiring?" another man asked from the back of the room. "When was that changed? Ever? The damn building was a tinderbox. Perhaps the fire started in the lower level. It could have spread quickly from there," he said.

"Nah," replied the chief, with some authority, "would have had to have been multiple electrical wires if that were the case. Too many points where it was ragin'. Can't imagine a single wire causin' that much damage so fast. Doesn't matter anyway. The fire marshal is due now from Concord and his job is to figure the damn mess out. You guys need rest. All of you go home except for Don, Bob, Chip, and Luke. We will need a crew at the fire site for the remainder of the evening. I need volunteers for the morning shift so these guys can be relieved. Any takers?"

A number of men raised their hands to volunteer to report at 7:00 A.M. to be of help. A few hours of sleep would be enough to function again at that hour.

"Get some rest, men!" barked the chief. "For those that are still wound up and can't sleep, there's beer in the cooler over in the corner. You guys deserve a brew! My father donated two cases, so help yourselves."

The firemen disbanded, except for eight or nine who took him up on the offer of a beer. They would continue to try to solve the puzzle of the fire. The conversation continued until 5:00 A.M. and then reverted to old stories of fishing and hunting.

At 3:30 A.M., the state fire marshal arrived to begin the investigation into the fire's origin. His conclusion, after weeks of detailed analysis, would be that the town hall fire in Harvest, New Hampshire, was indeed of suspicious origin.

✠✠✠

Nelson crushed out his cigarette before reentering the church house at 2:45 A.M. He rarely smoked because Lydia had hated it. He only lit up when he had a few beers, or was depressed or angry. He stood at the mantle in the darkened living room and cupped the urn with his hands—he kissed the side of it and then headed slowly for the bedroom with his bottle of scotch and a glass. As he sat on the side of the bed to undress, he picked up her photo on the bed stand and whispered, "Lydie, my love . . . the 'return to Raby' is near. . . . It began a while back . . . but now the plan is in irreversible forward motion. . . . I'm about to win the election . . . I can feel it in these bones. I'm sorry you're not here to share it—the commotion I've created with the fools in town . . . I love you and miss you very much." Nelson lay back, partially undressed. He was exhausted.

In minutes, he was asleep and snoring heavily. The empty glass was on the night table.

Twenty-one

Nelson's supporters, wondering if the fire would become an issue now that it was just two weeks before the election, quickly sought his input about what to do about rebuilding the town hall. They also needed to express their sadness over the fate of the historic building. When he returned their calls, he had a simple message. "I share your concerns. Should I win the election, we will be OK, I'm sure."

"It is sad that we lost the building. I saw the ruins the next day. It was terrible. We need to think about how to rebuild," he told one caller.

"Yes, we need to make sure we retain our history," the woman said, "The style of the building should remain the same when we rebuild, don't you think? Surely someone has the original blueprints of the old structure."

"Not sure about that," he responded. "The design may have been in the old structure at the time of the fire, and filed in the annals of the history room on the first floor. Actually, come to think of it, blueprints didn't exist back then."

"Oh, how sad," she said, sounding depressed.

"We will explore what residents have in their homes for history," he suggested. "We need to get through this forthcoming election first, and also await the fire marshal's report of the disaster. These things take time, but I can assure you that if I am elected, I pledge to make a replacement building a priority."

Nelson then added, "We need to rebuild an official hall in accordance with the history of the town," he said, feeling smug.

✠✠✠

Nelson was careful not to reveal what he knew was the truth about the town's history, since he was relying on Mrs. Perry's unpublished manuscript to reveal it at the right time. The documents his daughter and Libby had found in the attic of the village store had pointed him to the location of the original town hall. He surmised that other older residents in town had similar historic information that would be helpful. He would have Libby seek them out.

In response to another concerned caller, Nelson shared more details of his plans.

"I'm told from good sources that other older residents in town may have information that will be helpful concerning the early meeting sites in this little town," he said. "There may have been other community buildings that preceded the town hall as it relates to its present location. Perhaps we can find out where those structures were located," he suggested. He ended with campaign rhetoric, "I hope that you will vote for our Take Back Harvest Party . . . we need you good folks."

"You *will* be elected Nel . . . for sure," the man added. "We will help you reclaim the town . . . you have our vote!"

"Thank you," he replied. "Hope that you will tell your friends of our hopes and dreams for this little town."

"I will," the man added, "and good luck, Nel."

Another Palmer supporter called, concerned about where the town meetings would take place. Nelson could not answer the question; it was up to the selectmen.

"What will happen to the town meetings in the interim? Might you know, Nelson?" she asked gravely.

Nelson thought for a moment and commented, "I suppose they will meet in a local school, perhaps in the auditorium or in a teacher conference room at one of the schools. I think that would be advantageous, since there are no other large structures in town for them to coordinate town business. We hope that they keep the doors open to the public, as well. In a local schoolroom they would have to encourage dialogue," he said. "With my administration, I will make sure that there are never any secret meetings by government officials!"

He could literally hear the woman's sigh of relief over the telephone.

"You are a good man, Nelson Palmer. It was a blessing for us, when you moved here. Your heart is in the right place."

"I thank you for your support. Please drive a friend to the polls. Bring us some votes," he said. "We will need all the help we can find to get this little village back on track."

"You *will* be the next town manager," she said. "You . . . will definitely win. That's the buzz around town!"

For the first time during the campaign, Nelson was feeling the strength and incredible support of the locals. He knew that his Take Back Harvest Party's chances to win had increased in recent weeks—he and his friends were now in the running. He sat back in a chair at the kitchen table and sipped a cup of coffee. He could see out the side door of the church home and he became introspective and relaxed. He absolutely loved his home and the surrounding countryside. Cardinals, blue jays, sparrows, and chickadees frequented his property, especially in the backyard. Bird nests were everywhere in the tall pines, oaks, and maples. They seemed to sing all day long. The autumn leaves had faded and had all but dropped as November approached.

In Nelson's political agenda and in his own mind, the town hall was not a priority, at least not in its present location. The present ruins were linked to history only in the later evolution of the village, known as the town of Harvest. To Nelson, that building meant little in the true historic scope of things. It was an afterthought along the way and less valuable and significant than the centuries old, stone cellar hole that Nelson and Jason had stumbled across. It was clear in Nelson's mind, that few people in town really knew of the town's origins, history or forefathers, anyway. If they did, they would have held annual commemorative ceremonies on Memorial Day to honor the colonists' grave sites. The Perry manuscript was the key to that knowledge and only Nelson's relatives and his closest friends were aware of the document and the authentic beginnings of the real town, Raby. With Mrs. Perry, Jason Birch, and old man Parker dead, it was Nelson's responsibility and quest to publish the manuscript as a book of truth—a history of Raby.

Nelson smiled when he reminisced about the historic files that were lost in the fire. In the aftermath were the tax assessor's and planning board records, as well. The town would need to secure input from residents about their most recent tax bills or licenses. Since most residents were not happy with the town selectmen's attitudes in recent months, they weren't anxious to share their personal records with the existing officials, who appeared to be meeting in secret. Residents would be in no mood to assist the current administration or help them out with their now missing records. The majority of residents now were waiting for new blood to be elected, before they would share personal information with the town officials. They demanded credible representatives and the current regime failed that test miserably. The selectmen and their officials were unable to get the public to respond to requests for information. The town was about to go bust.

Nelson called a special meeting of the Take Back Harvest Party candidates. The election was less than two weeks away and he wanted to share his thoughts and strategies for a potential administration with them. He had a new idea for the town hall and they would be surprised by his revelations. With the campaign finance situation solvent from supporters' donations, and little more money needed for the remainder of the two weeks, he felt compelled to share with them, in confidence, his lottery winnings.

His fellow candidates were both astonished and pleased at his good fortune and pleased for him. He indicated that, with at least some of the winnings, he would be investing in the town's needs in the future. He also insinuated that the town's history was deeper and more dynamic than they had envisioned. He would not elaborate further at that meeting, but he indicated that he would share his newfound wealth of knowledge in time. He expressed his sincere desire that they all be elected—after all, they had positioned themselves and their agendas well and on their own—by door-to-door, grassroots campaigning.

✠✠✠

Nelson became the executor of the Jason Birch estate and cottage on the lake, which he owned through his holding company. After his friend's death, Nelson spent time at the cottage in solitude. It was a wonderful escape from the grind and stress of the day-to-day campaign. He made sure that the property was maintained and that the little boat and motor were not stolen from the dock.

Nelson sat in a folding chair on the small deck of the cottage. In the quiet of the day, he reminisced about his friend and knew that Jason would be proud of Nelson's almost-certain election. Jason had contributed his time and energy in the extensive campaign promotion. Political signs endorsing Nelson Palmer still adorned his front yard. They read ANOTHER VOTER FOR PALMER and TAKE BACK HARVEST! In a five-gallon pail to the right side of the deck was Jason's old fishing pole and tackle box. Nelson grabbed the cork handle of the rod and started the motor of the skiff. He headed out to the icehouse piers that Jason had once pointed out to him. In the same spot where Jason had once hauled out huge blocks of ice as a teen, Nelson caught many largemouth bass that particular evening. It was almost dusk.

The lake was serene and calm, and each cast of the line resulted in concentric ripples around the spot where the flashy gold lure landed. The *plunk* of the lure hitting the water's surface was the only noise Nelson could hear. The whippoorwills seemed quiet this particular evening. Water licked the sides of the small aluminum boat as Nelson shifted his weight on the uncomfortable seat. The lake was his and his alone, for the moment.

The night air was shattered by the haunting sound of a common loon. It passed to the left of the boat and settled in some reeds near the lake shoreline. Nelson knew that unique vocal tremolo call anywhere.

"Well . . . how about that?" he whispered. "Must be a nest of those guys nearby." The bird called out once more, as a warning to relatives. "I'll be damned," he said, "that surely must be a family of them over there." Nelson paddled closer to the area where he thought he might find them. The blade of the paddle was almost silent. Nelson strained his eyes. About twenty-five feet away he could see two adults with clear black and white markings. Surrounding the parents were two juveniles, this year's brood. One small guy attempted to jump on a parent's back. Nelson knew they often carried their young that way as protection from predators. The female resisted the juvenile's move—he was much too old for that. The evening was growing darker and the birds were mere silhouettes. The male called out again and the haunting sound reverberated off the surrounding hills. Nelson would go no closer. He knew that the adults would be migrating in late November before the lake would freeze. He relished the moment, hoping they would return safely in the spring.

He lowered the ten-pound, cast-iron anchor and sat and watched until it was near dark. He reflected on how gorgeous the state of New Hampshire was in landscape and wildlife. He was truly blessed to have settled into what he knew were his roots—Raby. His euphoric reflections were dampened only by the loss of Lydia. The couple had planned to grow old and die together. She was to share his passions in life—and he was to reciprocate. She would have been proud to know that Aunt Bess's historical genealogy knowledge was becoming true and in sharp focus.

Lydia would never have expected Nelson to get involved in politics to straighten out the town. She knew him as a man who thought politics was a hopeless gesture. Politicians were people who were not trusted. Nelson would never have guessed himself to be involved in local politics, either, but circumstances had forced him into it if there was to be change. *Change only comes through participation. Don't complain if you have no solution to offer,* he had preached to his children all his life. He now had plenty to complain about and to resolve. He quickly stopped daydreaming, pulled up the anchor, and lowered it gently into the little boat.

Nelson used a small battery-powered, secondary electric motor to return to the dock at Jason's cottage. He did not want to disturb the family of common loons. He knew that the wake from boats and their gasoline motors often wiped out nests where they raised their young. The loons, considered the oldest bird in the world, were shoreline nest builders and found it difficult to walk on shore. Their legs were too far back on their body, he had once read. They were named the "loon" in Scandinavia and it meant "clumsy." Nelson was not about to disturb the loons. He loved the birds dearly and he and his wife had enjoyed photographing them, as well. Nelson had bought her a 35mm camera and telephoto lens to accomplish the task. Her photos of loons and their young offspring adorned the walls of the church home.

Nelson was tempted to stay at the cottage that evening so that he could awaken to the morning call of the special birds, but decided instead to go home. He had many campaign tasks to work on.

"I will save nature's wake-up call for another morning," he said to himself. "There is too much to accomplish before the damn election." He knew there would be many messages on his answering machine.

Sure enough, there were many voicemails awaiting him, including several from Susan who needed to speak to him as soon as possible. She used the word "urgent."

Nelson took off his coat and placed Jason's reel and tackle box in the closet. He washed his hands and replayed the message machine nearby. Susan had left multiple voice messages for Nelson. This time he took notes of each caller's concerns, carefully jotting down their phone numbers. Susan's comments were most critical he felt. She needed to talk to him and sounded extremely concerned. She was normally pretty unflappable.

"Nel, the opposition is spreading rumors that you are a rich man who is *buying* the election," one message relayed on the tape. Nelson called her back as soon as he realized that her voice had a tremor in it.

"Susan? Nel here," he said. "What's up? You sound all flustered on the messages."

"Nelson," she responded with angst, "where the hell have you been? Fishin'? Those asses on the other side have been slingin' mud like crazy all day. They claim that you are secretly—a very rich man ... who is literally *buying* votes. . . . They think you are *paying people directly* to vote for you. Political graft! We don't need this shit so close to the election!"

"So . . . I'm *not* paying for votes!" he replied.

She continued, "At some point, you will need to come clean and let the general public know that you are the Lotto winner. They obviously can't understand how you are donating so much to town causes. The anonymity is apparently foiled. If the papers catch wind of . . . "

Nelson cut her off mid-sentence. "Susie Q, chill out for a while. Who cares about what the opposition slings around? They're desperate! They'll end up eatin' their words and lookin' foolish, anyway. Do you hear me, love? . . . They are desperate now. Time is short and they have lost popularity . . . actually, they never had it!"

"But Nelson, what if the newspapers print these lies? They will sabotage our concerted efforts, which we have achieved over the last few months. We have worked hard to make this all happen for you. Those bastards are lying about your intentions and even your credibility. You profess credibility. . . . Confront them!"

"Sue, I am not worried. Trust me, everything will be OK," he said, trying to reassure her.

"Well, they are shouting out things like you are 'tied to drug money and the mafia' and shit," she said with emotion. "Do you want that kind of crap to be believed as your reputation . . . now?"

"No . . . of course I don't," he said, pacing.

"Your recent donations to the town, the schools, the police and ambulance squads hint that you have mucho buckos, dude."

"So?" he replied. "What evidence do they have of my source of income or that kind of financial support . . . come on, will ya . . . Mafia and drugs? Really! . . . None! Right?"

"Yes," she continued, "but why not tell them of your lottery winnings so they understand where the coin came from? You appear to be hiding something . . . and you are."

Nelson knew that she had some good points, but he was reluctant to reveal his wealth just yet. He would in time, but wanted to reveal the information after the election was over. He still wanted voters to feel that they had elected him for his leadership, not his money.

"Sue, you have good ideas and concerns but I just can't do that yet. I wanted the town supporters to raise the campaign money that we needed, *on . . . their . . . own . . .* by volunteers who believed in what I, and we, stand for. . . . You! Me! And the others. After all, it is *their* candidates, me included, who promised to give them *a voice.* If I funded the campaign all by myself, and I could have, they would not partake in the process and voice their opinions. Look at what they did for us, all by themselves. They went door-to-door distributing flyers and working hard to get the votes. Do you think they would do that if I paid for the campaign? They would have merely sat on their butts, like before, to see who won."

"I see what you're saying Nelson . . . maybe I am upset for no reason. . . . I'm sorry," Susan said apologetically.

Nelson consoled her and added, "You and Doug come over this evening and I'll treat you to dinner. OK? We'll go out to eat so I can "buy" your votes—Mafia style," he said jokingly. Susan loved Nelson for his humor, confidence, and relaxed style of dealing with inconsequential issues . . . at least to him.

"Nelson, you are a funny man . . . a crazy and unpredictable man. You make me laugh. That is why everyone loves you."

"Come on over and we'll go from here," he reiterated. "We'll get some Italian food up the road, far away from the Harvest masses and asses."

"We'll be right over," Susan said, smiling to herself. Nelson could sense that she was a bit more relaxed. "I need to find Doug first. He's wandering around here lookin' for some masonry tools he misplaced."

Forty-five minutes later, they drove north to the restaurant.

At dinner, Susan, a bit hardheaded, still hoped to convince him to counteract the slanderous libel he was facing from the opposition. Awaiting appetizers, she would again begin trying to convince him there was an *issue* at hand.

"You're the boss Nelson, but I really wanted to alert you to the smut out there on the street. That is all I was trying to do on the phone," she added.

Doug seemed to agree. "If the residents who follow you believe what is being said," Doug added, "half the voters will think those jerks are right and believe that you are Mafioso and stuff."

"OK . . . OK . . . ," he said to appease both of them. "I will run a couple of TV ads that will reach most of the people who live around here. That should quell this silly shit and lies they are spreading. I can still defend myself from the slander without revealing my lottery winnings. OK? . . . Now, eat your meatballs!"

Susan nodded. "You're the boss . . . sounds like an ad might work. Thanks for listening to our concerns," she added. During the remainder of dinner, they talked about the land that they were clearing by the old foundation at the original Raby site. The dirt road was accessible and, in fact, was ready to be paved if Nelson wanted to do that. He hesitated about adding asphalt prematurely. It would make people focus on the old site and his potential agenda. Right now, it appeared to be an inconspicuous logging road.

Doug had shored up and refitted any loose stones of the foundation and he cemented what he could to secure a few unstable footings on one wall. In November construction and framing would begin.

Nelson concluded the dinner with Sue and Doug by telling them how grateful he was to them for their friendship and their work ethics.

"I will ride out there tomorrow to see all the good things you have done at the stone wall site. Thanks for keepin' me updated. Sounds like it's really comin' along and very accessible now."

They finished their spumoni ice cream and cannolis, agreeing to get together the next day to plan the TV ads. Nelson paid the bill and left a healthy tip on the table.

Twenty-two

Penny was pleased that her popular village store kept people from shopping for household staples up the road. "Daddy," she said one day, "we are really doing well. The deli is busy from noon on, and the little craft and gift corner is popular, even though the Thanksgiving and Christmas holidays are still weeks away."

"That's great, honey," Nelson replied. "The place looks great. I like the way you are displaying the historical newspaper articles above the shelves. It adds an ambiance that wasn't there when old man Parker ran it. By the way, how is the upstairs?" he asked. "Did you get the mess cleaned out? What a firetrap!"

"Sure did. We had a yard sale and moved most of it—a lot of it actually. Some old papers and furniture went pretty quickly. Lots of people buy that stuff and none of it was worthwhile to us. It's pretty clean up there now. We were thinkin' of rentin' it out, or at least a part of it. Maybe we could convert it to somethin' different," she suggested.

"Well, ya know hon, this ol' place was a general store for a long time. I think from most recent records that I've read, it also harbored a craftsman upstairs. I think the young fellow did wooden carvings and Shaker-like furniture to satisfy the local needs and homes. Some of his stuff still adorns the residences on the main drag. Mrs. Perry had some pieces of his work. The carved acorns he created were meant as a welcome sign to visitors. The craftsman also sculpted seabirds and eagles—a New England tradition. Wish I could remember the name of the guy!"

"Really?" she said with interest. "Perhaps we could rent it out to someone who does crafts like that and then sell his or her creations downstairs in the general store. Tourists would certainly buy those items as gifts and remembrances—don't you think, Dad?"

"Sounds like a great idea, hon, if you can find the right person," said Nelson. "I saw some loons the other day on the lake. They surely would sell if the artisan could sculpt and paint those unique birds. If that concept doesn't work, you might consider creating a small museum of the history of the town. There is surely enough space, and we could buy some glass and wooden cases to house the real historical items of this village. It would be great for school kids to visit and view the displays . . . ya know, learn about their local customs and heritage. We have been finding some artifacts at the old town cellar hole. Some pieces of pottery could be reproduced, and sold to visitors as remembrances of the town. The artisan could also be a potter, wood carver, or run a cooperage . . . whatever works for ya."

"Dad, you are just loaded with good ideas today. I'm inspired to make it work." She hugged her father. He was equally proud of her new direction and endeavor in town. She was part of the process of positive change.

Getting people back to the sentiments of the original town would take more than the election of her father, she thought. "Let's think about this some more, Daddy," she added. "You have certainly inspired my creative juices to do somethin' with that space upstairs. Let me talk to Ray, and get his input as well. Bet he will have some ideas. Wish he was home from Boston. . . . He is there all the time now. Business is booming and dinners with clients are way too frequent. Seems like we never see each other."

"You do that, hon. Talk to him and let me know what you folks decide. I'm here to help if you need me," he said pouring a freshly brewed coffee for the road. "You and Ray OK?"

Penny nodded yes, but quickly looked away from her father. She wasn't ready to share how distant Ray had become, and her suspicions about his long absences.

Days passed before Nelson stopped by again to chat with Penny for any length of time. The beer and cigarette portion of the store was slowly phased out and the caliber of the crowd that stopped by to purchase items was upgraded. His daughter planned to add a penny-candy counter and soda fountain, like the old days. After some searching at consignment stores and auction barns, Nelson found an old soda fountain dispenser for seltzer water and helped install the counter where customers could sit on stools and eat ice cream. Residents stopped by with their children for a frappé or root beer float. The atmosphere of the general store changed and the locals brought by friends and relatives from out of town to visit the little store.

Containers of fishing worms no longer resided next to the beer and milk in the cooler. The Parker store days were long gone. There was a separate cooler for outdoor sports-related items near the fishing and camping supplies. The Harvest Village Store now mimicked the famed village store of note, in nearby Putney, Vermont, which had drawn out-of-state tourists for generations. It remained one of the most famous village stores in all six states of New England. In time, Penny's store was popular, as well. During leaf-peeping season Penny had done well selling locally grown pumpkins and farm-grown produce. Tourists had scarfed up fresh vegetables along with multicolored gourds and ornamental Indian corn, which she had attractively displayed outside while renovations were going on to the interior.

Penny decided to place ads in New York and Boston papers for a resident artist or artisan.

In the first week, she had a number of responses, but few artists desired the remoteness of New Hampshire once the town of Harvest was described to them. Derek Mitchell, from New York City, who did sculpture, pottery, and painting, primarily in watercolor, sounded promising when he responded to her ad in the *Village Voice*. Nelson agreed to house her final choice of artist in one of his rental properties while he visited and toured the upstairs studio. Nelson charged Derek next to nothing for housing, a mere token of normal rental costs. The deal was done in days. Derek found the opportunity appealing and he and Penny hit it off from the moment that he arrived. The second floor of the village store soon became his studio. He had UPS ship his most important art supplies. The remainder of his possessions were transported in his van and he moved in before the end of the month.

Derek Mitchell was quiet and worked long hours. Soon he had painted ten watercolors and had fashioned a dozen wood sculptures of loons. His pottery creations were reproductions of the items that Susan and Doug found in the old Raby cellar hole. He was liked by everyone and quickly adapted to the town's need for artistic culture.

"Very nice paintings," Penny told him from the moment she saw him at his easel. "You do beautiful work, Derek, and they sell like wildfire downstairs in the store."

"Thanks for making my dream come true," he said to her. "I've hoped for this opportunity in New England for a few years now. Your ad was perfect, the studio the right size, and the timing magnificent, as well."

"Well, it is clear that you are talented and this second-floor studio should be satisfactory, right?" she asked.

"This is wonderful. You and your father have been very generous to me. It is comfortable and I'm adjusting well to the little community. It's a bit different than New York. Ever been there?"

"No," she admitted. "It looks great from afar, but I'm not sure I could handle all the commotion and confusion one sees on TV about the Big Apple."

He agreed, admitting that life in New York was fast-paced—that is why he had wanted to find a small town in which to be creative. She listened to his description of living on Manhattan Island. It sounded exciting, but lonely.

From the moment she first saw him, Penny found the man, with his thick, dark hair and penetrating blue eyes, dangerously attractive. Her family was the center of her life, as well as her store, but she found Derek to be a fascinating renaissance person. He was talented, dedicated, and carefree. A simple flower in bloom meant a lot to him and beauty was uncomplicated in nature and fodder for his creativity. He saw it before him in the surrounding landscape and reproduced it with ease in oils, watercolor, pottery, or metal. Penny admired his simple needs.

From the moment he laid eyes on her, Derek was taken by her form. She was older by seven years, but like her mother, was destined to be a beautiful woman at any age. He memorized her facial structure and painted her frequently. He was careful not to tread on the good fortune of his job, even though he found her extremely attractive and sensual. As a gift, he gave her a small portrait of herself, which she hid from her family.

Derek worked hard to keep his mind from wandering while meeting the increasing demands of the store; his creations sold out almost as fast as he finished them. After three weeks, she was able to talk him into stopping his work to share a coffee break. Then he would go back to sculpting and painting upstairs while Penny pretty much worked long hours alone downstairs. She hired high school students to help after-school with the cash registers. Ray was on the road almost all the time, and was of little help once the store was up and running. He called Harvest a hick town, even though Penny insisted it was changing for the better. He entertained clients in town and dinners often ran late, which frequently put him sixty miles from home, so he stayed over at Boston hotels on heavy traffic nights north.

One Thursday night in late October, while Ray was gone on yet another three-day trip, Penny was about to close the store. She noticed the upstairs light was still on and went up to turn it off.

"Are you still here, Derek?" she asked into the void of the stairway.

He called back, "Yes . . . still here, Penny, finishing a bird."

She stood at the top step and said, "Thought you headed out the back door hours ago," she laughed. "What a beautiful carving."

"Thanks," he said, holding the new creation up to the dim light above him.

"What is this one called?" she asked, leaning over his shoulder.

He could smell her fragrance as he said, "This one is a mourning dove, a very common New England bird. I know you've heard them early in the day; they often rest on telephone lines and tree limbs. They have a soft mourning sound and are known to pair for life."

"What do they mourn?" she asked.

"Have no clue if they mourn anything . . . life, I suppose," he suggested. "Maybe they know life is complicated," he added.

"Why complicated?" she asked. "They are simple birds. Is your life complicated?"

Derek looked away and said, "Sometimes you find what you want when you least expect it. 'When you don't look—ya find, they say.'"

"Yes, that is true sometimes. Sometimes you find . . . but cannot have!" she said, smiling.

"What do you mean? You, my lady, have everything," he said, holding the bird carving in the air once again. He rotated its body, then stood up. He placed the bird on the carving table and touched her hand. She grasped his lightly, then withdrew it quickly.

"I can't . . . I really can't," she whispered.

"I know. You have everything, right? A home, a husband, kids, and this wonderful store. Right?"

"Almost everything, except love . . . I don't have love. My life is this store because I need to occupy my time. Ray is not affectionate anymore," she whispered. "We don't have a closeness anymore."

"Why is that?" he asked with concern. "You are beautiful, smart, and caring. You are everything he should be looking for."

"Thank you," she said shyly, "But love is not a part of him any-more. He's too busy it seems. He doesn't notice what you apparently notice."

"Everyone gets busy . . . look at you and me. . . . We are busy as well," he suggested. He hugged her and felt her hug back. She sighed often, and then felt his warmth, unbuttoned her jeans and blouse, re-vealing her bra. He responded by helping her undress. He was excited beyond his wildest expectations, for he had expected nothing . . . ab-solutely nothing. She unbuckled his jeans and slid them down to the floor. He eagerly helped her remove his Jockey shorts as they knelt and kissed. To the side of them was a folded tarp for his painting that was new and unused. He held her with one hand and unfolded the fabric on the floor. A soft, padded duffle bag filled with art supplies was nearby. He laid her gently on the tarp with the bag positioned as a pillow beneath her head. He was overcome by raw lust and intent. She had come on to him and he was receptive. It was primal. He lay upon her, and gently kissed her now exposed breasts. Smiling she said, "This is exactly what I've needed. I thought of you all day, and I thought about this happening."

He was surprised by her candor. "I've felt the same way for days but have stayed upstairs for fear of offending you with my desires. I have needed to tell you how much I've felt for you," he whispered.

Derek was gentle, but firm. He elevated Penny's thighs and slowly increased the pulsing motion. She writhed in ecstasy from his obvious experience at lovemaking. It was primal instinct, and *he* was primal. She gyrated like she had never had impulsive sex before. It was beyond her wildest expectations. "Oh . . . oh . . . oh!" she cried out. "You . . . you feel wonderful inside me . . . you . . . feel like it should be . . . like sex for the first time," she said with enormous passion. She climaxed and continued to move as if she were just beginning. He experienced an orgasm as well, and neither one stopped. Again she experienced orgasm. "That's a first," she cried out. "*That* is a first!" she laughed playfully.

"What?" he said, sweating and out of breath. "What's a first?"

"Multiple orgasms!" she said. "I've never had multiple orgasms . . . heard that they were awesome," she said panting, "and . . . guess what . . . they are!"

He lay on her for a moment, holding her closely. She blew air into his face to cool him. Both were sweating profusely.

"Thank you," she said. "That was incredible. Can we do that again?"

"Give me a second, woman," he laughed, as he tried to catch his breath. He then began to slowly touch her all over and slid backwards, kissing her belly and thighs. Her head went back and her eyes closed. He performed oral sex on her and she climaxed in two minutes time. Most of her energy and his, was expended.

Derek then sat on his knees. He could not believe her responsiveness nor could she believe his. He had never experienced lust at its best before. He smiled and she smiled. They kissed and then came to their senses. She gazed at her gold watch and quickly realized the time—the children were home alone. She needed to get home. He watched her dress rapidly and then she grabbed his cheeks and kissed him good-bye. It was as if her "mom" psyche had kicked in, and all of a sudden, the primal aspect was overridden with guilt and responsibility—her children.

The mood shift was immediate. Penny smiled and ran down the stairs. Derek sat back on the tarp and heard her feet descend the final steps and cross the store's hardwood floor. He thought about the whole impromptu and sensuous scenario. It was spectacular to him and for him. He sat quietly for twenty minutes—alone in the dim light of the studio. The moon shown brightly through the only window, casting a blue beam at his feet. His eyes adjusted to the now subdued light. The carved birds had become ominous silhouettes.

Thinking deeply, he felt guilt. He had betrayed and violated Penny and Nelson's trust in him—Nelson's more than hers, since she willingly had desired the same evening's fate as him.

✠✠✠

When Ray called to check in with the family, their daughter answered the phone and said that their mother was not home yet.

"Not home?" he asked. "She must still be doing paperwork at the store. I will try and reach her there, honey. I will let you know where she is and what's keeping her, sweetheart."

"Thanks, Dad," responded ten-year-old Amy, with eight-year-old Chelsea by her side.

The store's phone rang with no answer. Penny's car pulled into the driveway at their home just as her husband called home again. The daughter answered again and said that her mom had just pulled into the garage.

"Good," he said. "Hon, I have to run. Tell mom hello and that I'll be in touch tomorrow. OK?"

"OK, Dad . . . bye . . . I love you!" the sad young girl said, hanging up.

Ray rolled over on his side in bed in the Boston Sheraton Hotel. The woman at his side was someone he had met at the bar. She was about ready to leave his room when Penny called him back at her daughter's request. As Ray said hello, Penny heard a woman's voice in the background. Penny hung up without saying a word after Ray's "hello." Her guilt from the evening with Derek rapidly dissipated. She felt simultaneously sad, sick, and joyful. She managed to compose herself and read *Willy Wonka and the Chocolate Factory* to the kids before tucking them in. They were happy to see their mother home and she hoped that they had forgotten she was late. Amy, the oldest daughter, kissed her mother good night and then said, "Mom, where were you? It was dark . . . where were you? You didn't call! You always call."

"Sorry, honey, I should have telephoned. I'm so sorry . . . I really am. Let me cuddle you for a while. I had things to catch up with at the store. That is why I was late."

She hugged her daughters and sang a lullaby until both girls fell asleep.

Penny showered and scrubbed herself, as if to purify her skin from the ravishing sex. Unlike Derek, she had no scratches on her back. He, on the other hand, was sore, and exhibited red streaks on his upper torso from her passion.

Penny crawled into bed and sat up against a fluffed pillow. She thought out loud for an hour, sometimes watching the TV, the sound masking her thoughts. She rehashed and rationalized her experience with Derek—the whole evening—over and over again. She envisioned Ray's unfaithfulness, and wondered how long he had been cavorting with other women. It was obvious that his desire for her had been waning for some time. They had grown apart and neither had wanted to admit it. Their marriage was only a matter of coexistence—basically for the children. Penny called Derek. She needed to tell him what had happened after she had returned home. They chatted for fifteen minutes and he expressed his concern for her. He ended by telling her that he felt wonderful with her, and that she was like no other woman he had known. She hung up, feeling much better, and soon lay back to sleep.

The next night she closed the store a bit earlier so she could spend three hours with Derek. The "cancer" of the erotic moments spread like wildfire. They became lovers from the first moment on.

Derek wondered if Penny would ever leave her husband. She had not discussed that with him. As an artist and free spirit, he was not concerned about his permanency in Harvest, New Hampshire. He cared deeply for her and knew he was falling in love. But he had never committed to anyone in the past, and she was different.

In the two weeks before the election, it was increasingly difficult for them to find time alone. Penny was needed to help with her father's campaign; Libby had given her a list of voters to call. Derek had to satisfy himself with seeing her during quick coffee breaks.

Twenty-three

On election day, Nelson Palmer greeted voters outside the polling place at the school gymnasium. The town used draped booths and paper ballots that required a pencil or pen to select each candidate. The polls were open on that Tuesday from 7:00 A.M. to 7:00 P.M. to allow working people time to vote.

Nelson felt good about his chances. Many residents entering the polling station expressed their desire for him to change the town. They needed his leadership to make the village a practical and cohesive community.

"Good luck, Nelson . . . you have my vote," one said.

"You'll win by a landslide," an older man told him. Many people continued to express their condolences to Nelson for the loss of his wife, even though it had been almost a year since her death. "My vote's for Lydia and you," one woman said. "We owe her that much."

"Thank you, ma'am. Thank you for remembering her," he said softly.

An older gentleman grabbed his hand and shook it firmly. "Nelson, we need you. You are a good man and will do this town good. Those SOBs have been rulin' this little place for decades. I thought I'd go to my damn grave before those rascals were booted out. Today will be the day!" he said, stammering. His Parkinson's disease was readily apparent to Nelson, and he hugged him.

Nelson said, "You will see that change today, sir. I promise. . . . If I win, you will see the change you want and surely deserve."

"Good, son," the old man said. "I've waited for someone to take charge . . . and you're the one."

"Thank you for the vote of confidence," Nelson said, smiling.

He greeted many more people waiting in line outside the doors of the polls. They all seemed to have him in mind for their votes. But across the street were signs supporting Nelson's opponent, Thomas Shaw. A few old-name residents chanted, "You can't buy the election, Nelson! People don't buy elections!" Few voters paid attention to the oppositions' supporters. There were too few of them to make a last-minute impact on voters.

At 6:00 P.M., Nelson headed home to watch the evening news. The actual counting of votes would not be completed for several hours and he wanted to see how the election would be covered on local TV. Awaiting him at the church home were Susan, Doug, Libby, Penny, and her family. Derek stopped by at Nelson's request. Even Ed Hammond and his wife had driven down from the north to witness the results firsthand. In anticipation of victory, they had placed celebratory banners in the enormous living room. Many of the helium-inflated balloons of red, white, and blue rose to the cathedral ceiling and were cast back down by the fans near its apex. American flags adorned the front door, the fence posts, and inside the front alcove of the reno-vated residence. It was as festive as anyone could have planned. There was to be a post-election party if all went well. Nelson was surprised by the atmosphere; he thought the decorations were premature. He had not expected to see so many relatives and friends there.

"Hey, buddy," Ed said, "the TV stations have you pegged to win tonight. The polls haven't even closed and they think that most exit polls show *you* as the winner . . . and by a landslide!"

"Wow! What a surprise to see you both. Thanks for comin' down."

"Can't rely on those exit polls though . . . they don't always pan out. Look what happened in Palm Beach County, Florida, for cryin' out loud." Everyone laughed, since Harvest didn't use the infamous ballots with chads in this election. As soon as they arrived, Amy and Chelsea, his favorite grandchildren, ran up to hug him.

"Hi, kids! How're my best party kids?" he said. They were a loving family and Nelson was close to the young ones. Derek noticed the closeness of the entire group. Penny paid little attention to him, not wanting her true affection towards him to be noticed. Derek misread her, and thought she was avoiding him. She almost seemed closer now to her husband that evening. *Perhaps,* Derek thought, *she and Ray are trying to reconcile their differences and work things out.* He absorbed the camaraderie of the evening and studied the family interaction. He became despondent; he did not want the family to be broken up by the discovery of his romantic involvement with Penny. By night's end, and after several drinks, he reached the hasty decision to move on immediately. He would pack what he could into his van that very night and head for the Maine coast where he had friends. He would leave Penny a note that stated that he needed the stimulation of the coastline and that he had overstayed his welcome in Harvest. He wrote that he loved her, but had to let her go and he listed the reasons—her family, children, and the continuity in the town. She was needed—to be there for her father, if he became elected. Derek's note also reminded her that if she ever left her husband, he would be there . . . waiting for her.

He left his forwarding address as Ogunquit, Maine. If she felt the need to contact him, she would be able to track him down fairly easily in that popular summer tourist town. Derek left the party quietly before the election returns were in. He needed to get his equipment and personal belongings packed in the next few hours. From afar, Derek looked at Penny one last time and smiled. She was hugging her dad. His heart sank. He knew that he would not see her again. She saw the look on his face and sensed that something was wrong. She resisted the notion to say anything more than a formal good night, and waved from a distance They could talk later in the week after Ray returned to Boston. But the moment of his departure and her failure to say something left her chilled. It was as if the blood was drained from her body. She just knew that he was saying good-bye . . . a good-bye without actually *saying* good-bye. She loved him and hoped he knew it. She turned away briefly and he was gone. Derek, the true love of her life, was gone.

✠✠✠

At 10:45 P.M. the results were announced for Harvest and the surrounding towns. The local TV reporters confirmed that Nelson and his Take Back Harvest Party were the winners by a landslide. There was jubilation throughout the Palmer church house. Champagne bottles were opened and the corks almost reached the cathedral ceiling. Friends, family, and campaign supporters hugged and kissed one another as they congratulated each team member. In the midst of the celebration, Nelson walked over to the living room mantel by himself. He touched the urn of his late wife.

"Lydia, honey, we did it," he said softly. "We actually won the damn thing and now the fun begins. I'm sorry that you are not here with me to share it. I know you would have enjoyed the process and been excited for this moment."

Friends and family noticed him by himself, but left him alone. "I miss you darling . . . I really miss your laughter and smile. You would have been smiling now . . . for sure."

Libby was watching him from across the room. She could see from afar the pain he was experiencing. Libby, although a strong campaign supporter, was close to Nelson, but not *that* close. She helped with his genealogy quest and kept the books for the real estate deals. If anyone knew Nelson Palmer, she did. But the relationship seemed business . . . all business.

When Nelson saw her sitting on a stool near the bookcase, he went over and gave her a hug.

"Are you OK?" she asked quietly. "Are you OK with all of this?"

"Yes," he responded, "I am fine. I just needed to tell her of the big win. She would have been proud of our efforts for sure."

"She *is* proud of you, Nelson. I am sure she is watching over you, and that she knows your joy. We all are happy that you won and want to be part of this wonderful change in town." Libby was about to say more, but all the grandchildren ran up to hug their grandfather again.

As they grabbed him around the legs, Nelson bent down and said, "You are part of history, you little guys. This big win for Granddad will make your life much easier and more fun. There will be lots to do here in Raby . . . I mean Harvest. There will be new soccer fields and festivals, and wonderful ice cream parties. Do you understand what I am saying?" he asked.

"Yes, Granddad," Amy replied with a smile. "Will you help me blow up another balloon, Granddad? Please?"

"Sure, honey. Where's that bag of special balloons? . . . I'll be back after I go get some more."

"Yippee!" the kids screamed.

Libby watched as he delighted in helping them blow up new balloons. She was happy for him and had grown to appreciate and understand Nelson's love for his family and his scheme for the town of Harvest. She knew her feelings were growing stronger for him and that, with time, she would need to share those feelings. Tonight, however, was not the time. It was his night to celebrate his wonderful accomplishment. Soon the other winners of the Take Back Harvest Party arrived at the church home with their families and the celebration went on well into the night. Media photographers arrived to capture the Palmers' celebration as presses were held to get the late results. His face would be on the front page of all the local papers the next morning.

✠✠✠

Penny entered the village store the next morning and noticed that the lights to the stairway and the second floor were off. Derek was always there ahead of her. She flipped the wall switch on and climbed the stairs to the art studio. Once she reached the top, it was readily apparent to her that Derek had disappeared. All that remained of him were five or six carved birds on the table to her left. One of the birds, a mourning dove, lay next to another dove, but it was positioned upside down, as if in death. She cried at the sight of the macabre position, since she knew that doves were a species that paired for life. A note to the side of the birds explained his leaving for Maine. She held it in her shaking hands and went to a nearby window to clearly read his poetic explanation. The tarp on which they made love lay to her right, folded. The art bag on which she had laid her head in passion was gone. She looked out the window of the second floor and stared off toward the mountain to the west. He had been kind enough to explain his departure and where he could be found. Ogunquit, Maine, was a mere hour and a half from Harvest and directly east.

She struggled with her thoughts of him. Although she loved him, she could not disrupt her family, especially the children. If in time her marriage was indeed over, she would find handsome Derek. For now, she felt that she needed to work on her home life. With her passion reawakened with Derek's prior presence, she knew that she was capable of feeling like a woman again. Her husband would certainly notice the difference in her. If he failed to respond in kind, she would consider other options. Because her children adored their father, she felt an obligation to be there for all of them. But her emotions for Derek would never wane.

Penny held Derek's note to her chest. Her pulse rushed from the thought of him. She cried for a while and then went back downstairs. Outside the back of the building, she lit a match and held the note in her hand. She ignited a corner of the paper and watched it burn slowly until it had been reduced to a small fragment, the charred remains floating to the ground like feathers. She returned to the alcove of the store and unlocked the front double doors for business. People had been waiting for coffee and she hadn't even made the carafes of regular and decaf yet. Piles of morning papers had yet to be brought in from the entryway. They were stacked and tied in bundles. Her father's picture was on the front page of each paper. They read, PALMER WINS BY A LANDSLIDE AND TAKE BACK HARVEST PARTY WINS BIG. Quotes from her father's interviews the night before claimed that there would be changes in the little town—changes for the good. Penny smiled at the photos of her dad. He looked handsome and happy. Group photos showed the supporters celebrating in the church house. The townsfolk now had an idea of what the new abode looked like on the inside. It appeared gorgeous in all the newspaper wire photos.

Some customers came in to congratulate her on behalf of her father.

"Thank you," she said. "We are very happy today."

"Were you partyin' all night?" a regular asked. "I noticed you were a bit late openin' up this morning," he added. "That's OK . . . you folks deserve it."

"I'm sorry," she apologized. "I was up pretty late and had some early morning chores to take care of here. I'll be more prompt tomorrow. Sorry that you had to wait for your daily coffee, Cliff."

"That's all right, Penny. We understand. It must have been a great celebration last night. You folks practically dominated the front pages of the papers. Nice photo of you and your dad."

"Yes . . . yes it was a great time," she said with a tinge of sadness, as she reflected on Derek's abrupt departure. Sadly, he was not in any photo. She had no photo of them together. How could that be? He had left before the results were final and before the photographers had arrived.

"We anticipate lots of celebration today, as well. Dad will stop by this afternoon to thank his constituents, so please stop back later. I need to get the balloons and signs up in the store window."

"I'll help ya," said Cliff. "Where's the tape and string, Pen?"

"Thanks, Cliff, this town has much to be thankful for," she said proudly. "Dad'll be good for this town. Finally someone will put the town first . . . and that is *my* dad," she said proudly. She handed Cliff the tape and some celebration signs of red, white, and blue.

Dozens of people stopped in to say hi to Penny. By noon, she would have her mind back on track and her thoughts of Derek would be reduced somewhat. In due time, all of the remaining carved birds that he had made would be sold . . . all but the two doves that appeared to have been a couple; including the one that had died. She would pack them away and hide the pair of birds in the back of the store. Only she would know where they were kept. She kissed each dove and then wrapped them in tissue paper before placing them in a shoebox.

Penny was ecstatic when her dad arrived at the store in the early afternoon. He stayed to say hello to many visitors to the store. His incumbent opponent never formally conceded the election or called Nelson Palmer to congratulate him. Nelson didn't care, since he was a very happy man and was looking forward to his swearing-in ceremony and inaugural address. For the first time in centuries, a Raby descendent was the leader of the town that was named for the family and the kindred town in England.

After the well-wishers left, Nelson took a close look at Penny's face. "Behind that smile, I can see that you are very sad," he said.

Penny's eyes filled with tears. "Dad, Derek left last night. He's moved to Maine.

✠✠✠

A few days after his successful election, at Susan's urging, Nelson decided to tape another TV spot. He wanted to thank voters for supporting his party and platform. He decided the time had come to elaborate on his lottery winnings because the pre-election ad had only mentioned that he had come into some personal wealth. This time he would be specific; he intended to reveal the amount he had won.

In his den, Nelson sat at a desk in front of an American flag—a setting similar to those from the oval office. He wore a suit and tie, instead of his usual denim or casual wool shirt, and had practiced the speech well. The brief oration was sincere and well delivered. He looked directly into the camera and said:

> My fellow supporters, as your new town manager, I wish to thank all of you who made my campaign a clean and effective run for office. As many of you already know, there had been speculation during the campaign that I had come into wealth. I admitted in the last TV ad, that this was the case. I would like to now clarify the issue of the windfall.
>
> Prior to the election, many months ago, I purchased some Lotto tickets right here in Harvest. Much to my surprise, one of my Quik Picks contained the winning numbers for that particular month. I won the lottery for the largest amount ever in the state—175 million dollars. As you can appreciate, my wife, Lydia, and I were flabbergasted by our good fortune. For legal and personal reasons, I elected not to go public at the time, but claimed it privately at the Concord Lottery Commission office some time back. I also felt that during the election, advance knowledge of the winnings would result in my supporters not thinking

that their role was important in the raising of funds to support the Take Back Harvest Party. It was important to have that support directly from the people. It is the democratic way.

He took a drink of water and continued:

As you know, I have worked hard in this campaign and our efforts, and all of our supporters' efforts, have paid off. People have shown pride in this little community and support for many planned activities related to our youth, our police and fire departments, and the rescue squad.

Our beloved town hall was tragically destroyed by fire some months back. We newly elected officials have been meeting in the local schoolrooms to conduct business as usual. I would like to announce that there are now preliminary plans to rebuild a town hall, but . . . not in the town center. The late Mrs. Perry, whom you all loved and knew well, had written a document about the town's history. It surprisingly revealed a location east of town where an original meetinghouse or public house for the town existed in the sixteen and seventeen hundreds. I am pleased to tell you that the late Jason Birch and I stumbled on the exact location during the campaign. We located the original foundation in the wooded area that Mrs. Perry had described. Amazingly, the structural integrity of the stone is phenomenal—considering its age. The new selectmen and I have agreed on a plan to build a new town hall on the original site. To assist in the potentially costly process and possible financial burden to the town, I will personally pay for the construction of the new building—that is, the amount over and above the insurance reimbursement of the recent fire. We have noted that the insurance for the old town hall that burned was inadequate for construction of a new town hall in today's economy. A new building would need upgrades according to prior codes. It is a public building that needs to meet state and federal codes—especially ADA disability requirements for access. The last town hall was not up to these standards.

Nelson's viewers were glued to their TV sets. He had captured their admiration and interest. He gestured gently, as he spoke with increasing passion.

Mrs. Perry's manuscript highlighted what was known of the older structure that we have discovered. It apparently was not all that dissimilar from the recent town hall. It mimicked the churches of the day and even had a steeple, we surmise. Back then, early settlers used buildings for multiple purposes. Community centers were used as churches as well. Meeting or public houses were the center of town.

I have researched the remainder of the Perry document in addition to other historical papers that Libby had found in the library archives. Their historical observations differed drastically from the archives that had been burned in the recent town hall fire.

Preliminary construction of the new town hall actually began last week and you will be able to watch the progress. We think that we can celebrate its opening next year. People in the trades, who wish to volunteer their time to the construction of the new facility, will be encouraged to participate. We want the building to be a community effort. Lastly, there are plans being formulated to create a park where the Harvest town hall was situated. It will have statues of prominent people who founded this town. I will personally contact an outstanding artist in Maine to assist in the bronze reproductions of those town fathers. I will have more details later. We are thinking of planting a permanent Christmas tree in the center of that park. The new Founders Park Committee seeks your input on the design. We also envision a holiday tree lighting next winter and in future years.

Your elected officials and I look forward to serving you. We want you to be proud of this town. I will be back to you with further details in due time. Thank you for listening and a pleasant good evening to you all.

The TV ad was aired for days and numerous times at night—especially during primetime TV. Town residents were surprised by the announcement about Nelson's wealth and the planned relocation and construction of the new town hall.

The new site was some distance from that of the building that went up in flames. Penny, who had watched the ad for the first time, was shocked when she heard that her father intended to commission an artist in Maine to create the statues. She knew from the description of the bronze work and the artist's location, that it had to be Derek Mitchell. Derek had previously told her that he had sculpted in bronze before switching to his woodcarvings and paintings. She wondered how her father planned to find Derek.

Twenty-four

The inaugural party for the Take Back Harvest candidate winners was over and the team began to get down to the tasks at hand. Because of the town hall fire, Nelson and the new board of selectmen met at the high school. The meetings were open to the public and the public was encouraged to participate in town-related decisions. Few of the old names attended the weekly meetings. The incumbents had been beaten badly and left without power or impact. There were rumblings that the victories of some newly elected officials might be challenged by recounts, but the issue was moot since all of the newly elected officials, who were affiliated with Nelson, individually had won handsomely. Most had received ninety-five percent of the vote. With the exception of one school board member, a moderate, all other incumbents lost the election.

"Listen to what the people have to say," Nelson instructed his new administration. "They have to have a voice in many of these decisions. A top priority for us will be the establishment of our new town hall. We can't meet in the local school forever and we will need to reestablish the town records and replenish the archives of the town's history."

The atmosphere in the town virtually changed overnight. Small businesses showed an interest in starting up in the revitalizing downtown, and local contractors and specialists were busy with renovations and new construction. Nelson's committee on town planning fostered new growth without the bureaucracy and restrictive bylaws.

People were encouraged to spend their money locally and to utilize local services. A sense of community evolved. The town had a renewed family atmosphere.

"We have seen tourism increase," one selectman said. "There appears to be a lot of people from out of state who have stopped to see our little town."

Nelson concurred, "You're right. The town is on its way to becoming a southern New Hampshire attraction. Even the well-known *Yankee* magazine wants to feature our community and our new look in a future issue. They called the other day. The magazine claims we are the New Hampshire 'town of the decade.' Imagine that! Who would have thunk it?"

"That's great, Nel," remarked another selectman. She was a proponent of establishing a chamber of commerce for Harvest—one that would increase the town's exposure to outside industry and professional businesses. The town also needed family practice doctors and dentists. "That kind of exposure is necessary to draw new blood into this emerging renaissance town." Board members agreed with her.

The local economy fostered a change in class structure in Harvest. It was apparent that white-collar residents were having a new influence. As professionals were now attending town meetings and participating in the process of planning the village's growth and other important strategic decisions, community affairs began to make sense and were well thought out. There were far fewer tempestuous encounters now that the new administration had settled in. The local sugarhouse tourist attraction and other restaurants doubled their businesses in less than a month. Even in winter, visitors actually headed to the town instead of away from it.

Libby met with Nelson almost daily in his rented office space. She entered the town manager's office one morning and said, "Have you seen the homes downtown—in particular, the ones that you don't own? People are repairing their fences and removing the trash from their backyards, and before winter. Imagine that! They seem to have pride in their properties and the town."

"I have noticed that," he said. "I have also decided to repaint the homes that my holding companies have purchased, although we may have to wait until spring to start. I wish to set an example for the town. Pretty soon, it will look like the attractive quintessential town of Ambler up the road. I love that little village, especially in winter, after a snowstorm. Do you think we could get Harvest residents to do that? Ya know, put all white Christmas lights in their windows?"

"Nel, you may be expecting a little too much in year one of your new term as manager. These folks need to adjust slowly. Some residents have never put up any lights during the holidays . . . let alone all-white ones!"

"Suppose you're right. Maybe I should wait a while before suggesting the 'glow of Ambler' idea." He chuckled and adjusted his reading glasses. He was working on a proclamation for the town. He wanted to honor his friends Jason Birch and Mrs. Perry with a special day.

As part of the rebirth of the town, the carillon in the church steeple was repaired by a local craftsman. It had been some time since the chimes had rung in the village. On Sunday mornings, the church next to the village store would ring the bells prior to the ten o'clock religious service. Nelson became a communicant of that congregation. The steeple was cleaned of pigeon droppings and the building itself would be refurbished and repainted in spring. The town, in general, would look brighter because of the overall revitalization.

Since it was November, they decided to organize an impromptu town Thanksgiving Day parade to mimic the traditional Macy's parade in New York. Santa Claus would appear at the end of the parade in a traditional sleigh that was placed on a holiday decorated flatbed truck. Nelson was Santa this year—a role he had generously played behind the scenes.

The Thanksgiving season was met with frequent end-of-the-year spontaneous gatherings and harvest festivals, well into November. Families participated in community events and bands played at most of the functions. Wreathes of bittersweet and autumn arrangements of fall pine cones and ornamental corn adorned the doorways of many historic homes. Penny's store had increased sales of late harvest pumpkins and gourds. Children were given free colorful helium balloons and American flags were draped in front of homes and fences. The town exuded pride and a renewed caring attitude.

✠✠✠

Penny never sought another artist to replace Derek in her store. She did not want to continue the tradition of a resident artisan—there was no substitute for him anyway. She would hold onto the memory of the excitement and love that they shared on the second floor. She began to use the space as a storage area again. The folk art for sale on the first floor were now gathered from many artisans who were area craftsmen—people who tried to imitate Derek's creations. Their crafts were well done and each, in their own way, appealed to tourists as New England souvenirs.

Derek Mitchell settled into the Ogunquit community in southern Maine. He rented a small studio to exhibit his wares. Penny was always on his mind but he felt that it was much too painful to deal with the memory on a daily basis. Having spent a couple of months on the seacoast, Derek was content just to carve seagulls in lieu of the majestic loons and mourning doves. Tourists bought the replicas of the seabirds, an animal typical of Maine and second only to the lobster. The detail of the birds was exquisite, especially the ones he captured visually and frozen in flight. He also painted red and white striped lighthouses and coastal ocean scenes using both watercolors and oils. The artwork sold for hundreds of dollars. For every sculpture that he sold, he put another one in storage. He hoped to do a show someday in a major seacoast gallery. His opportunity would be sooner, rather than later.

In Ogunquit, resided Olivia Horton, an elderly, wealthy patron of the arts—a frail woman who dressed elegantly every day. She wore a bit too much makeup and her perfume was often applied heavily.

"Derek, these sculptures and your paintings are some of the best that I have ever seen in this town," she remarked. She held her glasses close to the tip of her nose as she stared at each and every piece he had laid out for her preview. "I am a charter member of the art guild in town," she continued, fascinated by his works. "You must have worked hard all winter. We never see you out socializing anywhere.

"I would like the ladies in the guild to see this collection," she continued. "Are you open all week and would you mind if I invited the ladies over here?" she asked.

"Yes, ma'am, I'm open," he said. "I have the store open seven days a week for now . . . I have to catch those tourists on weekends and over the holidays," he said. "Please bring whomever you wish to the store."

"Derek, what is this over here, in plaster?" she asked, while pointing at the figure and stooping to stare at it.

"Ah, that one . . . that piece is not for sale," he said. "Why? Do you like it, Mrs. Horton?"

"Why yes, I do," she added. "It appears to be a nymph."

"It is like a nymph . . . she *was* like a nymph," he said, with a slight hesitation.

"Past love I suspect, that you pine for? Hmmn?" she asked with one eyebrow raised and a twinkle in her eyes.

"Why yes . . . it is a past, and *present* love," he stated.

"Where is she, boy . . . where is this delicate, beautiful woman?" Mrs. Horton pried, without hesitation.

"She's in New Hampshire, ma'am . . . uh . . . pretty far away."

"Why did you lose her, son? Screwin' around or somethin'? Boys are always losin' the ones they love."

"Not the case here," he laughed. "She's married and only a fantasy of mine. I could never have this woman."

"Son," Mrs. Horton asked, "don't mean to pry . . . but do you love her? Is she happy? Do you miss her?" she asked him while standing tall, as tall as she *could* stand. Her hands were on her hip, like she was lecturing him.

He hesitated, and then spoke quietly, "Yes. No. Yes! The answers to your questions are: Yes, No, Yes."

"You need to go get her, son—in New Hampshire! The state is our neighbor . . . a mere border away . . . for cryin' out loud. You need to have her near you—for inspiration and companionship."

Derek listened politely, as he smiled and nodded in agreement.

"I see the pain in your face, but she is the *beauty* in the plaster. Go get her!" she instructed him. "If you care enough to sculpt her, and this by the way is a phenomenal piece in front of me, then you need her with you."

Derek was ready to change the subject.

"Mrs. Horton, may I digress from the sculpture for a moment. You mentioned the art guild and a potential showing of my work a bit earlier in the conversation."

"I not only want to bring some of the girls over and have them see your works, but I also want to sponsor a show of this work. I have 'pull' at the Primrose Gallery in town, and they owe me a favor. I want you and your works to be in that gallery in early spring. Does that work for you, if I can arrange it? Do you have enough pieces to exhibit?"

"Why, yes . . . I'm sure that would be fine. Do you mean *the* Primrose Gallery, the one with Monet, Manet, and Picasso?" he asked.

"Yes, it is *that* gallery of which I speak. They have an anteroom, which is quite large. They feature locals on occasion . . . on rare occasion. It requires a vote of the guild members in town before a showing is approved. I will be happy to sponsor you. OK?"

"Yes, very OK," he said, beaming. "Thank you for the endorsement. . . . Thank you . . . very much."

"You deserve to have a show there," she added, "and be sure to bring the statue of the lovely nymph. Put a 'not for sale' sticker on it. What was her name, anyway?"

"Her name? . . . Her name is Penelope, but they call her Penny."

"The name Penelope has class," she said. "Penny doesn't. Call her what you want, but for the show, call the statue *Penelope* or *Mourning Dove*. Is that OK? It looks like a dove and a bird—it flows beautifully."

"*Mourning Dove* is what she will be called for the show," Derek said. "I used to sculpt doves in my last studio. That is uncanny that you would mention that name."

"Good," Mrs. Horton said, smiling. "By the way, you are a handsome man, Derek Mitchell. My husband, God rest his soul, was handsome, too. He had a mustache and beard like you. Just how did Penelope let you go, anyway?"

"She didn't . . . I ran," he said sheepishly.

"Well, no matter what. . . . She was a damn fool then!" she mumbled as she prepared to leave. "If I were younger," she said, with a whistle, "I'd be chasin' ya."

"Thanks, Mrs. Horton, you're kind," Derek said. "I think that Mr. Horton had *quite* a catch of his own."

"Looked like you, son . . . he looked like you. I'll be in touch."

"Thank you," he replied, kissing her hand. "Thanks for stopping by."

Derek sat down. He envisioned the Primrose Gallery and what was needed. He would begin to retrieve many paintings and sculptures that he had completed and stored away. He would need to pick his best works, even if it was to show the ladies in the art guild. There would be frames needed for the paintings. He had much work to do, if the guild members approved his exhibit.

The following week, the members of the guild viewed his selections. Without hesitation, they approved Mrs. Horton's request for Derek to have a show at Primrose.

The media promotion of the art show for Derek Mitchell included the nearby states of Massachusetts, and New Hampshire, and the coastal tourist areas of Maine. That meant that Kennebunk, Wells, Portland and Casco Bay, Maine, art aficionados needed advanced notice of the exhibit. Three weeks before the show, advertising flyers were mailed to his prior customers; he had provided Mrs. Horton with a database of contacts from the past. They were clients and admirers in New Hampshire, Massachusetts, and New York City, where he had begun his professional career. One prior customer, who resided in Harvest, found her personal invite in her U. S. Post Office box. She wondered if Penny had received one at the village store—for sure she would want to know of the forthcoming show that was scheduled for Derek.

"Penny," the woman said, "have you seen this invite? Your artist friend that was here a while back is having a show at a well-known art gallery in Maine. Were you aware of that?"

"No . . . no I wasn't. You mean Derek Mitchell? Can I see that for a moment?" Penny asked. Penny held up the embossed invitation with the Primrose logo. It said that the show was being coordinated and promoted by the Women's Art Guild of Ogunquit, Maine.

"Amazing," she said. "A real show! He apparently is doing very well there." She stared at a melting snowbank, which showed pockmarked gray patches.

"Look at the picture of him, Penny. It was shot in a studio, for sure. I'm happy for him," said the customer.

"Yes . . . me, too," Penny reflected with a sigh. "He really did nice work when he was here. He is missed by many fans and art collectors."

"Did you not get a flyer? . . . I'm surprised," said the customer. "They must have forgotten you, but I can't imagine how they would do that."

"I imagine that many people would not have gotten this flyer," Penny suggested. "We were just a small town in his professional life. He was not going to make it in the big time if he stayed here."

"I suppose you're right, but how could he forget *you* on the list? You fostered his New Hampshire beginnings. I'm sure it was an oversight, dear."

Penny knew why she had not received the invite. She just knew he had purposely broken off contact with her because of the pain of leaving her behind. He had graciously made no attempt to contact her after he left, to give her time to rebuild her marriage, since that was what she appeared to want.

The promotional flier had been mailed to some five hundred contacts of the Guild, as well as Derek's own mail list, extensive in its own right. Penny's name had been crossed out with pen, along with other addresses and clients that were out of date or invalid. It was obvious to Derek that he could not contact Penny, especially if he was to overcome his love for her. Mrs. Horton had noticed Penelope's name on the list, and wondered if she was the woman in New Hampshire that was the subject or model for the nymph sculpture called *Mourning Dove*. Instead of mailing an invite to her, Mrs. Horton decided to phone the woman named Penelope Browning.

Her call came into the village store later that afternoon, shortly after the customer had showed Penny the invitation. Penny was surprised at the overwhelming resurgence of feelings for Derek. The customer had left the invite with Penny and encouraged her to attend the art show in her absence. "I will consider it," she said to the woman. "It would be nice to see his new creations. It says here that he has some one hundred sculptures and many paintings of the Maine coastline."

✠✠✠

That same afternoon, Nelson called his daughter and asked her to come over after dinner. The anniversary of Lydia's death had passed, and he was sorting through some of Lydia's belongings. He told Penny he wanted her input on who should get what. "Since you were closer to your mother than your sisters were, you are the natural choice to help with all the decisions about Lydia's clothes and jewelry," he said. "Care for some home-brewed coffee and coffee cake? Libby brought the cake over."

"I think she fancies you, Mr. Palmer," Penny teased. "Could there be love in the wings there, father? Hmm?"

"She is a nice woman," Nelson said, "and very, very smart. All those years of workin' in the library, I guess . . . but I do miss your mother. Look at that box of stuff. Your mother had many things—I think you should go through them. I'll give you first choice, honey, before I call your sisters. Besides, you're the baby of the family and very special."

She smiled and hugged him tightly. He looked at her face, so much like her mother's, but drawn and tired in recent weeks.

"Why are there bags under those blue eyes, young lady?" he asked. "Is everything all right? You look tired. Are you workin' too much or are the kids getting' to you?" he joked, but with genuine concern.

"Fine, Daddy. I've just been workin' too long—too many hours, I guess."

"The marriage isn't working, is it, dear?" he asked gently. "I didn't really invite you over here to go through your mother's belongings. She had already listed who would get what before she passed on."

Realizing she could no longer fool her father, Penny thought a moment and said, "Is it that obvious?"

"Penny, a father knows . . . a mother knows! They see their kids at their highs and at their lows in life and can read their minds . . . not literally of course, but in general. Besides," he continued, "I saw the note . . . *the note* on the table in the store the night he left. He obviously loved you . . . and that is why he took off, right?"

Penny sat on the floor, folding in her legs like a child listening to a story. Her crossed legs supported her bent torso as she began to cry. Her head hung in shame. Her father knew her pain.

"You saw . . . the note? That was personal . . . that was a *personal* note," she said, sobbing.

"Honey," he said, stroking her hair, "I went to the store the night of the election celebration with Libby. She wanted to get extra items for the party and balloons for the kids. Hell, we were only gone fifteen minutes from the church house. Apparently no one noticed that we were gone, especially with all the champagne flowing. The note was downstairs originally. I took it upstairs so no one would see it, like *your husband*. Derek should not have left it there. Too many people could have seen it—the *wrong* people. I waited until now to say something because I felt it wasn't my business back then."

"Daddy . . . she saw the note? Libby saw Derek's note to me?"

"Yes, dear . . .she noticed it first . . . a woman's intuition, I guess. Thank God for that. I would have missed it on my own."

"Oh, God! What did she say?" Penny asked with outstretched and open arms. Her eyes were now red from crying.

"Honey, what Libby said is . . . 'your daughter needs you! Libby knew that if your mother was alive, you would have told her of the situation. Libby just knew that you had no one to tell. She's very perceptive, ya know," he said smiling. "I should have followed her lead. She also loves you."

Nelson hugged his daughter and then stood to refill his cup from the carafe. Penny declined his offer for a refill. As her eyes scanned the room, she realized the urn was missing from the mantel.

"Father?" she asked. "You loved Mom, right? I mean you loved her dearly, right?" she asked.

"Of course I did!"

"Where is she now? She is not on the mantel anymore."

"Honey. I felt it was time to stop mourning. There was no need to display her like a sanctuary. She would not appreciate that. In late spring, I plan to have her buried in a proper plot. When I go, I will be beside her. We will be buried next to this house, in the cemetery. For now, I have put her in a safe place in the bedroom."

"Dad? You didn't put her in the closet, did you?" she said, with a smile.

"Yes," he smiled back, hoping his daughter would not be upset with the less obvious location of the urn.

"You're right, and Libby was right. Had mom been with us today, she would have known of the current situation. She would have given me guidance and perhaps have halted the affair before it began."

"Well," Nelson offered, "You do have a father, too! You know, the *man's* perspective."

"Not the same. But since you know now, what is your advice?"

"Well, I have always said 'follow your heart.' If things are not working out in your marriage, don't be a martyr! You'll regret it. Also, don't stay together for the sake of the children. They will adjust and they will survive. You must think of your own health as well, mental and otherwise. These things take their toll on you mentally *and* physically. That affects your psyche, your smile, your personality, and can be more devastating than having a heart problem or cancer. It grates at you for years and is a slow death, much like a malignancy."

"Oh, Father, how did you get to be so wise and enlightened?" she asked. "I love you."

He hesitated, and with wide eyes and a twitch of the head he said, "Penny, I fucked up, dear, many times. I wasn't always married to your mother. I dated many women when I was young. I never followed my heart until I met your mother. I stole her from a man she was engaged to . . . a Harry Prindle . . . twit that he was. Your mother, and your father . . . followed their hearts. Old Prindle was kind of pissed about the deal, but who cares? Your mother and I were soul mates, OK? She was what I wanted and I went after her, and got her!"

"Daddy! You really did that? You stole my mother from another man? She was engaged for Christ's sake!"

"Damn good thing I did, or else you and your sisters would not have been born. And you would not be in this situation! Matter a fact . . . you would have been a Prindle, sort of," he joked. "Yuk!"

Penny stood up and faced her father again. The weight of her burden was off her shoulders. They embraced and he told her he was *there* for her—always, good or bad. She felt a closeness like she had never felt before with her dad. He had become her surrogate mother by default.

As she left the house, he said, "Prindle really was a putz, honey. You have to believe me," he chuckled.

"Oh, Daaaad," she said, smiling. "You are something else. Thanks for stealin' mom!"

After she left, Nelson poured a scotch on the rocks in the kitchen. He was exhausted by the experience, but pleased that he had met with his daughter. She was back to being her old self when she departed. He noted that her statuesque figure had regained her perfect posture upon leaving. He immediately phoned Libby and told her of their conversation. Libby congratulated him, then hesitated before adding, "We all love you, Nelson Palmer . . . your daughters and I. Not all fathers would have done what you did tonight—perhaps a bit late, but at least you did it."

"Well . . . I love you, too, Libby. You're a good woman. Intuitive and insightful. Let's do dinner tomorrow night. I would like to talk to you."

Nelson consumed two glasses of scotch. He would need them to sleep well that night. The night had been so long and time had flown by. He was concerned for his daughter and for the grandchildren. He knew that marriages were tough enough—when they worked out. He also knew that they were even more work when they were dying or dead. In this case, Penny's marriage was probably not repairable. For now he would be supportive of his daughter. She would need to be the decision-maker in the fate of her marriage to Ray. For that reason, Nelson did not mention the invitation he received to the Primose Gallery exhibition.

Twenty-five

Muddy lawns and an occasional flurry after a warm day made spring seem long. Nelson Palmer was busy between his new town duties and his work collating and organizing Mrs. Perry's documents. He arranged for the manuscript to be published in hardcover—later he planned to offer some as a soft-cover trade publication. Nelson hired editors, printers and binders to pull the project together. The tri-centennial anniversary of the original town, Raby, was approaching and he wanted the town to have the copies of the real testament of its birth by the actual date of the auspicious occasion. The title would be *Return to Raby: An Historical Perspective.* He kept the project quiet and even his speech on TV did not mention the word *Raby* in the rebuilding of the new town hall. People naturally assumed it would be the new Harvest town hall.

As Penny helped with the book's setup one cool and wet March evening, she got up her courage to ask about the bronze statues.

"Dad, I was wondering if you had selected an artist yet to work on the founders' statues. You mentioned a Maine artist in your TV speech. Father, dear, could the *artist* that you referred to be Derek?" she asked.

"Yes, dear, he is. Why?" Nelson asked. "That is who I have in mind for the bronze work."

"Have you talked to him about this?" she asked with trepidation.

"Yes. We've been in touch, and we will have more to talk about on Sunday," he added.

"Sunday? Are you going to his show in Maine?" she asked with confusion.

"Yes," he responded. "Did you get an invite? Libby and I thought it would be a nice ride," he said sheepishly. "Would you like to join us? We received the invite, as well. Libby and I would love for you to come along, but would understand if you did not go."

"Dad, I did get a call from a woman about the show way back when. She was pleasant and active in the Guild. I think she was the coordinator of the show. But . . . but . . . Ray is away, again, in Atlanta and I have the kids to think of," she said with concern. "I also don't know if that is a good idea . . . for me, mentally . . . if you know what I mean," she added to the unexpected conversation.

"Wow! You got a personal invitation by phone? You really rate. Why not get a sitter and come?" Nelson said, encouraging her. "Perhaps Susan will watch the children. I'm sure that she would baby-sit if you called her. She needs a break from the renovation work this weekend, anyway. Libby and I think that it will be fun. What do you say, honey?"

"Dad, I'll have to let you know. I will need to have the store covered, as well. I promise that I will look into it."

She was overwhelmed with the idea. She wanted to attend and see Derek, his new works, and just say hello. She had no idea if Derek would want her there and if her presence would disturb his first big show. She would mull the idea over and decide soon. She needed to call Susan about childcare if this plan was to work. She was confident that the store could be covered at the cash register. High school kids always needed the extra cash.

Nelson responded to the RSVP to Mrs. Horton in Maine by telephone. A secretary for the Ogunquit Art Guild recorded the number of people attending from each invite that had been mailed. The Nelson Palmer party RSVP was for *three*.

✠✠✠

As the gallery show opened, Derek stood chatting with some early arrivals, while Mrs. Horton and members of the Art Guild steered the elegantly dressed guests to the table with a champagne punch bowl and desserts. The centerpiece was a lovely floral arrangement of spring flowers ordered specially by Mrs. Horton.

The Nelson Palmer vehicle pulled into the overflowing parking lot and Nelson helped the two women in long dresses out of the car. The white clapboard building was surrounded by a typical New England white picket fence. The front and side of the building contained a porch with white-caned rocking chairs. It looked like a Southern mansion—sort of a white "plantation home" of the north. The deck of the porch was wide-board pine, old slabs that had been painted gray. Hanging baskets of artificial red and pink geraniums adorned the porch railing—the street number "one hundred six" was written in script over the jamb of the double-French doors. The building exuded class.

Penny was nervous. "I'm not sure that this is right. Perhaps you and Libby should go in first and I will wait out here for a while. I feel like this is trespassing—disrupting the event." Wearing only a light spring coat over her black crepe shift, she shivered as the breeze picked up.

"I'm sure that Derek will be happy to see you," Nelson replied, understanding his daughter's reluctance to proceed further. Libby coaxed her on and told her that they would only stay a short time.

"Penny, this is a wonderful day for Derek. I am sure that he will be glad to see old friends from Harvest. You are a friend of his and have inspired his creations. I think you will find him happy to see you."

Penny, still apprehensive, agreed to wait in the foyer while her father and Libby entered the show. She peered into the room from afar. It was packed; Derek was not in sight.

"Welcome," said Mrs. Horton to Nelson and Libby. "The name please?"

Nelson Palmer, ma'am, and two guests, thank you," he replied smiling.

"Oh, Mr. Palmer. It is such a pleasure to meet you and you also, Ms. Libby. I understand that congratulations are in order. Derek indicated that you won the town managership at home. I'm pleased to see that you came all the way from New Hampshire for this wonderful show. How do you do?" she added.

"Thank you. I did manage to win and Derek was there to cel-ebrate," Nelson replied. "It is a pleasure to meet you, as well, and to be here for his first show. Derek was a popular artist in our town for a while. This is a wonderful day for him and we thought that we would see how he has been doing in his new location, here in Maine. He is sorely missed in New Hampshire. He had quite a following, you know. Looks like they are all here!" he added laughing. He looked left then right across the room. Libby nodded in agreement.

"Oh, Mr. Palmer, that is wonderful. He has quite a following in *Maine* now, and so many friends of his have come from Boston and your part of the world. I noticed that there were *three* of you on the list. Was there a cancellation?" asked Mrs. Horton. "I hope not."

"Oh, no," he replied. "My daughter, Penelope . . . we call her Penny . . . is in the lobby getting a bit of air. She found the ride over from New Hampshire a bit long. She'll be in shortly."

"Penelope?" Mrs. Horton replied. "That is a beautiful name. I should see if she needs some water or something cool to drink," she said.

"That is kind of you. I'm sure Penny will be along shortly. Crowds sometimes scare her, I think,"

Nelson and Libby entered the main gallery area and began to look about the room. In the far corner was Derek, who was engrossed in conversation with two older women. He was describing the sculp-ture in front of them and telling how the metal was fashioned into the abstract art form that he had created to represent a bird in flight.

Mrs. Horton approached the front porch and smiled gently at the tall, willowy blonde woman in black. Three-inch heels made Penny look even taller than she was. She clutched her sequined handbag to her chest and stared away from the foyer and over the railing—it was a distant view of the ocean.

"You must be Penelope?" Mrs. Horton asked gently. "Your fa-ther said that you were a bit under the weather from the ride. Would you care for a glass of water or something, dear? Oh, pardon me . . . I'm Mrs. Horton, with the Art Guild. Are you OK?"

"Yes, thank you . . . I feel much better, Mrs. Horton. It's nice to finally meet you. I enjoyed our conversation on the phone."

"Me, too, my dear. . . . You must come in and see some of Derek's new creations," Mrs. Horton added with a smile.

"It was a bit of a rough ride today. Too many winding roads, I guess. I am very pleased to be here and to see this gorgeous building. It was nice of you and the Guild to promote his art— it was long overdue," said Penny.

"It was rather easy, actually," Mrs. Horton responded. "His works are wonderful and the public needs to see the variety of media that he utilizes." Mrs. Horton placed her arm through Penny's, as if to guide her indoors. They walked slowly through the portico.

"You are right, ma'am," Penny said. "He really offers something for everyone."

"Penelope, turn left past the doorway and I will show you a beautiful piece, which is so much a part of his style. Follow me, please," Mrs. Horton said, now holding Penny's left hand gently. Penny towered over the older woman but accompanied her into the main room. The two Waterford chandeliers illuminated the crowd below.

Mrs. Horton knew she was not yet relaxed, as evidenced by the sweaty palm and tension in her fingers. "Over here, dear," Mrs. Horton said. "This piece is called *Mourning Dove* and is a delicate nymph. Unfortunately, it is not for sale, but visitors today have been staring at it since the exhibit opened.

"Oh, my! It's really $300,000?" Penny gasped.

"The $300,000 price tag on the piece was my joke. It is not for sale," Mrs. Horton said with a laugh.

"It is beautiful," Penny said, staring at the likeness of herself. The breasts and flowing symmetry of the nude creation was modeled after her figure. Derek was the only one in the room who would know that level of detail.

Mrs. Horton stood and watched the reaction. She could see Penny's face light up as Derek spotted her from afar. He was still in conversation with an older woman and politely excused himself.

Penny stood silently and offered a tender smile from across the room. Her face was flushed from the encounter, even at that distance.

"Penelope, my dear, he still pines for you," Mrs. Horton said with a smile, and then excused herself to visit with another couple.

Penny was alone; her heart palpitating. She felt claustrophobic and held her breath. Derek walked toward her and for the moment, there was no one else in the room. It was merely her . . . and him.

Without a word they embraced. Nelson, Libby, and Mrs. Horton stood some distance, watching without appearing to stare. Derek grasped her shoulders gently, then kissed her on the cheek. He could smell her fragrance on her neck. It was the same perfume she wore when they made love. Her knees began to quiver and she felt weak in his arms. Tears welled up in her eyes. She closed them tightly, and two pearl-like droplets formed in the corner of each eye.

Derek said nothing and then pushing her back slowly, quietly said, "You are as beautiful as the last day that I saw you. It is such a nice surprise to see you here."

Penny grinned and told him that she missed his warmth and smile. She felt that the show was something she could not miss.

"It means so much to me to see you and feel you," she whispered. "You look wonderful and the gallery of your artwork is incredible. I have not seen very much of your works yet, but Mrs. Horton did show me your $300,000 nude of me. Am I really worth that much?" she laughed nervously.

"That sculpture will not sell for any amount. I could never sell your body," he laughed back. They embraced again and he noticed that one or two other women wished to meet him. He excused himself and told Penny, "Don't go anywhere. I have to work for a little while. Then we can chat. I see that your dad and Libby are here. They look happy together. Are they an item?" he asked with raised eyebrows.

She smiled and covered her mouth with her hand. "I think so," she whispered. "Mother would approve of Dad's choice, Derek. Distance should never separate two people in love. Right? She would have approved of us, as well," she added. He tilted his head to the side and nodded in agreement.

"Go do your work, Derek. I'll brief you on that later. Dad is happy . . . very, very happy. I am happy for them. They look good together, don't you think?"

Mrs. Horton interrupted them and reminded Derek that he needed to mingle. "Derek, this is Mrs. Harrington from New York. She wishes to speak to you. Also, Mr. Palmer needs to speak to you, as well. His bronze sculpture project could use more of your input."

"Excuse me, Penny. I'll be back, so don't go too far!" he told her. He squeezed her hand slightly and she smiled at him.

"I'll be over by my dad," she stated softly.

Penny walked around to look at his artwork on the walls. The theme was definitely the Maine coast and many oil paintings had either lighthouses or lobster boats as the focal point in them. She noticed a boat named *Penelope* and surmised the origin of that name. She chuckled at the possibility of her being named a "fishing boat." She seemed to be present in many of his pieces, whether they were sculptures or paintings. One watercolor painting was a cottage on the seacoast. It was reminiscent of an Andrew Wyeth painting, complete with weathered shutters on the windows, wavy grass, and wildflowers. The wooden street sign at the edge of the property was a piece of weathered barn board that said "Penelope Lane." It was obvious to her that Derek had never forgotten her. She was everywhere in the room. Only she was aware of what represented her influence in his life.

Penny looked over at the man that she was in love with and watched him work the crowd. People were buying his paintings off the wall.

A young woman approached Derek, evidently surprising him with a hug and a kiss. She was as beautiful as he was handsome. Penny thought that the embrace was far too long, especially when both Derek and the woman were smiling and laughing. They seemed so happy together. Penny felt her heart sink, and she quickly went from a state of euphoria to depression. She surmised that he had found a new love, and she was gorgeous. She stood silently by the punch bowl for a few moments, then feeling nauseated, she turned and headed for the lobby. Mrs. Horton noticed her leaving abruptly.

"Penelope, my dear, is everything OK? You look pale," she asked.

"I am fine, thank you," she said.

"Sit down here, sweetie," she said. "I saw you with Derek. You both looked like you were in love and happy. I have not seen him that happy since I met him," Mrs. Horton said warmly.

"He does appear happy," Penny replied. "I think he has found love again. She looks to be that beautiful woman over there, with him."

"Penelope, my dear. Don't worry your little heart. That, woman . . . you foolish girl, is his sister from New York City. She just arrived with her rich friends from the Big Apple. They have bucks to spend. Doesn't she look like him?"

"Really?" Penny said, feeling her blood return to her body. "He has a sister? I never knew that. She is very beautiful."

"Yes, dear, he has two sisters," Mrs. Horton said. "They both live in New York, but only one could make it to the show. This one, Sarah, is the younger one. The older sister, Rachel, is due to have her second child at any time."

"I didn't know that about him," replied Penny. "He never mentioned his siblings or family anywhere."

"You don't look so pale now, Penelope. Love is tough, isn't it dear?" she whispered.

Penny just smiled. She just knew that Mrs. Horton was aware of the relationship between herself and Derek. It was very obvious in his work and in their interaction.

As the reception continued for another four hours, Penny was able to wander back to her father and Libby. Derek always sensed where she was. His eyes often followed her peripherally. Her presence was magnetic. He quickly became bored with the trivial questions from the attendees.

The Art Guild had sold thousands of dollars of his art; he would be very happy with the total revenue after the Guild took ten percent of his earnings to cover costs of the catered desserts, coffee, floral arrangements, punch bowl, and a facilities fee. Before the exhibition was over, Derek talked with Nelson at length about how the founders' statues designs were coming, and they agreed Derek would call Nelson in a week or so and they would arrange to meet in Harvest.

At the close of the show, Penny hugged the artist and Mrs. Horton, and Nelson escorted the two ladies out of the exhibition to the parking lot. It was a long drive back to Harvest. Few words were spoken in the car and Penny lay down to sleep in the backseat. Libby and Nelson talked quietly during the ride. They could whisper about the day and how Penny reacted to the first sight of Derek.

"Ya know, Nel, she looked at *him* the way I looked at *you* when I first saw you," Libby said with emotion. "She is madly in love with that man back there, and when love is that strong, it is like a freight train. He obviously loves your daughter, as well. It was in his paintings and in his sculpture. It was everywhere."

"I know," he replied, as dusk descended on the highway. "So, you thought of me that way too, eh?" he asked. "Why didn't you say something?"

"Nelson Palmer, I was aware of you and you impressed me with your intelligence and the quest for your roots. The emphasis was intellectual at first. Besides, it was clear to me that you were already taken. You had a wonderful wife."

"True, I was taken, but I'm a bit vain . . . could use a compliment anyway, from time to time."

"Nelson Palmer!" she scolded, joking, "Not a chance I would feed your ego . . . back then."

"Really?" he asked. "When did you notice what a wonderful, human, sensitive, and considerate man I was?"

"Actually, Nel, it was when Penny told me of your intimate conversation in the church house, and also this afternoon. You never took your eyes off your daughter. Also 'Mr. Tough Guy' that you are, Mr. Town Manager, I saw the tears in your eyes when your daughter hugged Derek. You surely saw the love of a woman for a man and vice versa!"

"I didn't have any tears . . . no way," he retorted, defending his manhood.

"Oh yes you did, dear. I saw them through my own tear-filled eyes."

In the backseat, Penny blinked once or twice herself. She loved her father so much, but it was not the time to sit up and tell him. She would do it at another time, and soon.

Twenty-six

Planning for the 250th anniversary of the town of Harvest on Labor Day weekend started before the ground thawed. The prior administration had done little to publicize the event, even though they had appointed an organizing committee. The committee was dissolved after the election, and new members were asked by Nelson to take over the tasks. It was up to the volunteers, both new and old residents, to plan the three-day September celebration. Main events included a barbecue, parade, lobster bake, town dance, teen rock concert, and competitive games at the local ballpark. These festivities would also include an old-fashioned firemen's muster and hot air balloon rides. The celebration would be scheduled after the new town hall (which was taking shape at record speed) and the commissioned sculptures were completed. Nelson's secret plan was to dedicate the bronze sculptures of the original town fathers during the event. It would be his chance to unveil the *true history* of the town of Raby.

Penny was actively involved in the anniversary celebration program, and was assisted by many residents who served on subcommittees for individual activities. It took many meetings throughout the winter, so that people could be lined up to cook and assist with the logistics of each event, the parking, and the invitations to many dignitaries. The governor and state representatives of New Hampshire would be invited. There was protocol for state officials and that had to be followed in order to insure a successful event. Penny took the responsibilities seriously.

✠✠✠

Derek Mitchell and Nelson discussed the bronze works that the town manager wanted designed. At first, they spoke on the phone in February, and later at his art show. Derek mailed some preliminary sketches to Nelson, who called a few days later to tell Derek that he was needed in New Hampshire to fully understand how the art would be situated in the new park.

"I think we need to get together here, in Harvest, to view the area of the community park, Derek. Rough landscaping has begun and I could use your expertise in the layout of the bronze figures. Is it possible for you to come here to go over the site plans and to see what we have in mind for their location?"

"Yes, Nelson, that sounds good. I think that I will be free in a week. Does that work for you?"

"Sure," replied Nelson, "what day or days work for you? I'll pencil them in."

"I can probably be there on Thursday of next week. I will meet you at the church house. Is that OK?"

"Sounds great," he replied, "By the way, it was nice to see your show in Maine. I hope you did well by it."

"You have no idea how much art we sold. I guess my name was enhanced by the Art Guild and the Primrose Gallery venue. I certainly did better than I expected," said Derek, proudly.

"How is Penny?" Derek asked. "I really enjoyed seeing her at the show, as well. It was nice to see Libby there, too. You two look good together, Nelson."

"She is fine but a bit down—she's very busy with her store, the kids, and her volunteering in town functions. Libby is just fine. She's very helpful to me in business and a great companion."

Derek hesitated and then asked, "Why is Penny down in the dumps?"

"Well, she probably would want to tell you herself. I can give you her cell phone number, if you wish. She could use a friend right now. Here's her new private cell number. Touch base with her if you feel inclined."

"Please warn her that I will be in touch," he said thoughtfully.

Derek waited a day and then decided to call Penny. She would certainly want to know when he was meeting with her father in case Nelson hadn't told her.

The cell phone rang in her pocketbook. She retrieved it from among the other items in her purse.

"Hi there, mournin' dove," Derek said sweetly. Penny was elated to hear his voice.

"Derek!" she said loudly. "How are you? How did you get this number? It's relatively new for this prim and proper lady of a general store. Can't locate the damn thing most of the time."

"I have ways," he teased her. "A little bird told me."

"Oh yeah? What little bird . . . my father? It was him, wasn't it?" she asked, as she sat on a stool and crossed her legs. Her denim jeans accentuated her perfect figure.

"Yes, it *was* your ol' man. We spoke yesterday and he wants me to come out there next week. They are discussing the bronze work that week, so I was thinking of meeting with him next Thursday."

"Next Thursday? Oh that is exciting! . . . Will I see you . . . or will Daddy have you all tied up?"

"We should have time. I may stay the weekend and see friends from the days of my studio there. There should be plenty of time."

"Great . . . that is great," she said sincerely. "I need to see you."

"You do?" he replied.

"Yes, I need to talk to you . . . I . . . am finally separated from Ray. That's why I didn't call you right away. We recently decided to split. He said he needs time and space," she added. "We're selling the house. I need a fresh start and a larger place anyway. Daddy is letting me and the kids stay in one of his rental homes near the store."

Derek was happily surprised. "I'm glad that you finally came to grips with the situation. I don't know what else to say," he added.

"I have been down, Derek, but not about the marriage. It was dead anyway. I'm sad because the children are the victims. They love their dad. It's hard to juggle the activities, their school and their sports and hobbies."

Derek was only half listening to the details. He was lost in the moment of her being free.

"Are you there?" she asked.

"Yes, honey, I'm here . . . I was just thinking . . . too deeply I guess," he responded.

"How sweet . . . you called me 'honey'."

"I need to see you next week," he said. "Perhaps we could do something with the kids . . . together."

"Maybe," she said. "I just remembered. They are with their father next weekend. He is taking them camping in Greenfield, about twenty miles from here—a state park I think."

"So . . . you mean I can be with you, and have you all to myself?"

"If I can get the store covered, we may be able to get away," she said enticingly. "Let me see if I can get the high school kids to cover for me," she added.

"Penny . . . I have missed you so much. I can't wait to see you," Derek said, without hesitation.

"Me, too, Derek. I need to be with you . . . I *really* need to be with you."

"I love you."

"I love you, too."

✠✠✠

Nelson's attorney, William Mosley, called to tell him that the former selectmen wanted to settle the lawsuits that he had filed against them—the septic issue as well as the wrongful death suit concerning his wife.

"Nelson, they know of your power in town and wish to settle immediately. They are afraid that you will take all their personal assets if they lose. You have them very apprehensive and, to be perfectly honest, downright scared."

"Great," said Nelson. "I want them to squirm big time. How much are they offering for the septic aggravation that I went through? Is it the full amount?"

"No," replied Mosley, "but it's a good deal. They will settle for three quarters of what you wanted. That, Nel, is twenty-five percent more than I expected we would get from them. They will cover your legal fees as well, according to their lawyer."

"What about the wrongful death suit? How will they settle in *that* case? It is not as if I need their money. It's the principle of the thing."

"The insurance company for the town of Harvest will cover that, except for maybe punitive damages. The insurance company wants to settle the suit quickly. They are prepared to pay you the two million dollars that you sued them for. Apparently, the former selectmen and the snowplow contractors are prepared to publicly admit contributing to Lydia's death. Unfortunately the road manager is mentally incompetent to do the same or apologize for the disaster—the self-inflicted gunshot wound has affected his ability to respond to the issue."

"That *admission of guilt* is what I wanted in the first place. It wasn't the money. I just wanted them to admit that their callous negligence, irresponsibility, and ultimate inaction with the plowing issue resulted in my wife dying. They will need to formally apologize to me in every local newspaper, as well as on TV, with an advertisement. I want a letter as well."

"They understand that, Nelson. It was a condition of the settlement in the docket and suit," Mosley said. "You should get the punitive damages since the court will be sympathetic to your loss. After all, the selectmen are not paying out of their own pockets. It's the insurance company for the town that will pay the two million dollars."

Nelson thought for a moment. "OK, Bill, I'll seek the personal money, too. That will be part of the trust fund in my late wife's name. That way, it goes back into the town. You deserve your take of that since you worked damn hard on this case—you will get your percentage."

Mosley told him that using the money for the scholarship foundation in his wife's memory was a proper thing to do. It was also very "forgiving" on Nelson's federal income tax issue. Nelson would benefit from a tax break if he applied the entire amount to the Foundation—the same one he had established after the death of his wife. It would aid the fund bearing Jamie's name, as well. Mosley indicated to Nelson that he would be pleased to help maintain the paperwork and legal issues of the foundations, *pro bono*.

"Once these matters are settled," Nelson said, "let's discuss where we go from here. I appreciate your hard work on these suits. They have gone on for the better part of two years. I was prepared to go to court over these issues and I am glad those weasels are backing down in advance of losin' their asses.

"Well, then . . . while they are shaking in their boots, tell them that I also own the damn town. They don't know about the holding companies or the number of properties that I own. The bastards will eventually know that I own half the land and properties here—all of the ones that are worth buying!" he boasted. "I am the highest tax-payer in the town. I pay more local taxes than anyone combined. That means I basically own this friggin' place . . . all of it. I should call the place Nelsonville or Palmerville," he boasted, laughing.

Mosley let Nelson vent; he was enjoying Palmer's humor and sarcasm. He knew Nel was correct, since he had land holdings on the lake, downtown, the village store, and the surrounding woodlands. His famed church home was something that tourists drove by to see, even though it was still his private residence. His overall tax responsibilities surpassed even the largest businesses that operated in the geographical area. Nelson was the richest and most powerful person in the renaissance town. In fact, he was the richest person in the state of New Hampshire, thanks to the lottery and his subsequent investments.

"You're right, Nelson. You *do* own the town, but few people know of your holding companies—your total acquisitions are confidential. They just know that you are rich from your winnings."

Nelson thought for a moment and then said, "Bill, things here will change soon. I will have an announcement at the town's 250th anniversary in the fall. This town is changing . . . forever, and I am the catalyst and leader of the movement. The old names in this former shit hole are history. They will run outta here like rabbits by next winter. They are all idiots. Those people ruined this town in the past. If I have to, I'll shame the bastards out of this town forever. Their genetic progeny won't want to stay either!"

"Well, Nelson," his attorney said, "you already got rid of most of them. There are few of them left to harass. Why not let up a bit? You won!"

"I want every one of those cowards out of here. That is my mission. Contrary to what they think about the beginnings of this town and their ancient nonessential relatives, they know *nothing* about this town's history."

Mosley knew of his passion to correct the history. "Jeez, Nelson, you are fired up."

Nelson continued to vent. "I want them to know that their old names had little to do with the origin of this historic village. The history books have been wrong for centuries and I plan to rectify the situation."

"I plan to publish the true history of the town and distribute it to all our citizens at the celebration—the forthcoming anniversary celebration." Nelson finally took a deep breath.

Nelson's ranting had made Mosley realize that the man was on a passionate intellectual quest that went beyond his election. Mosley surmised that his legal expertise might be needed during the "transition of history," and he was pleased to be a part of the plan.

☩☩☩

Derek arrived the following Thursday and spent three hours with Nelson and the park committee to review his design progress. Each of the prominent founders cited in Mrs. Perry's manuscript would have a statue. Their actual faces were unknown, but Derek had simulated their stature and British features of the colonial days. The blacksmiths differed from the timber men, and the gentlemen differed from the hunters. Knowing what their trades were as early settlers allowed Derek to envision their clothing of that period. He supplemented what he didn't know through library research, thanks to Libby's help. Mrs. Perry's manuscript detailed each settler's role in the original town of Raby. Some were prominent statesmen appointed by the colonial governor or the king of England. After careful review, the committee approved his drawings.

"Now that we are done for the day, will you have time to stick around and see my daughter?" Nelson asked Derek directly. "I hope you two were able to touch base by phone." The young artisan indicated that they had spoken the previous week and planned to get together. He did not tell Nelson that he and Penny planned on getting away for a couple of days. Penny had suggested that they head to the White Mountains to get reacquainted. Derek, of course, was eager to see her. He would drive over to Penny's new home that evening. Derek reassured Nelson that he desired to see her and asked Nelson for permission, a rare symbol of chivalry and respect.

"I may stay for a day or two and then head back to Maine. By the way, do you wish me to do the bronze work here or in Maine? If I do the casting in Maine, it will be expensive to ship them here. Each one will weigh a ton," he said. "Time is of the essence."

"I would prefer that you work here, in Harvest. I can set you up with a building in which you can sculpt and mold as needed. There is a foundry not too far from here. If you need help with any aspect of the job, we can hire additional artisans to work with you. We just need to keep your actual work confidential. I want to surprise the town. You could stay at the late Jason Birch's cabin, rent free. There is no one in there at present. I use the property when I fish during good weather, but I'll be damned if I will ice fish. Too cold and too old!" Nelson explained. "Ice fishing is for numbnuts!"

"That would be nice and certainly an adequate abode for the little I need. It will take me what's left of spring and summer—actually about seven or so months—to do them if I have help. By the way, I'm not an ice fisherman either."

"No problem," Nelson said. "That should enable you to start soon. I'll be talkin' to ya. Let me know when you plan to be back here. I'll have someone clean the cabin for you. That way, it will be ready when you are."

"I really appreciate the offer. Once I get things settled in Maine and have someone watch my studio for me, I will be back."

Nelson told Derek to have a nice weekend and headed home. He already knew where Derek was going. Penny obviously was anxious to see the artist, and her father knew it. Ray had picked up the girls early and they would spend Thursday to Sunday night camping at the state park. That way the girls could spend quality time with their dad.

Derek arrived at the home that Nelson had provided for his daughter after the separation and expected divorce proceedings. He parked in the driveway and was greeted at the front door by a stunning Penny Browning. As she stood in the doorway, her figure and hair were backlit. She wore jeans and a flannel shirt. The evening was still cold from the late spring weather. She had a packed, overnight bag on the floor.

"I thought you would never get here," she said softly. "I thought my dad would keep you all day and night," she said hugging him tightly. Derek closed his eyes in passion and then kissed her tenderly. She was holding on for dear life. She did not want to let go of the man that she truly loved.

"I have made arrangements up north, in the White Mountains," she whispered in his ear. "All we have to do is drive a couple of hours. You will like the place I have booked. The views are beautiful and the accommodations are quiet and serene."

"Really?" Derek said, staring into her eyes. "You arranged for something up in the mountains? Tonight? I've never been to those parts."

Penny looked at him and studied his face and felt his cheeks. She touched his nose and lips gently with her fingertips. "Yes, tonight!

"I can't believe you came back here. Do you have any idea how much you have been missed?" she asked, while kissing his hand. She pressed it to her chest. "Feel my heart," she said. "It is racing. I was so scared to see you and now that you are here, I am so calm."

"I was wondering if you missed me as well," he said shyly. "But after seeing you at the art show, I knew that I was still in love . . . in love with *you*."

Penny leaned into him and said, "Get your bags. Surely you have a bag in that heap of a vehicle that you still drive. I'm surprised that it made it here," she teased him.

"Aren't we going in my car?" he asked. "I thought you wanted me to drive up north."

"We aren't driving," she said with raised eyebrows. "The limo will be here in ten minutes," she explained, surprising him.

"Limo? What limo? You ordered a limo to take us up north?"

"Yes, I did. It's a stretch—the kind that goes on—for miles," she laughed. "All you need are your clothes. I've got this basket over here. We'll take it with us. There is champagne, shrimp on ice, cheese and crackers and a bouquet of flowers. Bring yourself, your clothes, and a camera. You still travel with your camera, right?"

Derek was amazed by her advanced planning. She was a true romantic.

"Why . . . why, yes. I have the camera in the car. I can't believe that you arranged for all this. This is the most romantic thing that I have ever encountered," he said, while kissing her.

"A limo? I can't believe it," he said, while smiling. "You took a chance on me showin' up," he joked. "You could have been stuck with a solo limo ride north. Pretty confident I'd be here, weren't ya?"

She laughed, retorting, "I could find someone else, I suppose . . . someone thumbing on Route 10, perhaps."

The Lincoln limo pulled into the driveway and stopped behind Derek's car. A gentleman in a tux came to the door and escorted the couple to the white sedan in pristine condition. The carriage lights on the side of the limo glowed yellow in the twilight. The couple entered the plush, velour seats that wrapped around the interior like a living room couch. Soft music could be heard on the stereo system. Penny stepped in with her basket of goodies. The limo driver stored both travel bags in the trunk. A blacked-out window separated the driver from the riders in the back.

"Ma'am and sir, this button will contact me directly by intercom. Just press this button if you need me. The other button over *here*," he said pointing, "controls the sunroof, should you wish to see the night sky, and these buttons over *here* control the stereo and video system. There's an assortment of CDs and videos in here—from Mozart to Madonna. I'm sure that you will be able to select something that suits you for the trip."

"This is awesome. I've never, ever been in a stretch limo before," said Derek.

Penny smiled. She rested her head against the couch and pressed the sunroof control button for fun. The glass panel slid back into the roof and they were staring at the sky. She leaned into Derek's shoulder and looked up at his face as he tried to take in the beautiful interior and the view of the sky. Stars would soon be visible above them.

The driver pulled out of her driveway and headed out of town. He would take Route 93 north to the mountains.

Penny opened the basket of treats. She gave Derek the champagne to open and she placed the shrimp and cheese plate on the bar counter in front of them. She had purchased two special champagne glasses—engraved with their names—from a local jeweler. Derek aimed the cork through the open sunroof. It shot out like a cannon. They laughed and the driver was only momentarily startled. He had experienced that sound before, many times.

"That is so romantic," Derek said tenderly. "You planned all this and I brought you basically nothing. This must have cost you a small fortune."

"Not really," she replied, smiling. "This is a special event and I wanted you to know that I love you. Cost is no matter. Besides this is only the beginning," she said. He poured her some champagne. She also held his glass to be filled. They linked arms and elevated the glasses to lip level.

"Here's to you, me, and to us," she said.

"Here's to you, me, and to us," he repeated.

She held her glass up to his lips. He sipped from hers after he tried his own. She then drank from his. They laughed and talked, and ate from the array of appetizers that she had prepared in advance. In no time at all, the champagne was gone, but, no matter, the bar in the limo was stocked with basic liquors of the highest quality, and ice and mixers as needed.

"I'm a bit warm," she said while unbuttoning her flannel shirt. It was the champagne talking.

"I'm a bit warm myself, " he said as he unbuttoned her shirt and she his. She kissed his chest and then his lips. He was excited by the intimate atmosphere and alcohol effect. She felt his slacks and noticed he was aroused. She rubbed him gently while he was still clothed. He placed his hand in her jeans and reciprocated. She was totally responsive and became very excited. In a matter of a minute they were naked on the soft, deep blue fabric. He sat in the center of the back seat and braced himself. She performed fellatio on him until he could not stand it any longer. She straddled his nude body and lowered herself on him. He was erect and pulsating inside of her. She was slow to move her body . . . up and down and wiggling side to side.

"You like?" she said with passion. "How's this for a ride north?" she asked him. "You wanted to drive, Derek. Now you can!"

"Sweetheart, this is magnificent. I spent the day with your father, but my thoughts were on being with you. You please me so much," he said with passion.

"You, too," she responded. "There is no one like you, my love."

At night, the blacked-out window between the driver and the passengers was less opaque. The driver, who normally could not see back through the central rearview mirror, could actually witness his passengers' silhouettes if headlights were behind the limo. He was able to observe the naked woman elevating and lowering herself. The limo driver drove slowly, then faster, watching as much as he could. The erotic display was more than he could stand. The driver touched himself with one hand while driving with the other. It was like a live black and white video for him. They had only been on the road a half hour and she was already on top of the man. Limo drivers had often seen this kind of behavior before and often compared notes back at the office. But, quite honestly, this driver had never seen such an erotic series of motions. He was so excited that he almost went through a tollbooth without paying. He threw the quarters into the hopper and one of the coins missed the bin. The red light flashed and an attendant picked up the missing quarter and waved him on. The limo had already accelerated by then. The driver's underwear had evidence of his own excitement. He prayed that it would dry before they arrived at their destination north. He was afraid that his guests might notice.

Penny managed to roll to the side and Derek climbed on top of her . . . they lay diagonal across the seat as he thrust his entire body into her. Her legs elevated to the ceiling of the limo and straddled the sunroof opening. Derek and Penny kept in time with the CD that was playing a favorite tune, "Bolero," an erotic, lengthy song from the movie *10* with Bo Derek. The sensual piece challenged the lovers to endure the entire seventeen-minute song, even though there was no way that Derek or Penny could last that long. In a matter of a few short minutes they simultaneously experienced orgasms. She gyrated wildly, lifting her buttocks off the seat and elevating Derek into the air. Her moans and verbalizations could be heard through the darkened window of the limo. The driver had all he could do to stay on the road, especially with the sideshow and noise. Derek and Penny were oblivious to the driver, or anything else for that matter. Penny did not relent to Derek's fatigue and tried to get Derek to climax again. She was still writhing in ecstasy and had little problem satisfying her own self. By now Derek was exhausted. He knew he had missed her, but she had improved her ability to stimulate him beyond his wildest dreams. Never had he been with a woman that was so intense and stimulating. Her passion bordered on nymphomania . . . latent nymphomania. By now, they were both exhausted.

Penny smiled at Derek and he could see her face, dimly illuminated by the bar light.

"Do you think that I missed you?" she teased.

"I think, perhaps you did," he said, smiling and still naked next to her. He opened a side window to allow a breeze in. The windows were now steamed. She kissed his cheek and entwined her fingers between his fingers.

"How about round two?" she asked playfully.

"Are you kidding?" he asked. "That *was* round two and *three* perhaps!"

"Actually, I am a bit tired," she sighed. "Do you mind if I lie across your lap?" She placed her head on his moist lap, lightly touching him. "Good boy," she said to the now flaccid organ. "Good job."

Derek poured a scotch on the rocks while Penny slept in his lap. He sipped his drink and gently stroked her hair on the side of her head. He saw the features of her face, the striking lines of her jawbone, and the serenity of her relaxed face lying below him. She was stunning. Her naked body was curled into a fetal position, and he ran his hand down her leg to her calf. She was exquisite for a woman who had carried two children. He tilted his head back as he gently stroked her forehead, as if he was patting a dog. He could not stop touching her. She slept in total comfort. One half hour from their destination, the limo driver reminded them by intercom of their location. It was a short announcement, basically to alert them to get dressed. Both Derek and Penny would manage to do so before they arrived at the hotel. Derek did not know it, but the hotel of choice was the most historical building in the White Mountains—Penny had booked only the finest. The enormous white structure was the pride of the state of New Hampshire and the most popular in the North Country.

Over the weekend, they would wine and dine and relax in a room that had views of the surrounding mountain range. The acreage was nothing short of paradise. On Sunday, Penny and Derek were transported by limo back to Harvest. The ride back would be less amorous. They were far too tired to match the accomplishments of the ride up, as well as their escapades at the hotel. The perfect weekend was followed by the return to reality, and Derek needed to head back to Maine. Penny knew he would be back soon, since he had promised her dad that he would begin the next phase of the project. He would officially move into the Jason Birch cottage then. She felt sad as he left, but he assured her that he would call every day. He kept his promise.

Twenty-seven

In April, Derek moved to Harvest to work closely with Nelson on the statues. The lake in front of Jason Birch's cottage had thawed and patches of snow were visible only on top of the mountains. Penny and her children spent much time with Derek. Her uncontested divorce was proceeding rapidly. The biological parents shared the children every other weekend. Ray was now aware that his "ex to be" was seeing Derek. It did not concern him since he was considering moving in with his pregnant girlfriend in Somerville, near Boston.

Nelson and Libby were spending more and more time together, enjoying long walks in the country where they looked for jack-in-the-pulpits and violets.

His priority through the winter was to respond to residents' issues and to reduce the bureaucracy of the selectmen's agenda. They continued to meet in the local school. East of town, walls were up in the new town hall. The site of the original meeting house and its rustic foundation became a new supporting base for the wooden superstructure. Nelson had construction initiated before the snow began to fly. He had hired double the number of carpenters to frame it out and close it in before any major storms ensued. By February, the basic structure had been enclosed and windows and doors were installed. The workers were finishing the outside clapboards in spring, but the inside finish work would take all summer. A heating system had been installed so that the wallboard taping would dry and plumbing could be completed for the septic system.

"It's looking great, guys," Nelson said to a carpenter one day. "It is actually looking like a town hall. The people of this town will be excited when they see it finished."

The carpenter nodded in agreement and said, "This is the fastest we have ever completed a building. I can't believe that we started this winter and it is basically ready for the inside finish work. It has even been roofed with the gray slate that you requested."

"Yeah, that was a huge expense, that slate," Nelson responded. "With this nasty weather it's amazing that none of the men slipped and fell while they were working on the roof."

"One of them came close to doin' exactly that, Mr. Palmer. I saw him hangin' on for dear life. The stone was cold and slippery. He almost 'bought the farm', as they say."

"We surely don't need to lose anyone on this project. It's historic and important, but not at the expense of a worker becoming injured," Nelson said with concern.

The carpenter went back to work and Nelson donned a safety helmet. He wandered from room to room and studied the interior. He had contracted an architect to study other local town halls nearby and to design a structure that met the old style designs of the early settlers and their descendants. He was amazed by the crown molding and types of interior wood that highlighted the door frames. Lead and stained-glass windows adorned the tops of door thresholds. The oak and cherry woods of New England became built-in cabinets and bookcases. A separate room was designed to be an archives for the town's history. It was self-contained like a vault and fire- and flood-proof. The historical documents of the original Raby were to be housed in that room. They would reflect a true and accurate history of the town.

✠✠✠

Summer brought more and more people outside to enjoy the weather in downtown Harvest. They wandered on new sidewalks with their baby carriages and pulled toddlers in little red wagons. It had become a family town. The new town hall, a showplace, was finished and painted and became functional for the elected officials. Residents didn't care that it was not located in the town center. They accepted the newly created location as an historic area in the town's history. Plus, the stone foundation was authentic. That foundation was what gave the new building *strength*; the same strength that fostered the town's creation centuries ago.

Nelson, the selectmen, and the anniversary organizing committee were anxious to finish the detailed plan for the 250th celebration, which was coming soon. Derek's work was nearly complete, except for the final casting of the actual founders. That was a relatively fast portion of the creations, since the molds were now ready for pouring the molten bronze.

✠✠✠

As Labor Day drew near, preparations were finalized for the parade and the grandstand for the visitors and dignitaries was readied in place near the town center. The ball fields were cleaned and the children's activities and adult barbecues, lobster bakes, and firemen's muster were scheduled.

For the weekend events, surrounding towns sent their fire trucks for the parade and engaged in firemen's competitions. Beer flowed for the adults. The whole town participated in the Saturday, Sunday and Monday festivities. It was very obvious, even to outsiders, that the town had surely changed, and the new blood and new administration was responsible for that change. The atmosphere was electrifying and people could feel the energy. It was almost as if the town of Harvest was no longer in possession of its name or the demons of the recent past.

Nelson had hoped for that and had planned it that way. The highlight of the weekend would be a surprise unveiling of the sculptures. Nelson and the selectmen would also call for a special town election to follow the weekend celebration. The election would be unorthodox, since it was not November, but a valid, democratic endeavor after Labor Day to finalize the changes in town.

The bronze work now completed, the statues were delivered to the newly created town park and gardens. The sculptures were hidden from view in crates since Nelson wanted the event to be extraordinary. The wooden crates that housed his art were nailed shut. The night before their dedication, the crates were removed and the statues placed on their prefab permanent foundations. An opaque polyethylene drape covered each monument until the formal ceremony and unveiling. Security personnel were hired to make sure that the bronze works would remain secret throughout the night.

"What do you think, Libby?" Nelson asked. "Are you ready to see Derek's creations? It should be an incredible story for the future and for posterity."

"Well, Nel, when you do something, you surely do it big, my dear," she said. "I think this should generate the biggest news in southern New Hampshire in decades. It should be fun as well."

"Decades? You mean centuries!" he laughed, then continued his thought. "Actually, I think of this event more as an accurate portrayal of history. For years, the town has been in confusion. People have lived here in denial, for centuries. It is imperative to fix that error."

The printed and bound volumes of the Perry manuscript arrived before the anniversary weekend. Plans called for the book to be given away to everyone who attended the town celebration that weekend. He had ordered some three thousand books for the residents and another five hundred for visitors, tourists, dignitaries, and the news media. The hardcover book was handsomely bound in blue, with gold leaf and embossed gold lettering. It was a beautiful treasury of the town's real history . . . the *real* town history. Additional copies were printed in soft cover and would be sold at bookstores for years to come. The revenue would go toward the founders' cemetery maintenance fund, and an Ezra Raby scholarship for local kids who planned on attending college.

The week before the gala event, a semi had pulled up to the church house. The books were shipped in cardboard cartons containing thirty volumes each. Nelson hired men to move and store the books in the basement of the church.

"There," Nelson said, as the last box was unloaded into the church basement. "That should do it. We are now ready."

Libby looked at the massive 7,000-pound shipment and sighed. She had thought that the books would occupy a corner, not most of the cellar. "Will you look at this mess? It looks like a warehouse."

"Just look at the final product," he said, ripping open a box. He fanned the pages of the handsome production with his right hand. It was 700 pages of history, and all contained in one volume. "You edited this, Libby dear. Look what resulted from your months of toil."

"I know," she said with mock exasperation, " I think after that, I can be the town historian. I had to read the darn thing ten times." She was actually proud of the final quality production. She was smiling.

Nelson looked at her and smiled back. "You, my dear, are part of the reason why this project came together. You, by fate, are now *part* of the town's renaissance."

"I certainly feel like a renaissance myself," she said to him jokingly. "For years, I helped students research their town. I misled them. As the librarian, I should have done more research on my own," she added, feeling guilty.

"Don't beat yourself up, honey. Had Aunt Bess died and not told me of my roots, none of this would have surfaced. The damn town would have been the same as before—with an inaccurate history and full of . . . assholes!"

"Oh, Nelson, you old coot. Must you curse?" she said.

"Well, an ass is an ass," he said firmly. "Also remember, without Aunt Bess in Pennsylvania, I would not have met you, or this crazy town."

"You're right, Nel, and I thank God every day for that," she responded with a gentle touch of his hand. "I do love you . . . you old fool."

"Me, too," he replied. "Me, too."

The moving men returned as planned to move the boxes from the Palmer cellar to the downtown festivities on the Saturday of the celebration weekend. The selectmen would be responsible for the dissemination and distribution of the books at Nelson's dedication speech on Sunday afternoon. Meanwhile, the books were stored in a large rented van near the secured bronze statues.

✠✠✠

Chief Gooden called Nelson the night before the Sunday event and told him that the police force was ready for the final celebration. The parking and traffic flow pattern were already in place and would be implemented with precision. The chief digressed to verbally shower Nelson with accolades.

"Nelson Palmer," the chief said, "just look at this weekend and all you have done. You are an amazing man. You have changed this town forever. There is less crime and fewer problems with teenagers. The kids stay in at night and work on homework. They play hard after school and enjoy the new parks and sports fields. They are empowered with creative things to do. They are enjoying the weekend festivities."

"That's the way it should be, right?" Nelson said.

"I came here to find my roots, Darren, and I think I found the *town's* roots as well. It has been an amazing ride to transition. Can't believe that all of this change and vitality has occurred . . . through fate. It lay dormant in the people all this time."

"You did well, Nelson. It will be my pleasure to work the remainder of the weekend and watch the people have fun for a change," said Darren. "The 250th will be a great time. Thanks for all you've done for the town."

"My pleasure, Chief. Your force deserved more respect from this town, and now you have it. Kids respect you folks and that's a good sign."

"Yes," said Gooden. "It's much better all around."

Twenty-eight

What Nelson Palmer's genealogy search had revealed was that Harvest, New Hampshire, was not the incorporated town's authentic name. That was more dramatic than finding out his own heritage. He reminded himself daily that the original town was Raby, a unique town name that was also his ancestor's surname. It was deemed that title because of an originating group of Raby colonists that bravely came by boat from the northern English town of the same name. Many of their compatriots died in that endeavor to cross the ocean and seek the new world. They deserved to name their town after themselves.

Nelson's mission from day one was to set the record straight. In essence, he and young Susan were the only living, direct descendants of the original Raby name. Reverend Ezra Raby was their kindred relation. His relatives and their descendants had toiled to create a community that could survive the terrible winters, inevitable diseases, and floods. The history of their plight was clear to Mrs. Perry and beautifully documented in her book, and also in the remnants of the old stone foundation, which Nelson and Jason Birch had found by serendipity.

Nelson now knew Ezra's complete role and history, but the town didn't know the relevance of the man. Nelson also knew him as an honest man who had preached the gospel and twice married. He had fathered eight children, some of whom died very young. The tombstones shared their fates . . . most deaths were from the plagues of that early time period. They died prematurely and most likely from fever and pain. Not all of the colonists realized their dreams for which they were entitled—a new land of opportunity. They were known for their bravery and constructive efforts on behalf of the king once they arrived in America.

The historical account of the founding fathers, as related by Mrs. Perry, concluded that Ezra Raby not only built the foundation and church in which Nelson lived, he had also helped with the construction of the original Raby Public House, the one in the woods that Nelson and Jason Birch located. Ezra Raby arrived in America from England, trained only as a mason. He later became a man of God. He claimed to have had a calling. Mrs. Perry had alluded to that fact in her manuscript.

The town anniversary was now going on. Nelson had pondered history long enough. His thoughts and remarks were clear in his mind for dedication day.

For practice, Nelson had recited his speech to Libby. He had prepared the content of his dedication oratory with a reference to his family roots as well as the historical account of Mrs. Perry's book and the town. The research was a culmination of the efforts of many people. Lydia, Libby, Susan, Penny, and Nelson himself had accomplished the task.

Libby cried as he read the prepared text of his final draft. She knew that it would emotionally move the people of the town.

After the weekend of picnics, parades, and firemen's muster as well as other children's festivities, Nelson, with Libby and his committee by his side, stood and calmly addressed the crowd at the newly dedicated park. The sun shone on the podium on the most significant Monday in the history of Harvest. The park flowers and gardens were in fall bloom and the cobblestone walkway was now complete. Two United States flags and a flag of the state of New Hampshire bracketed his stoic figure. Penny beamed with pride as her father tapped the microphone to assure that it was turned on. Nelson breathed deeply and then began his dedication speech.

> Governor Branford, distinguished legislators, and town residents, ladies and gentlemen, children, and guests of this historic town, we celebrate the history

of this wonderful village, which has recently become a *renaissance* town. I say renaissance town because today is a *rebirth* of this village and its residents, not the actual anniversary of its founding. You have made this town anew by your votes on Election Day and by your volunteerism since the election. It is clear to the officials and your representatives that the town was once a town in sadness, a noncommunity of sorts. That is not the way it was originally founded. Historically, it was a community centuries ago. For years, the *town* has lied to you, by default. . . . I say the entire town, because in total it has been a mass of confusion over its own identity.

The residents listened intently.

The descendents of the recent past had no real knowledge of this town's history or its founding centuries ago. They cannot be blamed in total for their ignorance. The town records, and the people who were selfish one hundred years ago, basically stole the town from you and me—*they stole* history. Someone once said, '*history is . . . lies agreed upon.*' Well it rings true in this village. Some residents of the past took pride in claiming that *their* relatives were the founding fathers—this was an untruth—a distinct lie. Their relatives weren't the founders at all! Other dedicated people of the past were hardworking colonists, and the true founders. The late Mrs. Perry, our beloved longtime resident of this village, collated the real history of this town. She studied and researched it over her lifetime—up and until her death last year. The fact is—the original town where we stand today—was not named Harvest.

There was an immediate gasp from the crowd. They murmured among one another, wondering if Nelson had gone mad or had one too many beers. Schoolchildren looked at their parents in wonderment. They needed to know that their town history was taught incorrectly for decades. Their teachers had misled them all through school. Nelson continued:

> I hear your confusion. I want you to know that Harvest, as we know it, was not Harvest until a hundred or more years ago. Prior to that it was called a different name —Raby— spelled R-A-B-Y. The forefathers of this town were from Raby, a town in the north of England. They adopted the name of the town and brought it here. They loved it so much, that some of them took the Raby name as their own surname. The evidence for this historical revelation is real, and the gravestones in town do not lie. The men and women who founded the town were Reverend Ezra Raby, his family, and his shipmates. The few women who made the harsh journey were their wives. Some arrived later on additional voyages. Reverend Raby is buried with his family in the graveyard next to Lydia's grave. It is adjacent to my church home—the actual church where he preached.
>
> I came to this town from Pennsylvania to find my roots—to locate Ezra Raby and his family. I came here to find my heritage and not only found him, but a new town and *new town heritage* as well. This town is still Raby. It will always be Raby, New Hampshire, and should be called Raby."

The crowd was silent as everyone focused on his impassioned speech. They could see his tears. They could hear the tremor in his voice. He was overwhelmed by their attention. No one moved in the audience, even though a dog wandered aimlessly between people, seeking attention. Nelson's family was misty-eyed. The passion in his voice and the knowledge of his revelation impressed everyone that heard his poetic convictions. He had researched every aspect of the town and he could defend his thesis to the end. He was a true scholar of Raby.

My fellow residents, I had no desire to run for the office of town manager. I had no desire to do anything but live here, where my genealogical roots began. The turmoil in the town caused me to look deeper into the attitudes and issues of the past. The inaccuracies of the history, and the attitude of the elected officials that were not serving you, made me run for office. I ran for office *because you asked me to run.* Your currently elected selectmen ran for the same reasons. What went up in flames, the building on this very spot where we stand today was not the town's history or the original town hall. It was a surrogate sham. The real town hall for Raby is east of here—a mile or more. We will go there after this commemoration to formally view the new building. In a month we will formally dedicate it.

Today, we dedicate something different on this spot of earth. In this garden, we placed some benches for reflection, some flowers to smell, some epitaphs to read to your children, and some art to remind you of your true town history. I ask the men standing behind me to now remove the shrouds over the sculptures. Our resident artist, Derek Mitchell, created these beautiful renditions of the true founding fathers and mothers. Look to these bronze works for your own inspiration. That was a time when life was hard and death was real. In the middle of these bronze works stands Ezra Raby, a man of the cloth and a mason. He holds the Bible in one hand and a trowel in the other hand. He was a mason before he preached the good book. Surrounding him are three other men that were his contemporaries. They, too, settled this town and died here. A statue of a woman is symbolic of the mothers that bore and raised their young here. Many died as infants. Their families are also buried near Reverend

Ezra Raby. Visit their graves! . . . You may find your
own roots, as well. Your names may be the same as
theirs. Perhaps you are a direct descendent, as well!"

The crowd applauded wildly, as they thought of seeking their
own heritage.

Lastly, fellow citizens of this proud town, because of
your hard work and devoted effort to the positive
changes in this village, our selectmen will now pass
out the *real history* of this village, which even includes
a section on why we believe the name was changed
and the true history was hidden by the ancestors of
today's "old names." The books are free and compli-
ments of this revitalized town, from this point forward. Enjoy the history as told by Mrs. Perry. She
died not knowing that we would celebrate this day of
renaissance . . . *the return to Raby.*

The crowd, thinking he was done, again began to applaud loudly.
They were inspired by his tenacity, dedication to the truth and his
overall knowledge. He was devoted to making history correct and
just.

"One last thing," Nelson said, as he motioned for the selectmen
to now join him near the podium. "We, your elected officials, propose
that an election be held in two weeks to vote on the most important
proposal to ever be placed on a ballot in this village. The proposal is
that we return this town to its original name . . . Raby . . . its rightful
name."

The crowd erupted in applause. Persons who were sitting, arose
and stood to a four-minute ovation for Nelson Palmer. They were part
of history in the making and Nelson was their leader into the new
evolution of the town. They each were making a difference in the
direction of the town where they resided. He made them feel important by his compelling concept to change the name.

Nelson raised his arms to calm the crowd. The noise was deafen-
ing. He repeatedly thanked them. They were rejoicing and then respectfully quieted down to hear the end of his oration.

"Do I hear a second to the motion of changing the town name?" he yelled.

The crowd erupted in pandemonium and in unison yelled, "Second!"

"So be it!" he exclaimed back. "We will become the new residents of Raby . . . R-A-B-Y! Please be sure to officially vote for the change when the time comes."

A local band commenced a rendition of "The Star Spangled Banner" and continued to entertain from the flatbed truck. The residents danced and celebrated into the next morning. Fireworks exploded over the park and the residents and children rejoiced. Not one person was arrested for disorderly conduct and the rescue squad was never needed the entire celebratory evening. It was a civilized rebirth of a community. The town of Raby, New Hampshire, was reborn. It was truly a *return to Raby*.

✠✠✠

Libby spent more time at the church home than at her own house in town. The Christmas holidays were near and she helped Nelson decorate the church house. He reciprocated by helping her make her own home festive as well.

"Look at that," Libby said one night. "The church looks so beautiful with those lights about it. Even the blue spruce on the side looks like it was meant to be lit up year round." He agreed. Libby reminded Nelson that the town tree-lighting ceremony was forthcoming. He would be the master of ceremonies and had suggested the event prior to the election. It would be a simply planned evening but a real community gathering. They planned to sing holiday carols and the lights were to remain lit through the month of December and into the new year.

"You're right, Libby, dear. This entire holiday season will be very nice. Town events and family get-togethers will be festive. I hope that my daughters will visit, all of them. I invited Penny, Derek, and the kids over and she was to contact her sisters and get back to us."

"I think that it would be special if all your children could be here," Libby said. "Am I included in the family gatherings?" she joked.

"I was thinkin' of invitin' you, Libby. I need a date for the holidays," he teased. "Of course, you are a part of this. Do you have other plans that I don't know about?"

"No," she said, "I just didn't want to be presumptuous, ya know?"

Nelson took her hand and kissed her cheek. "Did you really think that you were not a part of our family Christmas?" he asked with tenderness. "You have been a part of this family since we practically met. Penny regards you as her surrogate mother. You are family now."

"Nelson, that is sweet of you to say that. I have had no one to share the holidays with for many years and I want to be family. It is fun to be a part of your town takeover and to watch the change in personal attitudes in this town. As I drove around yesterday, one could see that people are into decorating the town for Christmas. People care now and want to make their village a showplace for all to see. It is revitalized, and you are the reason for that."

"Libby," Nelson said, "you are family to me. You are a significant part of my kids' lives, and of this renaissance town. I feel like I've known you forever." He was reluctant to tell her how he felt, but tested the waters anyway.

"That is sweet of you, Nelson. Can I pick two pine wreathes for the front doors of your home?" she asked cautiously. "They would look great on the double doors."

"Sure," Nelson replied. "Feel free to decorate it any way you wish. Better than that, let's go together to the nursery. I think we will need a huge tree in the living room. Those cathedral ceilings are tall and a big tree will be needed. I would like all new ornaments this year, as well. We can hit the Christmas Gift Shop up the road and get all new lights and satin balls and bows. What do you think?"

"I think that you think like a man! Pretty darn old-fashioned. How about you pick out the tree and I decorate it? I have some other ideas for ornaments."

"Sounds fair," he said.

"Let's head up the road and see what kind of trees they have. With these tall ceilings, I will need them to deliver a tall one. It will be too long for the new SUV, for sure, and I don't care to scratch the heck out of the new paint."

"Yes, that's probably the best plan, Nelson," Libby replied. "You are no spring chicken, ya know? Trees are cumbersome and heavy."

"True, my dear . . . that is true," Nelson laughed. "Let's head north and see about a tree."

They drove up Route 10 and turned off onto a back road that went to a local tree farm. It was the kind where you can cut your own, or they would gladly do it for you. Nelson and Libby picked out a blue spruce that towered above them. The owner agreed to deliver the tree at no charge because he knew of Nelson's prominence in Raby and it was his way of thanking the new town manager for all that he had accomplished to date.

From the tree farm, Nelson drove to the Christmas Gift Shop a few miles west and set his friend Libby loose in the store. He sat on a bench in a corner of the store, dwarfed by large, artificial trees adorned with thousands of ornaments and figures. Libby picked out numerous unique handmade blown glass designs, colorful bows, and multiple sets of white lights. He smiled at her when she looked at him. On occasion he affectionately shook his head in dismay. He dreaded the confusion of the whole display in front of him. He became ill from the scented candles that permeated the store atmosphere. There was no escape from it. The Yankee Candle Company made gorgeous, festive candles, but the scent of each one seemed to mix and fill the air. Nelson was particularly sensitive to the artificial vanilla and strawberry vapor. A bayberry fragrance was also throughout the section where he waited. He motioned to Libby that he was stepping outside for a breath of fresh air. She sensed his boredom with shopping and knew he was sneaking out for a cigarette.

Outside the quaint shop, the bright sun bounced off the snowbanks nearby. He stood in the entryway and studied the snow-covered landscape. It was a fairly warm day for early winter and water dripped off the edge of the roof. He loved New Hampshire. It was the four seasons that had hooked him. No other part of the United States matched the changes in color, warmth, or scenery. New England was special in that respect. He lit up a cigarette just as she emerged from the holiday store.

"Ah, ya caught me, Libby," he said like a schoolchild.

"Nelson Palmer!" Libby responded, with a hand on her hip, "Those cancer sticks are nasty for you and you know it. Besides, I can tell at work when you sneak those things. Your clothes stink, just like the tobacco you smoke. It's a dead giveaway Nelson Palmer." He felt the well-deserved ridicule and knew she was only thinking of his health.

"Oh, well," he said. "That was the last one . . . I'm givin' them up forever," he said, squinting from the bright sunshine.

"OK . . . heard that before, I think," she said, disgustedly. "How 'bout if you promise to stop on New Year's? That's more realistic."

"You're on," he said to her. "New Year's, it is. That's a promise!"

Nelson took a long drag, held the smoke in his cheeks and then exhaled through his nose, just to irritate her. It made her smile, but she bit her lip in order not to laugh. He crushed out the cigarette he had hardly lit, in a bin intended for that purpose and helped Libby with the bags of ornaments. He opened the back of the SUV and the bags filled most of the storage space.

"You put it on my account, right?" he asked her.

"Sure did, Nel . . . you will have quite a bill there. Besides, you are the one in town with the bank roll," she joked.

"Ah," he responded in kind. "So, you want my friendship for my moola, eh?"

"No, Nel," she added, "I'm not after your money. These ornaments are for your house, right?"

He nodded in the affirmative.

"Then the bill is yours, right? she asked with a smile.

"Yes . . . it sure is . . . my bill," he said. "How much are we talkin' here, Libby? You weren't in there all that long."

"A thousand dollars!" she said. "Never let a woman loose with a free credit card or account."

"A thousand dollars? What the hell did you buy?"

"Well, once I got there, I knew you needed holiday gifts for the girls and their kids and the town hall."

"The town hall?" he asked with confusion.

"Yes, Nel. We need a tree for the lobby of the new town hall . . . your new Raby town hall. They had the perfect artificial tree with ornaments all set up. I bought the whole thing, as is. They'll deliver it."

"What? I don't do artificial trees! I do real trees."

"Mr. Town Manager, you will break the rules if you do that. Town fire regulations require that public places have noncombustible trees and ornaments during the holidays. It's the rules, sir! I thought that you would want a festive tree in the town hall . . . so, I bought one," she said smartly. "They will deliver it tomorrow."

"Ms. Libby, you are quite the woman, aren't you? I like your style. You got balls!"

"Mr. Town Manager, I do not need the male anatomy to make decisions," she smirked.

"Right . . . sorry . . . got carried away. I apologize," he said, holding his head down. "It was not an appropriate comment for a woman, especially *this* woman," he said, patting her head.

"Your apology my friend, makes you a gentleman. I accept," she said with a grin. "Let's get this stuff home before the real tree arrives at the church house." They chatted and laughed all the way home and Nelson enjoyed her company more and more it seemed. Libby was a fixture in Nelson Palmer's day-to-day life. He was amazed at how easily she fell into his daily regime of work, his family, and his pleasures. They had much in common. They worked and played hard and both grew increasingly fond of one another.

Nelson's extended family was beginning to gel and he also was happy in his life, again. He had found companionship . . . again.

Epilogue

The Palmer's extension phone on the nightstand rang. It was Susan.

"That is wonderful, Susan! When did he propose? I am so happy for you and Doug."

"He proposed last night. I'm getting married. Can you believe it, Nel? The old bartender is getting married . . . right here in Raby!"

"Where are you getting married?" he asked.

"The church in town—the one near the village store," she said. "We think that would be a nice spot. After all, I grew up near there."

"Well, hell, Susan. I have a church right here. Get married here, in my church home . . . right next to the late Ezra Raby and the family. It will be like he is there at your wedding. You *are* a distant Raby, ya know."

"Are you serious? It's a house now, not a church!"

"Susan, this is still a church, in a way. We'll bring in an altar and a few pews—right into the living room. They're still in storage from the renovation, remember? We can make it work. Once a church—always a church."

"Nelson, that is so sweet of you. Are you sure it won't be too much trouble? We could have the pastor come to your house."

"You betcha. Talk it over with Doug, and let me know. It would be my honor!"

Susan beamed. She just knew that her fiancé would agree to the new plan—he wanted Nelson to be his best man, anyway. Doug just hadn't had the opportunity to ask him yet.

Nelson immediately called Libby, who was thrilled with the idea. She planned to research the scriptures that were used in Reverend Ezra Raby's day. Surely, there were records somewhere. Perhaps Susan would want to use some of the passages in her vows or during the wedding ceremony.

✠✠✠

When Christmas arrived, the Palmer clan, including all four daughters and their families, congregated in the church home. The light snow fell across the hillside property, powdering the gravestones. Christmas Eve included a feast and an exchange of presents. The enormous fresh pine in the living room was decorated with myriad ornaments that Libby had purchased, and some she helped the grandchildren make earlier in the day to keep them busy.

Penny arrived with Derek. She pulled her father aside and whispered in his ear. "Daddy, I have some good news," she said, with a wide smile. "With my divorce from Ray final, Derek has proposed to me. Look at this ring!"

Nelson admired the diamond, then hugged her affectionately. "I am very happy for you both," he said. "It is obvious that you both care for one another. I know you will be happy."

"He fills the void that I once had," Penny replied. "This man is everything a woman could want."

Nelson whispered back to his daughter, "What about the kids? Are they OK with this?"

"Amy and Chelsea love him, and they still see their dad often. Derek is sensitive to their feelings. Even Ray has said nothing derogatory. I'm happy for that. He's not an issue at all."

"Congratulations, Derek. Take good care of my daughter. Don't disappoint her," Nelson said. "There is a reason why all this has happened. Many people don't believe in fate, but I do."

"So do I," Penny said. "The village store and Derek's arrival to this town is certainly fate."

Derek leaned over and kissed her.

"Ho, ho, ho, it's present time," said Nelson, as he handed each person a grab-bag present. In front of the fireplace in the church living room, they each opened their special presents. The grandchildren watched with wide eyes, after tearing their own open.

Derek had rigged his present for Penny. He made sure that one of the sisters took his secretly prepared grab-bag gift and then he asked Penny to trade. Penny exchanged gifts with her sister since it appeared much larger.

"Ah," she said shaking it, "what could this be? I'm darn good at guessing, ya know."

"Stop shaking the damn thing and open it, Penny," said her father. "You'll break the fragile thing. It sounds delicate. It's probably one of those pet rock jokes or something."

"Hush, Nelson Palmer! It's *her* gift. Let her guess," Libby stated with a smile.

"Whoever wrapped this one did a crummy job," Penny joked. "Must have been a man."

Finally, she ripped open the wrapping paper and stared at the long, wooden box. The packing material inside looked like straw. It was like a nest but the contents of the gift were well hidden. She teased off the straw protection and a stunning face appeared. She knew immediately what it was.

"Oh, Derek, you set this one up so I would get it. It is so beautiful, honey."

Everyone leaned forward to view the pure white statue as she carefully removed the sculpture from the wooden box. It was the priceless, *and not for sale,* sculpture that Mrs. Horton had pointed out at the art show in Maine.

Penny wept as she told each of her sisters the story. "It is called *Mourning Dove* and she is a nymph. Derek made it after he moved away from Harvest. It represents me, and the mourning that he and I went through. It is so beautiful. Thank you, honey."

Derek stood beside her and said, "You deserve to have it. It's for you, sweetheart. It is my gift to you. I could have sold it ten times over, but I chose not to do that, because it was always meant to be for you."

Doug said, "Derek, no one can outdo *that* gift. You're destined to get some lovin'."

"You're so sentimental, Derek," one husband teased him. "Such a sweet man."

Derek just shrugged his shoulders and winked.

"You're makin' us all look bad, Derek, you dog," came another comment.

Derek joked back. "I was *depressed* when I sculpted this," he said.

Nelson toasted everyone in the room. "This is a wonderful Christmas Eve. I toast all of you and your love for one another. Tomorrow is Christmas Day and we should all get to bed for the children. It is *their* special day. We'll see you all tomorrow at two. The turkey'll be done by then—buffet-style—to make it easy for the cooks. We love you."

The party of holiday well-wishers and relatives departed. Once the front door was open, the gently falling snow came straight down and caressed their winter jackets and hats. Penny and Derek stopped on the sidewalk to catch snowflakes on their tongues.

Nelson helped Libby clean up the evening remnants of food and glassware. They saved the heavy kitchen chores for the morning. They retired to the bedroom for the first time together. She curled up to him.

"This was a beautiful evening, especially for me, Nelson," she sighed, then added, "I love your family . . . and you, Nelson Palmer. I feel such a part of you and them."

"I love you, too," he said. "You are as much a part of this family as they are."

"Merry Christmas, sweet Nelson."

"Merry Christmas, my Libby."

Under the tree were their own presents, a stunning emerald necklace awaited Libby. Her gift to Nelson was a hand-signed first edition of John Fitzgerald Kennedy's *Profiles in Courage*.

✠✠✠

Derek helped Penny with the children's toys. He needed to put a couple of them together. They sipped wine, finished the toy construction, and placed the presents under the tree at 1:00 A.M. The kids were fast asleep throughout the whole endeavor. Penny grabbed Derek's hand and guided him into the bedroom.

"Thank you for the sculpture, honey. I owe you." Penny undressed and climbed into bed. "I have a little *present* for you," she said, giggling.

"Really?" he replied, climbing into bed beside her.

"Yes," she said. "Santa is about to *come* early!" The two embraced and kissed, then they made love. The morning light of Christmas Day would find them in each other's arms.

✠✠✠

The new town hall was dedicated and formally named, Raby Hall. Photos of Mrs. Perry and Jason Birch hung in the foyer.

The residents officially voted to change the name of the town. Nelson was reelected for two more terms. Nelson and Libby were married and lived in their church home. He fished when he could get the time. Susan and Doug were married and Nelson was the best man at their wedding in the church home. The local and promiscuous Tammy Prescott became pregnant again and moved to the west coast.

Penny and Derek also married and they had their own child a year later—a son. They named him Nelson Raby Mitchell.

Postscript

Posthumous recognition

For Grace (1924–1964)
an author unappreciated for decades,
for her candor, honesty, love, and desire to express
real life in literary form.

Acknowledgments

I wish to extend my sincere thanks to Marti Gorham, George Grove, and Tom Coughlin for taking the time to review the manuscript of this novel. Their kind comments on the back cover are deeply appreciated by the author. They are each noted authors or composers in their own right.

The fictitious "plea" to the colonial governor of New Hampshire for the establishment of a new town, in chapter 19 of this novel was adapted, in part, from the historic reference book, *The History of Brookline, New Hampshire,* by Edward E. Parker, published by the town, circa 1905. At one time, a town called Raby actually existed in New Hampshire.

The New Hampshire fishing records and fishermen cited and contained in this novel were derived from annual publications of the New Hampshire Fish and Game Department, as well as from the book, *New Hampshire Fishing Maps* by Charlton J. Swasey and Donald A. Wilson, 1998, Delorme Publishing, Yarmouth, Maine.

I sincerely appreciate the efforts of Tabby House in Florida in the final production of this novel. This is our third gratifying collaboration.

About the Author

J. P. Polidoro, Ph.D., is a director of business development for a company in the biopharmaceutical industry. He has been in the medical related field for thirty-five years. A reproductive biologist by training, Polidoro was awarded his M.S. and Ph.D. degrees from the Department of Veterinary and Animal Sciences, University of Massachusetts at Amherst, Massachusetts. His undergraduate degree was a B.A. in biology from C.W. Post College in Long Island, New York.

Polidoro is also a noted songwriter, guitarist, and performer. He has self-produced six albums of his own material to date. In the folk music world he is known as "The Good Dr. Jack."

Return to Raby: A New England Novel is Polidoro's third novel written on business trips cross-country and at his Laconia residence. His first, *Rapid Descent: Disaster in Boston Harbor*, a thriller-mystery about a doomed commuter flight from Logan Airport to New Hampshire, was published in 2000. His second, *Project Samuel—The Quest for the Centennial Nobel Prize*, is the story of the unscrupulous human cloning of Ted Williams, and was published in 2001, by Longtail Publishing (www.longtailpublishing.com).

Polidoro lives in Laconia, the lakes region of central New Hampshire, with his wife, Brenda, and two children, Stephanie (seven) and John Perri (six). He has three grown children (Michael, Chris, and Kim) by a previous marriage.